THE KINGSFORD MARK

To Darlock House, set high on wild, wind-swept Exmoor, the ancestral home of recently widowed John Kingsford, ex-M.P., comes Carlo Graber—young, wealthy, knowing only the life of the world's playgrounds for the rich—determined to unravel the mystery of his own birth. The moor gives Carlo a rude welcome, the vagaries of its moods matching his own wild and impulsive nature. Here he falls in love with Birdie, a farmer's daughter, and for the first time knows tenderness and understanding. Slowly, too, he is drawn into a strange love-hate relationship with John Kingsford, a man who through the decoding of the diaries of Parson John Kingsford—his great-grandfather—discovers, and plans revenge for, the great betrayal of his life. Against a pastoral background, brilliantly observed, this story tells of the timeless compulsions that twist and shape the lives of John Kingsford, Birdie and Carlo to an explosive climax, the echoes of which spread far beyond Darlock House.

THE
KINGSFORD MARK

*

VICTOR CANNING

THE
COMPANION BOOK CLUB
LONDON AND SYDNEY

THE COMPANION BOOK CLUB

The Club is not a library; all books are the
property of members. There is no entrance fee
or any payment beyond the low Club price of
each book. Details of membership will gladly
be sent on request.

Write to:
The Companion Book Club,
Odhams Books, Rushden, Northants.

Or, in Australia, write to:
The Companion Book Club,
C/- Hamlyn House Books, P.O. Box 252,
Dee Why, N.S.W. 2099

Made and printed in Great Britain
for the Companion Book Club
by Odhams (Watford) Ltd
60087205X
8.76/305

Chapter One

NORTH-WEST over Squallacombe and Ricksey Ball the low sky, a sheet of beaten lead, was scored suddenly by a snake's tongue of lightning that struck eastwards towards the cloud-darkened heart of Exmoor. A hailstorm swept down Hangley Cleave, beating viciously at John Kingsford's face, forcing him to turn his back. He moved away, up the moor slope, towards the distant ridge road.

Although only a few days into October the royal heather bloom was dying fast under the ravages of the worst autumn he could remember for many years—more than that, John thought; the worst year in other ways that he had ever known. He would be glad to see it dead and gone. Skip, the sheepdog, moving ahead of him whined, its pelt hedge-hogged by the wind blast, trapping the hail in a sudden grey scurf. Hail, rain and wind hissed through the air and beat a tattoo against his back as he headed for the road gate.

He turned eastwards along the ridge road. It was nearly three miles back to Darlock House. He had gone about a mile, the road losing height gently as he went, when he heard the sound of a car coming up behind him. He stepped back on the grass verge to let it pass. The dog sat at his feet and shivered.

The car came slowly up to him, windscreen wipers fighting against the rain which had now taken the place of hail. It stopped alongside of him. It was a new station wagon, mud-splattered, and piled high at the back with luggage. The nearside window was wound down. There were two people in the front. A woman was driving, a scarf tied over her head, and the collar of a fur coat turned up around her neck so that he could see little of her face. Alongside her, on his side of the road, sat a youth of about seventeen. He had an over-plump, tanned face and wore a glossy peaked cap of navy blue and a thick leather jacket.

The youth said, 'Excuse me, sir—could you help us? We are lost and looking for Darlock House.' His English carried only the faintest trace of an accent.

John Kingsford nodded. 'You're not far off it. Down the road another mile. On the left you'll see the drive gates.'

The woman leaned forward suddenly and looked up at him across the youth, and said with a smile, 'You're John Kingsford, aren't you?'

'Yes, I am. You stopped the right man for directions.'

'I know your brother. You are very like him.'

A fierce rain squall swept down the road and the buffeting wind almost made John lose his balance. He held the car's door handle and said, 'This is no place or weather for introductions. We've been expecting you. Mrs Hurrell will look after you.'

The youth raised his head and looked intently at John Kingsford, and then slowly smiled. 'You could squeeze in. We could give you a lift.'

John shook his head. 'I've got the dog. No, you go on— and welcome to Exmoor. It isn't always like this.' He made a motion for the youth to raise the window.

He watched the car drive off. The woman he had not been able to see well, but the youth looked as though he could do with some long walks in this kind of weather. He moved on, thinking about his brother, the Very Reverend Robert Hugh Kingsford, Provost to the Bishop of Avon, two years younger than himself, full of good works and good intentions—and persuasive. That definitely, otherwise Miss Grace Lindsay—the woman driving the station wagon—and Master Carlo Graber who wore a seaman's cap and clearly needed exercise would not now be heading for Darlock House to take over the old tower wing, though tower was too grand a name for it. Well, he couldn't see that their stay could do anything for him. Nothing could help him, except the common salve offered by time and fading memories to all men who had met loss and had to learn to live with it.

He walked on with Skip at his heels. To his right he saw a pair of ravens take the wind and sweep with an easy mastery of the gale high over Darlock moor and down the long combe that cradled the stripling river Mole where it dropped towards Heasley Mill and North Molton. Without wanting to remember, he saw them both riding the combe from Radworthy, where his great-grandfather, old Parson John, had often preached, to the top of Mole head. He and Elizabeth, both not long met but already the knowledge in them of what was to come, waiting to be put into words, into the days and nights and the years of being man and wife. The memory was vivid, too vivid . . . soft late Spring weather and the larks singing high. He had told her Parson John's saying that from where they were you could spit into the trickle of water at your feet and in the fullness of time know that it would flow down the Mole to the Taw, and so out to the Atlantic by way of Bideford estuary. Then, if the wind were good and strong at your back and you were a good spitter, you could clear the ridge road from Devonshire into Somerset and hit the meagre top of Sherndon Water. Your spittle would then go down the stream and into the Barle above Landacre bridge, and so on to the Exe below Dulverton and finally reach the English Channel. They had both spat into the water at their feet but had failed miserably, laughing together, to reach the Sherndon Water. A young fair-haired girl on a

7

black mare, and a not-so-young dark-haired man on a chestnut gelding. . . .

He moved on, thinking of great-grandfather Parson John. He had died in 1922, at the age of eighty-two—sixteen years before he, himself, had been born. He had never known his grandfather, and scarcely known his own father who had been killed in World War Two four years after his birth, two years after the birth of his brother Robert. From his mother and others he had heard many stories of the old parson. And now, as he sat most nights, as he had done for the last months, deciphering the old man's diaries, his great-grandfather had become an almost tangible companion; alive in the room, talking to him and, though remote from his own loss, a comforting presence. A few lines from the entry he had made the night before floated into his mind. *Pony went lame at South Molton so I left it at the George Hotel, refused another mount since it was a fine frosty night and walked home with Skip. Coming across Darlock moor we put up a covey of black game. Tomorrow I go to Barnstaple to see Mr Weaver over the plans for the addition to Darlock.*

The extension had long ago been made to Darlock. Grace Lindsay and Carlo Graber would be settling into it now. Of black game on the moor there were only a few left. But there was still a dog called Skip, had always been from the old man's days, the name shared by many different breeds in the passage of time. Tonight he would sit again in the old man's company, transcribing the simple letter code, broken years ago by his Very Reverend brother who had soon tired of transcribing the diaries which had been begun in 1869 when his great-grandfather had been twenty-nine years old.

The white posts of the drive gates came up through the rain and John Kingsford turned down through the avenue of low, wind-twisted beech trees to Darlock House which lay with its back to the high ridge behind, and faced the steep combe which fell away to the twisting valley below, where the Sherndon Water took to itself the flow of the Kingsford Water coming down from its source at the top of Hangley Cleave. Wind and hail swept up the drive in a cold welcome.

*　　　　*　　　　*

Mrs Hurrell and a maid served dinner. Within a few minutes of meeting, Grace Lindsay had guessed that Mrs Hurrell ran the house. She was a slight, straight-faced woman, long past middle-age, her sternness of manner betrayed occasionally by a surprising smile and a sudden warmth in her grey eyes. That she thought the world of John Kingsford was clear. To learn later that she had come into the family as a young maid of sixteen was no surprise to Grace. The world, she thought, was fast losing a place or the patience for both of them. Darlock was a little island which the greater world ignored, something in its way as alien and primitive as the moor which gave it rough shelter; thinking it, she recognized at once a familiar intolerance in herself, an impatience with people who had nothing to offer her. Or rather, she could be frank with herself, could never know what she would like to be offered since she did not know herself. Even before her sister, Margaret, had died and left her more money than she had ever dreamt she would possess she had drifted; and, lately, mostly at the heels of Carlo. And how typical it was of Carlo, on their first night here—where they had come at his urging, sprung by some idle quirk, some memory of something his mother had once said about the place—that he should pretend a headache, not to come down to dinner, wanting nothing except to be left alone in his room. This from Carlo who had made her organize and arrange everything so that here they were at the beginning of winter the occupiers of a whole wing of this house and here they would stay until Carlo tired of the place. Thank God if there was one thing predictable about Carlo it was that he had never—like his mother—been one to stay long in any place. Thank God, too, that when he soon became eighteen she would be quit of responsibility for him and released from her promise to her sister.

John Kingsford said, 'I hope the boy's all right. He should eat. Mrs Hurrell could send something up for him.'

'That's kind. But it's not necessary. He's just over-tired. We've done a lot of travelling lately.' The boy should eat. All boys should eat. Keep their strength up. Keep fit. That would be a Kingsford philosophy. Grace sipped her burgundy. It was good, perfectly served. That, too, the Kingsfords would know about. Then, with a moment of self-irritation, she chided herself for the irrational stand she was taking against John Kingsford and all he and his forebears represented.

To her surprise she knew from his next words that this tall, dark-haired, compact man had sensed some of her feeling.

He said, 'I shouldn't have thought Darlock was your kind of place. I can't think what you are going to do here. We've little to offer. It's the beginning of the worst part of the year. You can ride, and hunt, of course . . . if that's your fancy?'

'I'm afraid not. But we shall be all right. Carlo wanted to come. Simply I think because his mother talked to him about the place. And when he gets an idea into his head it's hard to put him off.' Impossible. He could be an absolute swine when thwarted.

'I remember her. She came down for two or three weeks years ago. Not long before Bob went up to Oxford. How was the Very Reverend when you saw him?'

'Charming. Very much the churchman.'

He laughed. 'Good old Bob—even as a boy he went in for that kind of thing, robes and censer-swinging, ritual, and all that stuff. Though he could be a proper hellion when he wanted. Rode like a madman, too, though he had the worst pair of hands in the country.'

'Hellion?'

'That's one of Mrs Hurrell's words. It describes any boy with the wind up his tail and bent on devilment.'

She laughed. 'It describes my dear nephew, too, at times.'

'Well, we must try and keep him busy doing something useful.'

Prompted by his last words and speaking before she could consider any question of tact, she said, 'I didn't know until your brother told me that you were no longer a Member of Parliament.'

'That's so. Kicked out of my constituency at the last election. Only a handful of votes against me. Close run—but there it was.'

There was no regret in his voice, though she knew he had been a member for over ten years.

She asked, 'Will you try again?'

'I don't know. I don't think so. It was never really my kind of life. I've no real political ambition. Mother pushed me into it. It was my father's old constituency—and she was a great one for tradition. She felt my father would have liked it.'

Grace would have liked to ask him more, but she realized that for all his easiness of manner it would need only one ill-considered question to harden him, make him close up like a clam. She knew from his brother that a month after losing his parliamentary seat, he had lost his wife. No seat, no wife—and there had never been any children, and now he sat by himself in this big house and probably pretended to find plenty to do. It was a pretence she was well used to acting herself.

As he started to tell her something of the estate and the farms which lay to the south of the moor which were let to tenants she looked at him and considered quite calmly whether he was the kind of man she would want, a man to fill her void and so his own. She couldn't think so. He might take another woman at some time, she felt, but never again look for love. He was the kind who loved once, and when that had gone . . . well, some men used women as a convenience—she had been used herself as such—and some just soldiered on, worshipping a memory. No, he was not for her. Imagine being mistress here, where the draughts fought against the central heating, perched on the edge of a wild moor with the wind coming in from thousands of miles across the Atlantic, where bad weather was king and you couldn't walk a hundred yards without hearing the sound of running water and sinking up to your ankles in boggy ground? Pray God that Carlo would soon take against it. Why, in God's name had he been so keen about it?

John Kingsford's voice came to her, '. . . the old Kingsford home used to be on the other side of North Molton. The house is a ruin now. It was Parson John—my great-grandfather—who bought this place with a legacy he inherited from an aunt. He moved up here while his father was still alive and when he married he brought his wife here. She was an heiress and between them they enlarged the place. But the tower wing which you're in was put up by Parson John some years before he married. He loved the moor. What my great-grandmother thought of it isn't recorded, but she had a town house in London and each winter she travelled a lot, though the old parson didn't often go abroad with her. Although he took Holy Orders he never had a regular living but he was always ready to stand in for any local parson who needed help. But at heart he was a farmer, and a moorman.'

Later that evening alone in his study John took from his files the letter which his brother had sent him about the hiring, as he had called it. Hiring—it was a good word and an honest one, dating from the end of the war when the family had been going through a bad patch. The house had been too big for the small family. His mother—a practical woman with a fatherless family to brood—had decided to let the tower wing during the summer to visitors. Usually they had been families with young or teenage children who hired the wing for a month or two at a time. The children of some of the hirings were now old friends of his.

. . . the name Graber, as such, will mean nothing to you. But you will possibly remember a Margaret Lindsay. She came down for about three weeks as the friend of a family—their name escapes me —who took the hiring for two months. She was—if my memory serves me right—a flighty piece as they say. Graber was a Swiss banker, not entirely I'm told without a certain dubiousness of character. . . . John smiled to himself, as he had smiled when he had first read it. The Very Reverend had deliberately acquired a nice line in pomposity over the years. *The boy Carlo was their only child. Graber, who was much older than his wife, died some years ago, and Margaret Graber last year. The boy I am told by his aunt—Grace Lindsay—had been somewhat spoiled by his mother (very well endowed with this world's goods by her late husband) and has an extravagant and volatile nature. But, so Miss Lindsay informs me, he is at heart a well meaning, good natured lad. Though, I fancy, she will not be sorry to welcome the end of her guardianship and be left in peace to enjoy the generous legacy which was willed to her by her sister. She seems, Miss Grace Lindsay, that is, a capable, self-contained woman who gives me the impression of nurturing some feminine dissatisfaction of a more fundamental nature than, say, a broken*

heart. I sense some esprit lacking in her which has perhaps warped a little the capacity for any warm communication with others. But (and I note your smile as you read this) enough of the pontificating. Cut the dialogue and come to the 'osses. They are set on the hiring, and I cannot see that in your present circumstances it could do you anything but good to have, no matter at what remove, some fresh faces and voices around Darlock. Besides, too, you know how Mrs Hurrell loves company and enough work to fill her days. You have had two bad blows, my dear John, and although I know you will be keeping yourself busy I do not—speaking as a pastor of souls—think you can do your own soul anything but good to have a little noise and bustle and coming and going around Darlock. You might even turn mildly missionary. I understand that Margaret Graber was over inclined to the bottle after—if not before—her husband's death, and this may have contributed to the boy's unsettled state. You could exorcise him with a few weeks of moorland life and exercise. Expose him to the spare and noble virtues which life on the edge of a wilderness demands from all who would survive into fine manhood. I see you smile again. But write and tell me that you will agree to the hiring and I will communicate dates and all necessary instructions. Domestically, Mrs Hurrell, I know, will be delighted. Financially you can mark your own price and, since I know you have no need to 'scratch around for a bob or two', donate it all to a favourite charity.

He put the letter down, remembering now, as he had remembered when he had first read it, the face of Margaret Lindsay quite well over all the years—a pretty, laughing, yet slightly weak face; fair-haired, a tall, well-built girl in her early twenties. The family she had been with escaped him almost totally, but Margaret Lindsay he could never forget because she had been the first woman he had ever seen entirely naked. Some years older than himself, she had scared him out of his wits at first and then awakened him to a fumbling burst of passion. Well, it was all now water under the bridge; Margaret Lindsay, who had married a

Swiss banker much older than herself, and had taken to the bottle, was dead. . . .

He put the letter back in its file. Like most long established families the Kingsfords were inveterate letter hoarders and some of them—like his brother—inveterate letter writers. He pulled from under the desk the small leather-bound box which held Parson Kingsford's diaries, a collection of black-backed, marble-edged notebooks, many of them worn and stained, the ink of their entries faded, the lettering of the coded words (such a simple alphabetical code that his brother had broken it in a couple of hours) precise and neat for a man who had been so large and broad-handed as the parson, a man more at home on a horse than in a pulpit. He would work for two hours and then go to bed. Self-pity had gone, but memory bit like a slowly healing wound. To escape the present, and well aware of it, he went back into the past, riding to Barnstaple with Parson John to see Mr Weaver the architect.

When Grace Lindsay went into Carlo's room before going to bed, he was sprawled in an armchair reading. Music came softly from a transistor radio on the table at his side. By the radio was a supper tray.

Grace said, 'Don't stay up reading until all hours, Carlo. You've had a long day.' She nodded at the tray. 'You've had something to eat, too, I see.'

'Some cold meat and salad. Mrs Hurrell brought it up. I like her.'

Grace smiled. Carlo's judgments were always simple. I like. I don't like. Few degrees between the two.

'Why do you like her?'

'She's a happy woman. You can sense it all around her.'

'You should have come down to dinner—then you could have given me your judgment on Mr Kingsford.'

Carlo dropped his book on the floor, and lit himself a

cigarette. The silver cigarette case had belonged to his father, the shabby lighter was from some cheap bazaar.

'I know about him. But it is not so simple.'

Grace waited for more, but when Carlo remained silent she said, 'Yes. Go on.'

Carlo ran his hand over his smooth dark hair, then laughed. 'You always want to know what other people think about people. Why? Can't you make up your mind for yourself?'

A little piqued, she said quickly, 'That's good coming from you. You change your mind a dozen times a day about what you think.'

'No I don't. Not about people. Only about things. Why don't you go to bed? You look tired. But even when you are tired and a little cross with me you still look beautiful n your own *noli me tangere* way.' He stood up and took her hand and kissed it. 'Goodnight, my dear aunt—and thank you for bringing me here. I'm sorry I bullied you about it.'

Grace laughed, touched by his fast changing mood. When he wanted to, he could be charming and loved to air a slightly old-fashioned courtesy.

'You're an impossible boy.'

'Not boy—almost man. Would you like a nightcap before you go?' He nodded to an expensive, white leather travelling bar which stood on a table by the window.

'No thank you. Goodnight, Carlo.'

When she was gone Carlo opened the case, took out a glass and a bottle of whisky and poured himself a neat drink. He stood for a moment before sipping it, listening to the high wind beating against the heavy sash window. There was rain in the wind, and some of it had been driven through a crack in the warped frame on to the oak window ledge, already stained from past intrusions of the weather. He was of middle height, large-framed and with a stockiness which lack of exercise and excess of good living had turned to a youthful corpulence. His face was round, plump, and suntanned from lying on summer beaches. When he smiled it was a pleasant, open face. But, in thought, as now, there was an almost petulant, near bad-tempered cast to it that set deep folds of slack flesh below his dark eyes.

He sipped his drink and went back to his chair, reaching out a hand to switch off the radio. Chin tucked into his chest he stared at his outstretched feet and began to whistle softly to himself.

There was a knock on the door.

He called, 'Come in.'

Mrs Hurrell's maid came into the room.

'Mrs Hurrell says, please, have you finished with your tray, sir?' She was a girl of about his own age, sturdy, thick-set, with short brown hair, her face pleasant and weather-flushed, and her words rich with a west country accent.

'Yes, I've finished. And will you thank Mrs Hurrell very much from me?'

'Yes, sir.'

He could tell that she was a little shy and nervous with him. She was a big, well-built girl in all departments . . . solid, he thought, a sturdiness in her which could hold her against any moorland gale.

He gave her a grin and asked, 'What's your name?'

'Vera, sir. Vera Thorn.'

'That's a prickly name. Are you prickly, Vera?'

The girl laughed. 'Not that you would notice, sir. That is, I hope not.'

'I'm sure not.'

Then, as she turned away holding the tray, he reached out and pinched her bottom. The girl jumped and for a moment the tray was in danger of falling.

With a momentary flare of emotion Vera said, 'You

didn't ought to do that, sir! If I'd dropped this lot Mrs Hurrell would have been in a real tear.'

Carlo laughed. 'Mrs Hurrell's no dragon.'

Moving to the door, Vera said, 'That's where you'm wrong.' And then with a giggle she went on, 'You'd better not try that on her. Nor on me again.'

'You shouldn't have tempted me.'

The girl gave him a long look, face unmoving, and then, with a broad smile, went out.

The moment she was gone the girl was out of his mind. He finished his whisky and lay back deeper in his chair, staring at the closed door as though he now waited for the next entrant, for the next amusement. But there was no need for waiting because the next entrant had already taken her place in his thoughts, and she was no stranger.

He sat thinking about his mother, the background to his memory of her a warm, loving sensation touched with a familiar soft pity. She had been a stupid, impulsive, weak woman. In drink—as he had guessed at an early age—she had found an escape into a fantasy personality which pleased her more than her real nature. With more drink even that comfort was lost and she became incoherent in thoughts and words, pitiable and sometimes abject, though no matter at what stage never able to impair the genuine affection and love he had for her. Of his father he seldom thought. He had seen little of him as a boy— a figure which came and went, travelling, trafficking, always busy, always bustling with importance and replacing affection with gifts and indulgences. When he had died he had not been able to find more than a polite, outward show of grief . . . had no reason to do more because by then he had known that the man was not his father.

Hearing the gale still strong outside, sensing the rambling rooms and passageways of this house spread around and below him he was full, if not of contentment, then of calm happiness because he knew from his mother's own mouth, though it had been a mouth that spoke from drink-roused memory, that he had been conceived in this house. This was his place, the starting point of his life.

The morning after her drunken revelation it was clear to him that she had no recollection of anything she had said. 'It was the older one. John Kingsford . . . though he never knew. I had my pride, too . . . bloody Kingsfords. . . .' Then she had drifted away into rambling incoherencies about Darlock House and the days she had spent on Exmoor. He knew her well enough to understand that sober she would never have revealed her secret. Her own pride and a genuine concern not to disturb him would have kept her silent. And, for exactly the same reasons arising from his love for her, he too had known that he must never let her even suspect her own indiscretion.

Not, he thought, as he lifted his feet and rested them on the edge of the table, that he cared a damn. So, John Kingsford had thrown a casual leg over his mother, and forgot it the next morning. *Droit de seigneur*. . . . So, he was a Kingsford bastard when, if his mother had been of the right class, he could so easily have been a Kingsford heir, nursing love instead of contempt . . . maybe envy? Perhaps. But what did it matter? Curiosity had brought him here. Just a simple itch in the mind to see and know this man; this John Kingsford who had not long ago lost first a safe Conservative seat—an achievement which called for special gifts certainly—and later his wife. When he had told his aunt a short while ago that he knew about him, but that it was not so simple as knowing about Mrs Hurrell, it was really an evasion because he had no intention of telling her the truth. He was sure he would not like him because the man was not his type. Kingsford was one of those strong, physically hard men, farmer, country gentleman, who stuck animals' heads around the walls of their house, rode to hounds, preferred hard weather to good, liked the feeling of walking miles in wet tweeds, worshipped fresh air and exercise, couldn't sleep comfortably on a soft bed, and probably thought that the young people of today were a bloody useless lot and not overclean.

Slowly he began to giggle to himself. Who cared what four legs got sweaty and tangled to create you? From the moment you were born you were on your own and, particularly with plenty of money, life was full of little divertissements.

*   *   *

John Kingsford heard the clock in the distant hall begin to strike twelve. He went to the study cupboard and fixed himself a nightcap and then sat down and began to read through the set of diaries entries he had decoded that evening. By the time he came to the last one he had finished his drink. For a moment or two he considered having another and then was firm with himself, knowing that drink would not help sleep because he had briefly tried it in the past.

He read the last 1871 entry he had decoded.

Sunday, 1 October
Left Darlock at 6 o'clock and rode down to Romansleigh where I had promised to take the Harvest Festival service. The rains of the last two days had the roads awash, but today the sun shone. There were flocks of golden plover returned to the high fields above Fyldon—as early as I have known for many a year and a sure sign of a hard winter. The Vicar was still abed with his fever so I dined alone with his wife and her two daughters, nice girls, Jane and Amantha, who were subsequently very jolly, for their mother allowed them wine with their meal.

Preached one of my old sermons and—to be truthful—an

indifferent one which I promise myself to better when I have the time. However, I consoled myself that it was fitting as the congregation too was indifferent and seemed not much uplifted despite the good harvest which is now all safely in.

Coming back over Alswear Great bridge the far side of the road was a foot deep for some way with flood water from the Mole. On Fyldon Hill caught up with old Tom Darch driving his battered old shandrydan on the way home to Buttery. He tells me that his daughter, Hannah, who has been many years in service over at Castle Hill with the Fortescues is giving up her place soon, which is vexing him. He called her 'a terrible head-strong wench with a brain full of fancies'.

Came in with the rising moon to Darlock and found Weaver waiting for me about the alterations and with clearly every intention of staying the night which at first did not please me. But after dining and a manful application of port he proved good company. He sat at the pianoforte for which he has a nice touch in such a big, clumsy man, and sang some songs and ditties, a few of such a nature that they would, I am sure, have banished all indifference from my late congregation.

Bed at 3 o'clock.

He smiled as he finished reading. It was difficult for him sometimes to keep in mind that his great-grandfather at that time had been only thirty-one years old—six years younger than himself. Most of the time his diaries read as though he were fifty or sixty, not a comparatively young man who had been well known in the district for roving eyes and gallantry towards the fair sex.

He switched off the study lights and walked along to the main hall. Oil paintings of the Kingsford men and their wives and children hung around the high dark-panelled walls. To the left of the steep run of balustraded stairs hung the painting of his wife, Elizabeth. It was a full length portrait of her standing outside the main doorway to the hall, the stone steps in full sunlight, the porchway behind her in dark shadow against which her hair flamed like a blown fire as the wind took it. On the step at her feet sat Skip. She was smiling, the greeny-blue tints of her eyes alight and the set of her lips giving her a smiling, almost mischievous look . . . a lively, spirited face, not beautiful but warm and pleasant and in many ways still a girl's face, reflecting the pleasure and excitement of being alive, eager for all life had to offer, untouched by any shadow of care or self-importance.

Each night as he came to the foot of the stairs his ritual was established. He stopped and looked at her; sometimes only for a few minutes, sometimes for much longer before switching off the hall light and climbing the stairs. In the early days there had been nights when he had found it agony to stop looking at her, to make the break and pass on. Now, because he was well aware of the uselessness of self-pity, he curtailed his indulgence severely allowing himself a few moments only to look at her face. Then, before memory could swamp him, he passed on. She was dead and he had to go on living—in the present not the past. He switched off the hall lights and went up the stairs. There was, he told himself, nothing special about grief. It was a commodity always in full supply for humanity.

Curiously there came into his mind the comment in his brother's letter about Grace Lindsay . . . *of nurturing some feminine dissatisfaction of a more fundamental nature than, say, a broken heart.* Well, death was more absolute than a broken heart. And if nurturing grief or dissatisfaction—as he saw clearly now Robert had meant—beyond their proper bounds was unhealthy, then he had come perilously close to it.

Walking around the gallery that overhung two sides of the hall below, the sound of radio music coming softly along the corridor which gave access to the upper floor of the tower wing made him pause. Down the passage a thin slit of light showed from the almost shut door of Carlo Graber's room. At the same time there came to him the faint smell of cigarette smoke which he recognized as Turkish. He clicked his tongue, momentarily irritated at the youth's taste, at his even smoking at all. Recognizing his own stuffiness of attitude, he moved on to his own bedroom. Then, in his bedroom—to which he had moved from the main bedroom after his wife's death—he remembered for the first time in long years that it had been to this room that Margaret Lindsay had come to wake him from sleep.

Chapter Two

DURING THE NIGHT the weather changed. Carlo was awake early and soon out of the house. As he stood on the stone entrance steps Skip came across the lawns and joined him. The steep combe that ran down from the house was still in shadow but the southern flanks of the far valley were in full sunshine. The wind had dropped and the morning was cloudless. Sheep, like plump maggots, moved slowly on the far hillsides, crawling over the dun, rust-coloured moor pastures. A handful of ponies with a scattering of this year's foals now well grown moved in a thin, straggling line across the crest of the opposite ridge, a black flowing frieze sharp against the blue.

Carlo, who was no habitual early riser—bed usually claimed him late unless some purposive urge took him—enjoyed the feeling of being isolated and alone, free to wander around the place to make his own judgments and appraisals. He explored at random, accompanied by Skip at his heels.

Darlock House was T-shaped. The long upright of the T reached across the hill at right-angles to the slope. The drive from the road, tree-lined, came curving around the foot of the T and then ran up to the main doorway half-way along the block. The crosspiece of the tower wing making an angle with the main run of the building faced west. Its only claim to being a tower was that it rose a floor above the main building and there was a low, stone parapet around the roof which had been crenellated. It was an ugly house, stone-built and slate-roofed, crouching against the hillside. The main façade showed clearly that it had originally been a simple, small farmhouse to which many additions had been made over the years. The lawns were neat and small, and the flower beds few. At the foot of the drive before it turned along the front of the house was a large shrubbery of rhododendrons through which ran a small stream.

The stream, Carlo discovered, ran up the side of the drive, narrowing and then dying away almost at the drive gates. A side path from the drive took him down to the back of the house where there was a small courtyard, one side of which was formed by a low stable-block and a run of outbuildings. Over the half door of one of the stables a horse hung its head and blew through its nostrils as Carlo passed by. A man—later to be known as Mr Hurrell, or simply Tom—crossed the yard with a wheelbarrow full of stable muckings.

Carlo went into the house through the back door and found the kitchen where Mrs Hurrell and Vera were working. It was a large, warm, spotless kitchen.

Mrs Hurrell gave him a smile and a nod and said, 'You're up early, sir. Almost beat me and Vera. Couldn't you sleep?'

'Oh, yes, thank you Mrs Hurrell. Like a baby. Nothing on my conscience to keep me awake.' He grinned. He had known even at their first brief meeting that he could get on with Mrs Hurrell. Women were always easy so long as you had the sense to spot exactly where their limits were drawn.

Mrs Hurrell said, 'Nor you should have at your age. What would you like for breakfast?'

'Oh, just some coffee and toast.'

'Lord, that's no proper fodder for a young man. I'll fix you some eggs and bacon.'

'Well, if you think I should.'

'Good. You can have it with Mr Kingsford. He's already started.'

Carlo hesitated. 'Will that be all right?' Under the terms of their taking the tower wing they were self-contained, with their own dining-room and sitting-room. That Grace had had dinner—as he could have done— with John Kingsford last night was simply a welcoming courtesy.

'Why not? Mr Kingsford won't mind. He's not the touchy sort at breakfast. And you haven't really met yet, have you?'

'Not really.'

'Then you go and join him. Vera'll lay another place.'

She told him where to find the breakfast room and he went in and joined John Kingsford. The life he had led with his mother had long since smoothed out any boyish shyness or lack of self-confidence with strangers—if indeed he had ever had much since he had always had an easy, natural self-assurance.

After introducing himself, Carlo said, 'I'm sorry that I didn't feel like coming down to dinner last night, sir.'

'That's all right, Carlo. Sit down. Glad to see you up so early. Best part of the day—and it's going to be a good one. The glass is going up.'

He would, thought Carlo as he sat down, think that the early morning was the best part of the day. Most people would have opted for the evening or the night. He said, 'I'm sure it is—but sometimes it's nice to stay on in bed.' It was not a thrust, just the faintest flourish of innocuous comment, designed deliberately to evoke, and so gauge, the response this man would make.

John chuckled. 'I wouldn't quarrel with that. There were times at your age when my mother or Mrs Hurrell used to haul me out of bed. To be quite honest I might have been up a little later, but I've got to go off to Taunton for the day.'

Carlo marked the response as adequate, and as Vera brought in his breakfast said, 'Aunt Grace and I came through there yesterday. Then we got hopelessly lost. It was lucky we met you, sir. We might still be wandering around. I must say Exmoor didn't give us a very warm welcome.'

John laughed.

'She'll make up for it today. But beyond that I can't promise. Do you like the country?'

He could have said that it depended on the country and the season and his own mood. People threw conventional questions at you, and then scarcely bothered to listen to the conventional replies.

He said quietly, 'No. I'm not a countryman.'

'Well, that's a frank answer.' For a moment John was a little puzzled. He wanted to ask why, in that case, Carlo and his Aunt Grace were here, but before he could say anything further Carlo said—

'But that doesn't mean I can't like it. That's why we came. I'd like to like it. I've always had a feeling that I'd like to, perhaps, farm or run an estate. But my mother was always against that. With her it was usually Paris or Rome or the South of France or Bermuda.' He smiled, knowing that he was making things right, sensing his initial frankness had been over-blunt for this man's taste and he had no reason to antagonize him. 'And always, too, the same old things, and she liked to have me with her.'

'But what happened when you went away to school?'

'I didn't—not after my father died. I had tutors.'

'I see. Well, perhaps we can do something about finding out whether you would like country life. Do you ride?'

'A little.'

'Shoot?'

27

'I've had lessons. Clay pigeon shooting at Monte Carlo. But I don't like killing animals and things.'

'No reason why you should. But things have to be killed, one way or another—otherwise you wouldn't be having bacon with your egg.' He smiled, quietly amused by Carlo. 'Both of which are going cold—so eat 'em up, lad, or Mrs Hurrell will think you're sickening for something.'

Giving his attention to his food Carlo—for whom breakfast was normally an almost non-event—found, whether from his early rising or the mild stimulation of being face to face with this man, that he was enjoying the eggs and bacon. Maybe, he thought, he did have the makings of a countryman. But he seriously doubted it.

*   *   *

Carlo gave the lightest of knocks and walked immediately into Grace's bedroom. She was sitting up in bed, reading, a silk shawl draped over her shoulders. On a side table lay her breakfast tray.

Twitching the shawl over her nightdress and her half exposed breasts, she said without feeling, "My dear Carlo —as though you hadn't heard this before—it's very polite of you to knock, but you should then wait until you are called to enter. Since you've caught me naked more than once I can't think why you persist. I should have thought you'd seen enough naked women by now to have become quite blasé about the female body.'

Carlo sat on the end of the bed and grinned.

'I like it when you talk like that. I never know whether you're angry or just saying what you think I expect you to say. Anyway, you have a very beautiful body and it's always a pleasure to see any part of it. But as for my true feelings . . . well, half a breast is better than a whole one, the suggestion of nakedness more stimulating than nakedness itself. To go further——'

'Don't. I dislike you even more when you put on that mock pompous act. What are you doing up so early, anyway?'

'Catching the best part of the day. Didn't you know that? Mr Kingsford told me. I had breakfast with him. I think he's going to try and make a countryman out of me. That'll be nice, won't it? I'll buy a farm and you can keep house for me.'

'God forbid. When you're eighteen, you're on your own. Then you can buy all the farms you like and buy all the housekeepers you like—and anything else that takes your fancy. Like coming down here in the middle of winter. I suppose some time or other you will tell me why?'

'Probably—if the occasion arises. Though I don't think you'll find it very exciting.'

'But there is a reason. Come on, Carlo—admit it.'

'A small one. Perhaps we'll get around to it one day. But for now, I wondered if you wanted the car this morning?'

'No. I've got some letters to write. And anyway, there's nowhere I want to go.'

'Then you don't mind if I take it?'

'Not at all.' She smiled, and added, 'I'm only surprised you should ask me. I suspect you when you're over-polite and particularly when you have that grin on your face. Carlo, my dear Carlo, what are you up to? I'm no fool, you know. You've landed in trouble before and I've hauled you out. It doesn't amuse me any longer.'

Carlo stood up and shrugged his shoulders. He said, 'There's not going to be any trouble. I'm going to be the perfect country gentleman. I think you forget sometimes that my mother was English and all I know of this country is London and a few other stupid places. Now, I'd like to see some more of it, and since my mother used to talk about this place, I thought it would be a filial gesture to begin here.'

'Tell that to the marines!'

Carlo gave her a mock bow, and said, 'No mystery, no secret—just a nice gesture.'

Grace laughed and waved him away. 'Get out of here—and don't drive too bloody fast. A broken neck is something I can't fix for you.'

Going up the drive in the car Carlo relished the feeling of good humour and well-being that possessed him. It was, he thought, a bit like having had a few drinks, but better because the uplift lasted longer with him and the aftermath was usually reasonably placid. He liked his aunt, though he thought the word an inadequate one to describe their relationship. She was more like a much, much older sister, entirely loyal and reliable. When he got into scrapes —and there had been a few bad ones since his mother's death—she got him out of them, usually at the price of a mild lecture. He liked her sense of humour, which could be sharp and biting when he really annoyed her. Driving, he wondered idly why she had never married. Men there had been because he had known some of them. Some she must have known quickly were complete bastards. Perhaps that was why she chose them. Because she didn't want to be caught up permanently by any one man. Why not, he wondered? She would make a good wife. She was little over thirty and her body—which he had seen naked on a few occasions—was well-shaped. Maybe a bit full in places but that was no drawback—*au contraire*. She was of far more than average intelligence and well read, though she had a weakness for sloppy romances which she was careful not to leave lying about and of which he would not have known except for the challenge a locked drawer or case always presented to him. She often got angry, but was never flustered. Somewhere, someone or other had given her a raw deal, he felt. Her face in repose was gentle, a calm, almost beautiful face, framed by smooth dark hair, and with brown, frank eyes. Sometime he must find out what had happened to her—maybe after this. It would be a nice little exercise to amuse himself with when he had finished here.

But finishing here was the main thing now. First of all he wanted to know about John Kingsford, really know about him because that would reveal, surely, some new truths about himself. Kingsford had been 'the onlie begetter'. (But what happened when you went to school?) Christ . . . he had got more from a series of tutors than he could ever have got from school. And of tutors he had had all kinds. Some had given him book learning, and one a real love of books so that he always had some other world into which to retire. Others—for they changed often—had opened new worlds for him which would have made his mother's hair stand on end. Yes, that's what happened, Mr John Kingsford. That was school. And then, when the whole Darlock scene bored him, he would tell Kingsford the truth, and that it didn't matter a damn, thank you very much, and then spit in his eyes and say thank you for nothing. . . .

The picture of such a moment was so vivid in his mind as he turned out on to the ridge road that he giggled with pleasure and put his foot down hard on the accelerator. Clear the way! Here comes Carlo Graber Kingsford! Here comes Toad of Darlock House! Here comes the fruit of fornication. Here comes Carlo, laughing Charlie Kingsford, in his chariot of fire, unleashed horses under the bonnet, smoking up the high, blue empty skies of Exmoor. . . .

A ewe that had strayed over the moor wall and was grazing on the grass verge stepped into the road twenty yards ahead of him. Carlo swerved, missed the sheep by

31

inches, nearside wheels spinning up gravel and turf, straightened the car and, foot going down hard again, headed for the top of the ridge where the great shoulder of the moor cut sharply against the blue sky.

For the next hour he drove as the mood took him, fast on the long straight stretches of road, taking the car up to ninety miles an hour, relishing the speed and the power he commanded, and then suddenly easing off and dawdling, sometimes pulling into the side and looking at the country. He was going nowhere by design, and the feeling of vacuity was enjoyable. He went north to Simonsbath and then along to Exford and finally found himself in Withypool. He parked the car, lit a cigarette and walked back on to the bridge over the river Barle. He leant over the parapet and watched the coloured flood water from the previous day's rain racing bank high. A pair of grey wagtails was flirting about amongst the boulders on the river bank. He watched them, not knowing what they were, but liking their swift bobbing and flirting movements, his eyes pleased by their bold grey and yellow plumage. A girl came over the bridge on a motor scooter. He turned at the sound of the engine and watched her. She wore a white crash helmet with a red stripe down the centre, a white raincoat and high brown boots. The crash helmet, he thought, looked ridiculous, but the face underneath it was pretty. He turned back to the wagtails, wondered what they were called and decided that he must buy a bird book and find out. Whenever he had travelled with his mother and later with Grace, he had been an inveterate buyer of guide books, museum catalogues and street maps. He had never been anxious to ask people for information. He liked to discover things for himself.

When his cigarette was finished he went back to the car and drove slowly away, choosing the right fork instead of the left at random at a road divide just outside the village.

The road began to climb steeply towards the top of the moor, the deep valley of the river dropping away on his right. A mile out of Withypool the road took a sharp bend over a stone bridge that spanned a little rivulet under the flank of the hill. There was a layby just beyond the bridge. In it was the girl with her motor scooter. The machine was propped on its stand and she was kneeling by the back wheel.

Carlo drove into the layby and pulled up. He got out and went round the back of the car to the girl.

As she straightened up, he said, 'Trouble?'

'Yes, a rotten old puncture.' Her voice was easy, self-composed and nothing like as heavily touched with the local accent as Vera's.

'Bad luck. Where are you going?'

'South Molton. Shopping and a few things.'

'How far's that?'

'Six or eight miles.'

'No problem. I'll give you a lift there and we can get a garage to do the puncture. That all right?'

'Oh, sure. Thank you very much.'

He smiled. He liked her easy, matter-of-fact attitude. She had a puncture. Someone came along and offered her a lift. Nothing unusual. No big deal. No big display. He liked people who took things as they came. He lifted the tail gate of the station wagon, then went to the scooter, switched off the petrol and made sure the petrol cap on the tank was well screwed down. Cars and engines he understood. Although he could drive like a maniac, that was at his own risk and decision. Stupid risks like petrol running all over the inside of a car were only ignored by fools.

He lifted the scooter into the car and wedged it safely, leaning against the back seat.

'There we are.' He opened the car door for her and then

went round the station wagon and got in beside her. As they drove off she began to unstrap her safety helmet.

He said, 'Do you have to wear those things?'

'It's the law.' She pulled off the helmet and shook her hair free. It was brown hair with deep, almost rusty tints. There were greenish flecks in her brown eyes and the sun-burnt, smooth face was just touched with faint freckles below the cheek bones. She opened her raincoat, gave a little tug to her jumper to tidy it and settled her jean-clad, booted legs comfortably.

Carlo said, 'My name's Carlo—Carlo Graber.'

'That foreign or something?'

'Swiss father. English mother. Do you come from Withypool?'

'Just outside it. Great Cotters. That's a farm.'

'You work on the farm?'

The girl laughed. 'Not much. Only when I have to. I'm a secretary. Well, shorthand typist. Just lost my job in Dulverton. That's partly why I'm going to South Molton. There's a job going there. Carlo . . . I like that. Sort of romantic. I'm Ethel Mavis Carter—pretty awful, isn't it? But nearly everyone calls me Birdie.'

'May I?'

'If you want. Do you live around here?'

'No. My aunt and I are just staying for a while—at Darlock House.'

'What, Mr Kingsford's place?'

'Yes.'

'Oh. Are you related to him or something then?'

Carlo laughed. 'Not so that you would notice. No, we just rented part of the house. Do you know Mr Kingsford?'

Birdie shook her head. 'No, not really, not so as to be asked to tea. But everyone around here knows him. He had some bad luck, didn't he, his wife being killed in a car accident up country somewhere?'

34

'Yes, that's right. How come you lost your job in Dulverton?'

Birdie chuckled. ' 'Cause I'm fussy. I don't like bosses that lean over you, breathing heavy and trying to look down your blouse while you're working. You know, the wandering hand brigade—and old enough to be your grandfather.'

Laughing with her, Carlo said, 'Hope springs eternal in the elderly breast. What about the not-so-elderly?'

She grinned. 'What—like you?'

'Could be.'

'If I have to—I'll think about it and send you a postcard. Is this your car or your aunt's?'

'Hers. But I can have it whenever I want it.'

'That's the kind of aunt to have. . . .'

Driving, and talking to her, Carlo was slowly aware of a feeling of unexpected contentment. This girl's easy, straightforward naturalness was refreshing. Most of the girls he had known until now were sophisticated and usually selfish bitches with an eye to the main chance and always calculating . . . calculating what you were worth, what you were good for. Few of them seemed able to be easy and natural; or, worse still, because this usually led to his getting into scrapes, were too easy and natural. Birdie—a nice, simple, straightforward country girl with a mind of her own. He was, he thought, enjoying his first day at Darlock House.

*   *   *

Grace had lunch by herself in their private dining room which looked westward beyond the side lawn to a dark plantation of fir trees which covered the side of the steep combe running up to the ridge road. At half-past eleven Carlo had telephoned Mrs Hurrell saying that he would

35

not be back to lunch. Momentarily Grace wondered what had made him so thoughtful. Usually he was the last person to bother about telephoning to save anyone else trouble. After lunch she went up to Carlo's bedroom and unpacked his cases and put his clothes and stuff away in the wardrobe and chest of drawers. Always when they travelled she did this valeting service for him. The only thing she never touched—and there had never been any comment between them about this—was a battered pigskin case which had belonged to his mother, the key of which he always kept in his own possession. She had very little curiosity about what Carlo kept in the case. Curiosity about Carlo or his private possessions held no strong appeal to her because she knew Carlo so well now. Whatever the case held could tell her no more of Carlo than she already knew. One day, the conviction had grown with her over the years, Carlo would make his mark in life—whether it would be a bright or a black mark would, she felt, depend on some small, insignificant thing, the turn of a card, the fall of a leaf, the look in a girl's eyes, or some chance remark or gesture that happened to seize his attention. There was no solid, single character called Carlo, dependable and predictable . . . only a succession of characters or roles which he dropped into according to mood, casually, or, less often, some presentation which he would maintain for long periods to serve some purpose of his own, seldom ascertainable. Although he was often exasperating, she had to admit that he never failed to entertain, either pleasurably or unpleasantly. Because he would soon control so much money she knew that whatever he did as a man would probably gain him the excuse of being an eccentric; a soft judgment always forthcoming from sycophants.

Having tidied his room, she put on a coat and a silk scarf round her head and went out for a walk. If Carlo decided to stay here long she told herself, then no doubt it would be the first of many such walks. If that happened she would have to keep her sanity by going up to London now and then for a few days at a time. She walked up the drive and went lefthanded along the road from the entrance gates. The beech hedge that topped the road wall was beginning to turn colour, a few dark fruits still clung to the dwarfed growth of whortleberry bushes that clothed the old wall. The afternoon was dying and a chill breeze was beginning to blow, piling drifts of high, grey-edged cloud across the sky. She felt lonely, adrift, an alien in this world. Then, since self-pity always evoked a ready opposition in her, she laughed to herself and suddenly remembered, though she was not sure whether correctly, the lines of the poet Herrick . . . *such discontent I ne'er have known since I was born than here, where I have been and still am sad in this dull Devonshire.* . . . Though whether she was in Devonshire she did not know since at dinner the previous evening John Kingsford had told her that the road was the boundary line between two counties, Somerset to the left and Devon to the right. But where did that leave anyone in the middle of the road?

Thinking of John Kingsford, her eyes were suddenly taken by the yellow and bronze beech leaves which put her in mind of the hair of his wife. Mrs Hurrell had pointed out the portrait in the hallway to her that morning. 'Poor lamb, so sudden it was, and she with everything to live for. . . .' There was no denying the truth that Elizabeth Kingsford had had everything to live for. All the good things from the first moment her eyes had opened. The portrait was full of it. This is me, alive and enjoying life . . . self-confident, no worries. . . . Not only self-confident, but no prey to doubts, probably unable to understand why everyone else could not be the same. 'A proper lady and the apple of Master John's eye.' Mrs Hurrell's final accolade for any woman.

37

Aloud, Grace said firmly, 'You bitch!'

The epithet was for herself, not Elizabeth Kingsford. Envy, even for the dead, turned her sour, and self-propriety demanded the truth from her. Self-pity was an old enemy. She shut her mind to all she had been thinking and walked briskly down the road. After a while she came to a crossroads, marked by a grey post with white direction arms. She turned left and within a few yards passed an unpretentious building with a sign reading *Sportsmans Inn*. Some way beyond the inn a car came up from behind her being driven fast. As it went by she recognized the station wagon, and had time to see Carlo driving with a girl sitting beside him. The car was going so fast that she was sure that Carlo would not have recognized her. Not that it would have mattered either to her or to Carlo. She smiled to herself. Carlo liked girls, though there was no regularity of type in the ones he found and often, as she knew, nothing in many of his choices except a desire—need almost—for feminine company. The number of young men who had ever come anywhere near friendship with him would not have exhausted the count of the fingers of one hand. What kind of girl he had picked up raised no curiosity in her. In good time she would be told about it. What would it do to Carlo, she wondered, if waiting in the future there was some girl he would really fall in love with?

*   *   *

Carlo had enjoyed his trip to South Molton. He had dropped Birdie in the main square and then taken the scooter to a garage to have the puncture repaired. Then he had wandered around the town for a while, spent some time in the small museum and more time in the old church which dominated the town, its tower visible for miles around.

When he met Birdie again he learnt that the job she had gone to see about had been filled. She was not concerned over this. There were plenty of jobs going and—clearly, Carlo guessed—she was in no real hurry to find one. They went into the Goose and Gander Hotel and had a couple of glasses of sherry each, and sandwiches for lunch. After this they had picked up the scooter, put it in the back of the car, and then driven round for an hour or so, listening to the car radio or talking, both of them relaxed and levelly content with each other's company so that it was difficult for Carlo to accept that they had only so recently met. They fitted each other, Carlo accepted, as though they had known one another for a long time. That was an experience which had seldom happened to him before with any other girl.

Sitting now in the car in the little layby where he had originally picked her up, he knew that he was not going to attempt to touch or embrace her. They both knew it, he felt. She was an attractive girl with a self-assurance that matched his own. That took all nervousness or clumsiness from their relationship. They would move, when the moment signalled it, to a common rhythm.

He said, 'Why don't you let me drive you back?'

'No. Somebody would see us at Withypool or up near the farm.'

'Does that matter?'

'Not really.' She half turned and grinned at him. 'But when I find something nice I like to have it all to myself for a while.'

'Yes, I know what you mean. Like a broody hen.'

Birdie laughed. 'What do you know about broody hens?'

'Nothing. Here—' He fished in his pocket and brought out a small, gift-wrapped box and handed it to her. 'I got something for you. I thought it was the right thing for a Birdie.'

He watched her as she unwrapped the little package. She did it unhurriedly, turning once and giving him a small frown of inquiry. That was what he was coming more and more to like about her, the calmness, no hurry, no false trills or little insincere flashes of wonder which other girls would have thought were expected.

Inside the wrapper was a small fancy box which held a silver brooch, a plain bar surmounted with a silver swallow, wings spread. He had bought it at a boutique in the town.

Birdie said, 'It's nice. I like it, and thank you. But you shouldn't have bought me a present. Seeing how you helped me, it should be the other way round.'

'It's not a present. It's just a way of saying thank you for a nice time.' He watched her, waiting to mark some gesture which he knew would have come from most girls to signal the licence of a kiss or a caress in return for the gift, and was pleased when Birdie made no such sign, but calmly put the brooch back in the box and neatly replaced the wrapping paper. That was how it should be, he thought, with the proper ones, with the ones who could match his own certainty of insight.

He got out of the car and lifted the scooter from the back while Birdie strapped on her helmet. As she did so, he said, 'Does this place have a name? I mean this little bridge and corner?'

'Why?' She got astride the scooter.

'You know why.'

She smiled. 'Yes, I do, Carlo. And it's nice, I think. But you don't have to set great store against it. It's called Portford Bridge. And if you come round here too fast of a dark night you could break your bloody neck.' She kicked her machine into life and above the engine almost shouted, 'So, if you're going to be coming this way often—just watch out.' Then, for the first time according him any open sign of intimacy between them, she put the tip of an index finger against her mouth and then lightly touched the back of his right hand with it.

Carlo watched her drive away, marking her progress all down the long hill curves of the road until she passed from his view, knowing, as he knew she knew, that this was only the beginning. There was no need to arrange anything. The certainty of meeting again had been with them almost from the first few minutes of their encounter that morning.

At dinner in their private dining-room that night Carlo said nothing to Grace of his meeting with Birdie Carter. He simply told her that he had driven around, getting to know his way about the country and had had lunch in South Molton. After dinner, Grace went up to the tower wing sitting-room and Carlo wandered into the kitchen to talk for a while to Mrs Hurrell.

Leaving Mrs Hurrell he wandered round the house, making himself familiar with it, lingering in rooms where he knew he would give no cause for questioning if discovered, and with others contenting himself with a quick opening of doors and a rapid survey, fixing each one in his mind. There were only three rooms which were locked, one which he was later to discover was the gun room, John Kingsford's study, and a bedroom on the top floor of the main run of the original house. None of them he imagined would offer any difficulty if he wanted to examine them for the locks were old and of conventional types. Somewhere on the ring of skeleton keys which he carried in his mother's old suitcase would be keys which would fit them.

*   *   *

John Kingsford arrived back from Taunton at nine o'clock. He ate the cold supper which had been left for him by Mrs Hurrell and then went into his study, cleared up his correspondence and some estate matters and then settled down to Parson John's diary.

Not himself a man who had ever been inclined to keep a diary, he wondered as he worked, and not for the first time, what it had been in the character of his great-grandfather which had—clearly quite compulsively—in the midst of an active and mostly outdoor life forced him each night or early morning to set down his doings with such regularity. That the old man—a young man then—felt compelled to record his life must point, he felt, to some aspect of character which was missing in him. Odd, but then there was a tradition in the family that marked Parson John as someone out of the ordinary. There had been tales and rumours about him, now become almost a dim folklore, which still persisted in the country roundabout. It was odd, too, that the diaries should have been deposited with his solicitor before his death with instructions that they were not to be handed back to the family until fifty years after his death. He and Robert had been in their thirties when this had happened. Neither of them then had had time to spare on them—particularly when they discovered they were in code. It was only some years later that the Very Reverend, spending a holiday at Darlock, twisted an ankle, and with forced time on his hands decoded the cipher and transcribed the first few notebooks.

John worked on the diary until eleven o'clock when a small point in one of the entries made him break off.

The entry read—

Friday, 13 October

Riding back from Simonsbath this morning met with Frederick Knight who tells me that he is thinking of treating with the General Omnibus Company for the purchase of some of their French mares which, having gone lame from London stones, he is sure could be worked sound on Exmoor. Since the coming of his father, John Knight, to the moor to start the reclamation of the old Royal Forest the family have not lacked for new ideas, nor for money to pursue them though, so far, it must have cost them a fortune. Folk around talk openly of the moor as Knight's Folly. My father at the time of the sale of allotments made a bid for one of them and was ever after thankful that he was outbid. Much as I love the moor, I am heartily thankful, too, that except for the small parcel around Darlock all our farms and lands are to the south of the moor.

Ate a bacon and bread sandwich at the head of Span Bottom and finished my flask of brandy. As I sat there an old dog fox came up the combe. The wind was with him and he was only twenty yards away when he saw me. I have seen the old rover before for he is easily recognized by a limp in his near foreleg. He stared at me for a few minutes and then made off over Fyldon common where I saw two crows come down and mob him.

To the mine at Heasley Mill where I saw the mine captain, a rough spoken Yorkshireman but of a reasonable nature and we easily settled the trouble which lay between us about some of his men poaching the Mole with lanterns and salmon spears. The men responsible, it seems, departed from working at the mine some three days since and have gone up to Bristol.

Coming back up Fyldon Hill it started to rain heavily just as I caught up with Hannah Darch who was until recently with the Fortescues at Castle Hill. She is a well grown young woman with a civil way of speaking and a pretty manner which I fancy she has caught from being at Castle Hill where she tells me she was a parlour maid. I made her get up behind me, telling her I would take her to Buttery. So we rode double horse down to the ford at Deercombe corner but before we reached Buttery she would get down and walk the last half mile to the farm as she did not think it proper that she should come home riding behind a man of the cloth. She is a good looking young woman with dark, large eyes and raven hair to match. That old Tom Darch and his now departed wife should have spawned such a hand-

some creature late in life is a wonder, for Tom is a twisted oak and his wife, good soul that she was, a bent old crab apple.

At Darlock I found waiting for me, delivered that forenoon by carter from North Molton, the little Spanish bureau which I bought at the sale of furniture from Northcote Barton last week. It is a pretty piece inlaid with many coloured woods and an embellishment of brass edgings fancifully wrought in a running design of birds, fruits, and flowers. Altogether an elegant creation of fine workmanship fit for a queen or princess which thought, as I write this, determines me that when I marry I shall give it to my wife. It is my earnest wish for a multitude of reasons that the lady should manifest herself soon. Corinthians 7:9.

The reference to St Paul's epistle made John smile. Parson John had been a man of healthy appetites and all his life was known to have been delighted at the sight of a pretty face. As it happened, and the family records showed, he was to have a few months longer to wait before the lady did manifest herself—the daughter of an Exeter merchant who was to bring him a considerable fortune in her own right and by whom he was to sire two boys and four girls. But it was the reference to the little bureau which most interested him. It had been duly presented to the parson's wife and had stayed in the family since, being gifted down to each mistress of Darlock in turn. The bureau was now in the London flat which he had taken when he was first elected a Member of Parliament. Sometime, he thought, he must go to London and make arrangements about the flat. He needed it no longer. The bureau would come back to Darlock where it belonged.

Chapter Three

CARLO joined John Kingsford for breakfast the next morning.

With a slight lift of his eyebrows, John asked, 'Have you decided to join the ranks of the early risers permanently?'

Carlo smiled. 'I'm considering it, sir.'

'Take it easy—or you may find yourself turning into a countryman after all. What did you do yesterday?'

With suitable omissions Carlo told him. He finished, 'I also bought some maps of the district and a couple of guide books. I like poking around and finding out things for myself. My mother—' he paused fractionally watching John's face and saw no shadow of any reaction, '—travelled a lot, but all she could ever remember of any place was whether the hotel was good or bad. She wouldn't go near a museum or a church. I had a look round the church at South Molton yesterday.'

'Did you now. Old Parson John was very fond of it. He preached there a few times.'

'Parson John?'

John explained about his great-grandfather, and went on, 'He left an old case full of his diaries. They make good reading and are full of local interest covering the years from 1870-odd to around 1880. He wrote them in a very simple code which my brother, the Very Reverend, broke. I've transcribed them so far up to the winter of 1871. Perhaps you'd like to read what I've done so far?'

'I'd like to do that very much, sir.'

'Good. I'll get 'em out for you some time.' He grinned and added, 'There are no dark family secrets I wouldn't want you to read. The old boy had a quick eye for a pretty face, though.'

Carlo—quite apart from his main interest in this man—wondered whether there wasn't a natural shyness in him which, added to his recent upsets, made him appear stuffier than he really was. This morning he was relaxed and friendly. As they talked his mind toyed with the fantasy that had his mother married this man he would have been born a true Kingsford, and Darlock House would have been his home. He would have been Master Charles—certainly not Carlo—to Mrs Hurrell and the rest, gone to the same public school as John Kingsford, been brought up here like all the past Kingsford boys, and would have loved the moor and the surrounding country, ridden to hounds, got tight at hunt balls, fished, farmed and—no doubt—wenched around the place until the right girl came along. Thinking of this last, he had a sudden picture of Birdie. Her family had been tenant farmers at Great Cotters for ages. If he had been born here he would have known Birdie long ago. But if he had fallen in love with her—he could imagine the look on this man's face if he had said he wanted to marry her. That wouldn't have gone down well! Wrong sort. . . . Well, it hadn't been like that, and he wasn't sorry about it. He liked his life and the way he was. The moor, the country around, Darlock House, and the Kingsford way of life were no more than objects of curiosity to him—like foreign cathedrals and picture galleries, the mountains and lidos of Europe. He just wanted to know about them all. Knowing was one of his chief passions.

John said, 'I've got an hour to spare this morning—why don't we get some stuff from the gun room and see how well they taught you to shoot at Monte Carlo?' He cocked an eyebrow humorously. 'I promise I won't ask you to kill anything.'

Carlo held down a spurt of resentment. Monte Carlo—in God's name what could you learn about shooting there? The implication was clear. It was only here, in England, around this moor, country born and bred, that you learnt things like that. Bloody snob!

With an apparently pleasant eagerness, Carlo said: 'Oh, yes, I'd like that, sir.'

After breakfast they went along to the gun room which John unlocked. He picked out a well-used double-barrelled 12-bore, a handy knockabout gun. Until he knew Carlo's form—and maybe not then—he was not handing out any Holland and Holland or one of his pair of Purdeys from the locked steel cabinet at the end of the room. As an afterthought—remembering the first time he had been allowed to use it at the age of twelve—he took down a German Walther, a .22 long rifle with a five-shot action repeater, fitted with an adjustable micro peepsight. Carrying the guns, ammunition and a clay pigeon trap which had seen better days, they went out of the house, across the front lawns and down into the narrow combe to the shooting point which faced the steep bank of the opposite side of the valley which was topped by a small plantation of firs.

Carlo knew that every move he was making was being watched. While he approved, he could be resentful. He had been well taught and he knew the gun safety rules. As with everything he did, he tolerated no sloppiness. Do it and do it well—if not, leave it alone. Additionally he had no desire to shoot either himself or anyone else by accident.

John set up the clay trap and said, 'Call "Pull" when you're ready. I'll put up a few singles first so that you can get the feel of the gun.'

On the first clay Carlo missed, swinging through much too fast. He missed the second and third but noted that

John Kingsford had kept them all on the same trajectory. He granted him decency marks for that. With the fourth, he scored a hit. Four more followed all on the same line and he put down three of them.

Watching Carlo, John acknowledged that—out of practice though he might be—he had been well taught, and he had a nice natural action, a good straight left arm and a natural balance as he swung through. His eye was good and he had—not all that common—a sense of oneness with the gun that gave no hint of aiming or hesitation.

John said, 'All right, Carlo. Now they'll come any way. Doubles, singles . . . and the doubles can range from about two feet apart steady or swing away from each other to an angle of about forty degrees.'

From that moment John mixed them and Carlo put up a very good score indeed considering that the gun was strange to him. Better, in fact, John told himself than he could have expected from many people who considered themselves good shots.

When they ran out of clays, John handed Carlo the Walther.

'You fired one of these before?'

'No, sir.'

John explained the piece to him, and then pointed across the valley. 'There's an old ash stump about half-way up the bank—see it? I painted a white circle, about the size of a plate, on it years ago. You can just make it out. The range is just under a hundred and fifty yards. It fires a shade high and a shade right. Now—down on the ground, it's a bit damp but that won't kill you. Let's see if you can put three out of five inside the plate.'

John watched Carlo. The youth took his time. There were plenty of others who might have been flustered and impatient, eager to make a showing. He liked Carlo's self-contained manner. Clearly he was the kind who didn't

48

rush his fences. If he had settled to do something, then it had to be done well.

John raised his field glasses and watched the pale, weather-worn, now almost grey circle on the ash stump. He could remember the spring morning years ago when, supervised by a maternal uncle, he had come down here and painted the circle before firing the rifle for the first time. There had been no father to teach him. He had fallen to a bullet from a German rifle. No real memory even of the man. An uncle was one thing, but first moments like these should always be linked with a father.

Carlo fired.

As the stump chips flew, John said, 'Two inches off the plate at three o'clock. That's the right pull.'

Carlo fired again.

John said, 'An inch outside, ten o'clock. There's quite a breeze coming up the combe, that put your correction out.'

After a moment or two Carlo fired again and scored a hit on the plate, an inch inside the rim. He put the next two shots in an inch-grouping just below dead centre.

As Carlo stood up, John said, 'Well done.' Then with a grin, he went on. 'All right—I take back whatever I may have been thinking about Monte Carlo. Any time you want to come down here you can—but you let everyone in the house know where you are. The gun room key is always hanging on the board in my study if I'm not around. Don't let it go to your head, but you could be a first-class shot if you wanted to.'

Back in the gun room Carlo said, 'What about cleaning the guns, sir?'

'Oh, old Hurrell will do that—unless you want to save him a job.'

'I'd like to do it.' Carlo paused and then said, 'Although I don't like shooting animals and birds, I like guns, just as

49

I do engines and motors. There's something about precision and design. About things that do a job properly. I think I would like to be an engineer or designer of some kind.'

'There's nothing to stop you, is there?'

Carlo laughed. 'Only myself, I reckon. You see, there's so much else to do in the world that appeals to me. I suppose it would be better if I were poorer and had fewer choices.'

'You'll find something. You've got plenty of time.'

When John Kingsford had gone, Carlo settled down to his cleaning job. As he worked, he knew that some time or other John Kingsford would later quietly make an inspection of the finished job. Nothing could stop him doing that because that was the way he was. And the way John Kingsford was, presented now some very interesting contrasts between them. They were poles apart. He was moved to a quick rejection of all the man cherished. . . . John with his spartan view of life, his devotion to the principle of masculinity and manners, the manners of a country gentleman and the firm virtues of his kind. He had probably lost his parliamentary seat because he was fifty years behind the times politically speaking . . . the damn Trade Unions, bloody Communists, people don't know what work means these days, just out for all they could get and ready to strike at the drop of a hat if it wasn't all given to them on a plate! Carlo raised the Walther rifle and aimed it at the mask of a fox hanging on the wall. Useless vermin—shoot 'em, I say. And all this quiet, dignified mourning for his wife. Never be another like her. Couldn't be, not in this world. Brood on his loss for ever. Never marry again because how could there be another who would ever half-fill her place? Pure self-indulgence—as though wives weren't being lost every day, as though any one woman was unique! Death strikes—so what the hell? Plenty more where that one came from. New supplies always in stock.

He lit a cigarette and put his feet up on the working table. And yet . . . there were times when he liked the man, found something attractive in him, though it was damned hard to put a finger on it. He was sure that John Kingsford would have liked to have caught him out in some mistake or carelessness over the shooting. Surely a decent sort would hope that you would know your stuff? Already be on your side. Still he had to admit that the praise given had, in Kingsford's terms, been high . . . *you could be a first-class shot if you wanted to.* You had to be bloody good to get that. Well done, Carlo. He suddenly laughed out loud.

His job done, he locked up the gun room and—because he guessed John Kingsford would be in the study and he did not particularly want any more contact with him at the moment—he went into the kitchen and found Vera there alone. He gave her the key to take to her master and made a mock move to pinch her bottom which made them both giggle.

In their sitting-room he found his aunt reading the morning papers. He kissed her and then poured himself a large glass of sherry and lit a cigarette.

Grace said, 'For your age you drink too much and you smoke too much. You have other faults, too, but I won't weary us with them. However, now having put you in a good mood I wonder if you would like to drive me to Barnstaple this afternoon? I've made a hair appointment.'

'Delighted. Though why do you want your hair done? Nobody's going to see you up here.'

'You're quite right. But a woman just gets the habit. And I like my habits. They make me feel comfortable with myself. Do I fancy you could be in one of your sunny, provoking moods?'

'I was considering it.'

'Then reject it. What was all that banging and shooting noise this morning?'

'That was me. My first lesson in becoming a country gentleman. I had a shooting session with Master John. He thinks I might have promise.'

'Promise? But you used to win prizes at——'

'I know. But country gentlemen don't like boy wonders. I missed a few clays to put him at ease and plugged a few outside the target with a rifle.'

'You're a bastard, Carlo.'

'I know. I'm thinking of becoming a professional one.'

'Go away and leave me alone.'

'That's your trouble. You always want to be alone. Why don't you get married? You'd be a good catch. Plenty of money and more than most women in the way of——'

'Carlo—' Grace interrupted him quickly, '—knock it off.'

'Sorry, Grace. I was just making conversation.'

Grace eyed him for a moment or two, and then said, 'All right, I'll tell you what I'll do. I'll promise you to get married within the year—on one condition.'

'Which is?'

'That we pack up and leave this place for good within the next two days.' Grace waited for him to reply, but he said nothing and she sensed that his teasing mood had swiftly gone. There was no surprise in her at the sudden change. Sudden changes were all part of Carlo's nature. She went on, 'No deal?'

'Certainly it's no deal. Why on earth do you want us to leave here?'

'Because I don't trust you, Carlo. And I don't believe any of the reasons you've given for coming here. You're brewing up for something. God knows what. Maybe you're not even sure yourself—but there's some maggot working in your mind.' She smiled suddenly. 'Don't give me that black look, Carlo. I don't mind your stupid scrapes with girls and . . . well, drunken high spirits. But we've had one really bad go, haven't we? I don't want another—and that's what I have a feeling could happen here.'

'What bloody rot.'

'I hope it is. Now, buzz off and read a good book or, better still, take a long walk across the moor. You're putting on too much weight.'

To her surprise, though it was far from the first time that Carlo had surprised her so, his face cleared and he began to laugh. Then he came up to her, raised her hand and kissed it, and said, 'I love you. One day when I'm a grown sensible man I hope to marry someone just like you, someone with the good sense to bash me over the head when I need it.'

*   *   *

That evening while transcribing Parson John's diary John came across a passage which read:

At Bampton this afternoon met with Sir Hamish Riark who was until recently at Northcote Barton. He has now bought himself a considerably smaller house at Dulverton which he says much suits him and his wife, though if the truth be told the real reason is that it much more suits his pocket and dwindling circumstances. He is always much buoyed up with the prospects of the various ventures into which he plunged from time to time with all the impetuousness and bad fortune which attend his forays at the card tables and bloodstock sales. He is, however, a man of cheerful and kindly disposition and impossible not to like. On hearing that I had bought his little Spanish bureau at the Northcote sale he described to me the manner of the opening of a small secret drawer which it contains. On reaching home I followed his instructions and discovered the drawer. It is opened by the turning of the last of one of the small gilt roses in

53

the running motif which forms a band round the base of the bureau above the legs. A half a turn of this rose, placed where no idle hand could carelessly wander, springs free a section of the ivory inlaid panelling dividing the four drawers in the front of the bureau. The cavity is commodious enough to hold a jewel case or a pair of pistols. Riark told me that his mother maintained that the Spanish nobleman for whom the bureau was originally made always kept therein his secret correspondence with the agents of Queen Elizabeth in whose pay he was for many years. This I doubt, but it is a pretty story which I shall pass on to my wife. The cavity is closed by pushing the panel back into position against its own spring which in turn causes the rosette to return to its original position.

If Parson John had passed on this secret to his wife—and he almost certainly would have done, thought John—then she had not passed it on to any of her children for he had never heard of the drawer before. But more immediately in his mind again from the reading of the entry was the bureau itself, now in the London flat in Sloane Street which he and his wife had used when his parliamentary duties meant that he had to be much of his time there when the House was sitting.

Leaning back in his chair, he realized that he really should do something about the flat. In the last six months he had not been near the place, seldom thought about it. His brother had a key which he had given him and sometimes used it. But not often he was sure. The Very Reverend had plenty of friends he could stay with. As for himself, he knew that he would have no further use for it. He had no intention of standing for Parliament again. The best thing to do was to take away any small pieces of furniture, pictures and like stuff which he would wish to bring to Darlock, and then let the place. That meant a trip to London to mark the items he wanted and then the making of arrangements for their removal and finally putting the flat in the hands of an agent. Until now he had almost shut the existence of the flat from his mind because it was there he had been told the news of Elizabeth's death.

That night he paused in front of the painting of Elizabeth and the memory of his agony was a shadow. Not normally a fanciful man, it seemed to him for a moment or two, as her eyes were held by his, that she knew and approved, and had been waiting for this moment.

The next morning he was not joined at breakfast by Carlo. He was amused, but not surprised. The youth had his points, but he was clearly not a stayer. However, later when he was in his study telephoning to make arrangements for a visit to London, Carlo came in and asked for the key of the gun room so that he could take some target practice. John said, 'I missed you at breakfast. And you missed Mrs Hurrell's kippers. She has a married sister who lives in Hull who sends them down now and then.'

Carlo shrugged his shoulders, and grimaced. 'My loss. But I took a sleeping pill and never surfaced.'

'Sleeping pill? What on earth for?'

'To stop thinking. Don't you ever get like that, sir—when you lie there and start thinking, and your thoughts begin to go round like a squirrel in a cage? The only thing to do then is to drug the little beast.'

'Sometimes, yes. But I don't take sleeping pills. They're not good for you. Certainly not for young men of your age. My advice to you is to cut them out. If you keep going hard through the day, you'll sleep like a log at night, believe me.'

For a moment Carlo eyed him, his smooth, brown overplump face flat, expressionless. Then his mouth moved with a flicker of amused triumph and he said, 'But that wouldn't solve anything, would it, sir? I'd still oversleep from fatigue. It's a puzzling world, isn't it?'

Before he could stop himself John laughed and then with a wave of his hand said, 'All right, Carlo, you win. Take the key and get out. That's just the kind of answer my brother Bob would have given.'

Carlo took the German Walther rifle and went down to the firing point. He put five consecutive shots into the centre of the painted circle and then refilled the magazine. While he was doing it a bird came over the edge of the combe and settled on the tip of a fir branch twenty yards to the left of the target stump.

Carlo, while he objected to killing animals and birds with a gun, saw no reason why he should not indulge his sense of mischief. He lay down and aimed at the branch six inches to the left of the bird's position. Mr Rook, he told himself, was going to have a surprise. He fired and hit the branch a few inches to the left of the bird which jumped into the air and flew off protesting.

Later, while Carlo was in the gun room after having cleaned the rifle, John Kingsford came in to find the young man standing in front of a framed map on the wall. The map consisted of large-scale Ordnance sheets which had been pasted together to cover an area of about ten miles in radius centring on Darlock House.

Carlo turned and said, 'What does this blue line mean, sir?'

The uneven blue line formed a rough equilateral triangle with Darlock House not far from the centre.

'That's the Kingsford Run. A sort of cross-country course. You'll see it cuts across roads, never follows them. Goes along streams, moor tracks and so on. Every Kingsford boy has had to do it since the old Parson's time.'

A little puzzled, Carlo asked, 'Do what, sir?'

'Make the run. You could choose your own time of year and you had to do it before your eighteenth birthday.' Seeing Carlo's puzzlement, John added, 'It's just a family tradition. No sense to it, except that. Or, maybe, it's like some tribal thing. A test of stamina which you had to pass before you could call yourself a man. All the way round is somewhere around twenty miles and precious little of it flat going. But until you'd done it . . . well, you weren't really a Kingsford.'

For a moment or two Carlo was silent. He should have expected it, of course. Tradition, proving yourself a man, a tribal rite . . . could you beat it? You were born a Kingsford boy and then the rituals began. Christened in the same church, handed over to a nanny, sent to the same public school as your father, became a country gentleman, learnt to shoot, hunt, fish and all the manly exercises, looked after the family farms or went into the church or politics . . . got married and eventually were buried from the same church whose icy font waters had marked the recognition of your immortal Christian spirit. And somewhere along the line you had to do the run. What bloody nonsense.

Disguising his real feelings, he said, 'Was there any time limit set for the run?'

'No.'

'Then I don't see the difficulty. You could take all day if you wanted.'

'Of course you could. But you didn't. Come and look at this.'

John moved down the room to the side of the window. Hanging against the wall was a long narrow piece of polished mahogany. Listed on it in gold lettering were the various names of Kingsford young men. Set against each name was a date and then out on its own a time in hours and minutes. The first name read:

Robert Henry Kingsford. 1896. December 3rd.
2 hours 47 minutes.

John went on, 'There's never been any question of

57

taking it easy. You were out to beat all the Kingsfords who'd done it before you.'

Carlo let his eye go down the list. He saw that this man standing by him had done it in two hours thirty-eight minutes. To his surprise he saw also that the record was held—in two hours twenty-seven minutes—by his brother, Robert, the Very Reverend. Remembering the comfortably fleshed figure of the churchman, he showed his surprise.

'I would never have thought that your brother . . .'

John laughed. 'Bob? At seventeen he was all skin and grief, and he could go like a greyhound.'

Before he could stop himself Carlo said, 'Has the event ever been open to outsiders?'

'Oh, yes. Now and again others had a crack at it. Of course, their names never went on the board. That's just for family. As a matter of fact, too, nobody has ever beaten Bob's time. Why? Do you fancy having a go?'

The man, Carlo guessed, might not have deliberately thought that he wanted to do any such thing. But in his voice he felt that he caught the edge, not of a challenge, but of a veiled certainty that he could be written off as wholly unfit for such a run. Without any impoliteness, somewhere deep in this man lay the solid stratum of rejection. Masking his own feelings, Carlo said casually, 'What do you think I'd get round in, sir?'

John hesitated. To be unkind was no part of his nature, but truth was something he never shirked, so he said frankly, 'In your present shape I doubt whether you've got a chance to beat four hours. It's hard country, uphill and downhill, boggy marsh ground, rocky ground . . . really tough going. I should forget it.'

Carlo smiled. 'I think you're right, sir. It's not my scene.'

As John left the gun room he was vaguely aware of a

sense of disappointment. The youth had spirit and he would have expected it to have been flushed into the open. Any normal chap would have taken up the challenge. He'd half-hoped for that from Carlo. He didn't know why, but he had.

In the gun room Carlo stared at the map. The route meant nothing to him. He had no picture of the ground which had to be covered. John Kingsford. Two hours thirty-eight minutes. Robert—two hours twenty-seven minutes. Well, good for the Church. He didn't suppose he had a hope of beating that. But it would be very, very satisfying to nick a couple of minutes off John Kingsford's time. Why not? If the Very Reverend could turn from a greyhound into the portly priest of today, there was no reason why overweight, over-smoking and drinking and pill-taking Carlo Graber couldn't thin down. Oh, hell—why should he bother? It was childish just to rise to that kind of bait, since bait he knew it was even if John Kingsford might not. No—it wasn't for him. The whole thing would be a bloody, egotistical bore. . . . Still, it might be interesting to walk around the course, to give himself something to do. He'd need a few maps.

Carlo went into the hall and looked up the number of Birdie's father in the local directory. When he rang the farm Birdie answered.

'Birdie—this is Carlo. What are you doing this afternoon?'

'Wash my hair, maybe. I dunno.'

'I could meet you at Portford Bridge, just after two. I've got to go to Barnstaple. Interest you?'

'I'd rather go to Exeter. Barnstaple's dead.'

Carlo grinned. Birdie was never going to be led.

He said, 'Why not . . . I only want to buy some maps.'

'Okay. Just after two.'

*   *   *

59

Over lunch, Grace said to Carlo, 'I'm going to London tomorrow for two or three days.'

'What for?' asked Carlo.

'Because I've been asked by Mr Kingsford if I would like a lift up and back. He's got to go up on some business.'

'Why on earth should he ask you? Anyway, you've only just got here.'

'There are things I can do. Also I don't find this place as interesting as you. I need a break now and then.'

'But you've only been here a few days.'

'I know. I suppose with time the intervals between breaks will grow longer. Anyway, you don't care whether I'm here or not. You can always amuse yourself.'

'That's true. Well, I don't envy you the trip. You'll be as bored as hell having to make conversation with him. You've about as much in common as you would have with a man from outer space. Anyway, that's your business. Do you mind if I have the car this afternoon?'

'No. But why don't you buy a car of your own? It's the first thing most young men want.'

'I'm not most young men.'

Grace smiled. 'What you mean is why should you buy one when you can always have mine. There's a good streak of Graber carefulness in you, Carlo.'

With mock dignity, but enjoying the double meaning beyond her comprehension, he said, 'My father was an upright, honest gentleman who knew the value of money and never wasted it on frivolities. I am merely trying to model myself on him.'

'Well, good for you, Carlo. Do I hear faint applause from on high?'

Carlo grinned. 'What you can hear from up there are jackdaws walking on the roof.'

'What do you know about jackdaws? You couldn't tell a hawk from a handsaw.'

'No? I've bought myself a book about British birds. Soon I shall know all our feathered friends around here. I intend to become a naturalist.'

Grace laughed. 'You're mad!'

Pouring himself another glass of wine Carlo said, 'Only —as was the character you've just quoted—when the wind is north-north-west. A common wind around here. When it's southerly then I know the difference—with a little help from my book—between a hawk and a heron. And I don't mind telling you that there are a lot of things I am going to learn here. Why on earth do you think I came?'

'I haven't the faintest idea. And what is more I haven't the faintest idea what you are talking about. But then I'm used to that when you are on your third glass of wine at lunch.'

Carlo gave a little giggle and raised the glass to her. 'Never mind, you may in time. Anyway, here's to the last time.'

He sipped at his wine.

'Now what on earth are you talking about?'

'Something you will applaud, dear aunt. While I am here, I have decided to give up smoking, sleeping pills, and all intoxicating drinks. This is my last glass of wine.'

'Good heavens—do you really mean that?'

'Absolutely. A man should respect the body God gave him.'

Grace, amused and puzzled—Carlo often had whims but they usually sprang from some good reason even if he seldom revealed it—put her hands together in mock prayer and said, 'Amen'.

Carlo said, 'I would like it if my new regime were kept as far as possible a little secret between the two of us.'

'If you wish it, Carlo, of course. Some time perhaps you will tell me really why you've decided on this. You're up to something . . . I only hope it's something healthy.'

Carlo finished his wine, drew out his cigarette case and said, 'Now for my last cigarette—and then I'm off.'

When Carlo had gone, Grace sat over her coffee thinking about him. She was quite used to his talking in a stilted pompous way at times. Usually it meant that he was in good spirits and, often, planning some mischief or private enjoyment. She was sure that there had been some positive reason behind his almost bullying her to come here. That reason, logical or idle, would make no difference to the way he implemented it. He would chase a girl or shop for days to find some particular type of tie or shirt he wanted with the same dedication. His desires and his mischief came in small or large portions, but the intensity of his concentration was always the same. She was quite certain that he was mad in the sense of being passionate. When there was something on his mind it occupied all his mind no matter what it was. He was far more like his mother than his father. When her sister had wanted something, then that something was the only thing in the world that existed for her. And how often had she chased after useless things, and useless men . . . and in the end she had been lucky to want and get someone as solid (and wealthy and understanding—for she had had a drink problem when they met) as Graber. Yes, mother and son were very alike even to the unconcealed delight they showed in other people not knowing what they were after, or possessed, or had done. So many things in life were a giggle; they allowed the giggle to escape from them, but never the secret cause which created it. Still, what did it matter what they were? There was deep down a goodness in Carlo which she acknowledged and respected. And, as long as she lived, she would cherish love and gratitude towards her sister who had without any bidding come to her when she needed help and had given it to her freely and with great bounty. . . .

Chapter Four

JOHN KINGSFORD and Grace left for London soon after breakfast. When they were gone, Carlo took the maps he had bought at Exeter into the gun room. They were Ordnance Survey maps, the scale roughly two-and-a-half inches to the mile. Sitting at the table Carlo marked out the route of the Kingsford Run in pencil. When he had done this, he split the route into sections of two- or three-mile lengths. These sections, beginning at the start point —which was a bridge on the river Barle about three miles north-east of Darlock House on the Exford road—he intended to walk separately in the following days in order to make a survey of the route. Later, he decided, when his training programme was under way he would run the route in larger sections separately and—making allowances for the slower pace of the whole run—get some idea of what would be required from him in order to beat John Kingsford's time.

Now and again as he worked, he would sit back in his chair and stare dreamily at the map, relishing the pleasure of having this new project to occupy him. He couldn't pretend that it had anything to do directly with his real purpose in coming here. Curiosity was largely the basis of that.

Curiosity was enough, too. Give it time and it produced unexpected off-shoots. Like this thing now. Anyway, he was a Kingsford, although no one knew it. So he must act like a Kingsford . . . purely for his own satisfaction. He would do the Run and beat John Kingsford's time.

The idea, once in his mind, was not to be rejected.

The whole Darlock thing, of course—as Grace had unknowingly sensed—was a piece of idle mischief, a mad ploy which had slowly grown in importance. Largely, he knew, because nothing else had cropped up, since the idea had first come to him, to supplant it. It was something to do. It passed the time. But now this Run business had arisen. It was a challenge to which his nature responded with powerful delight. Irresistible delight, otherwise—with all the money he wanted, and much more to come when he was eighteen, and no inclination to devote himself to any particular useful work or profession—he could have gone on moving idly and luxuriously along the pleasant route which he had followed with his mother. When it was all over, he would find for Grace some outrageously expensive present to make up for dragging her down here. Not that she would be impressed, but it would make things right with himself towards her. Anyway whether a present pleased or touched a woman was unimportant. It did something much more fundamental. It marked the giver as a suppliant for favour or forgiveness, either of which—whether granted or not—produced an illusion of power in the woman. And once the illusion had been created it needed only guile and intelligence to exploit it. Birdie, yesterday, had been wearing the swallow brooch.

Birdie was still sizing him up, he knew. She had to be because she knew nothing about him or his intentions with any certainty. She was content to depend on convention and keep a weather eye open for the first of any actions which she would recognize from experience and so classify him. During all the time they had spent together—and they had not got back to Portford Bridge until eight

64

o'clock—he had neither said nor done anything which was exceptionable. He had got his maps, taken her to the cinema, and then bought her a very ordinary meal in an undistinguished café. She did not smoke, so—he imagined —had not noticed that he no longer used cigarettes. She had had a glass of white wine with her meal, and he had taken a Coca-Cola, without any comment from her. Birdie he liked because of her even acceptance of things. Birdie he liked because one day he wanted to make love to her. Birdie would know this, and be a little puzzled because he seemed in no hurry to make any preliminary advances. Most young men would. Rush their fences, as John Kingsford would say. He was in no hurry because there was a higher, subtler form of pleasure to be gained from his own way of approach. When he had drawn up at Portford Bridge and they had sat for a few minutes in the car before he took out her scooter she had reached out for the radio set, turning it on, and sliding nearer him across the wide bench seat. Not touching him. Waiting, he knew, for a corresponding movement from him to bring them together. She would know then whether to rebuff or encourage him. To baffle her, he had taken her hand, raised it to his lips and kissed it, saying, 'Thank you for a nice time.'

Without embarrassment, Birdie had said, 'I say. That's very Frenchy sort of stuff. But nice—after the all-in-wrestling stuff most chaps go for.'

'I'm not most chaps. I have my own way of doing things.'

'Yes, that's true. That's what makes it interesting. But underneath it all adds up to the same thing, doesn't it? But don't get me wrong, Carlo. I like it. It's nice to see someone doing their own thing. Not just copyin' others. . . .'

He could hear her saying it now, the burr and roll of her accent giving a rich tone to her words, marking them with their own gentle magic and earthiness . . . the stuff of the moor around them, the farm where she lived . . . cows slopping in across the yard for milking; the herded, ungainly sheep being rounded up by lean black and white dogs . . . the simple, close-to-the-land life. But Birdie, he sensed, was far from simple. She was waiting, and watching him and whatever he did he guessed she would match, and whatever she gave would have to be a true gift because there was no doubt in her mind of her own value.

He locked the gun room and took the key back to the study. This was the first time he had had the chance to be in the room alone and with time on his hands. For the moment he was content to give it only a general survey. John Kingsford and Grace would not be back from London for two or three days. The staff here, since they were early risers, went to bed soon after ten and slept at the back of the house. He was going to have all the time in the world to poke around. He looked at the curtains of the one big mullioned window. They were brown velvet and when drawn would let out no light. But he would check that some time from the outside.

The desk was flat-topped with a morocco leather inlay. On the desk was a leather-covered looseleaf book. Before John had left that morning he had told him that he was leaving the Parson John diary out for him to read, but had asked him not to take it out of the study. Well, that was convenient because it gave him a reason to be in the place whenever he wanted. He turned a few pages, just glancing, and saw that Kingsford's handwriting was in a fine, precise renaissance style. Something which he would not have expected.

A sentence or two came up under his eyes:

> . . . and was told by the landlord that the body of the Hawkins boy was recovered from under the rock fall this forenoon. He is to

be buried at Radworthy and I shall take the service since for the next two weeks I have agreed to oblige the rector who is away to Exeter on a diocesan conference and then goes to Seaton for a week. It was less than a month since that the boy and his father were up at Darlock slating the new roof to the stables. . . .

Woke this night in a fine sweat from a bad dream. The Devil seizes any chink to invade our sensibilities. Read the Holy book until the dawn came . . .

Quick sympathy for the Parson made him smile. Where dreams were concerned, bad ones, he was himself a connoisseur. Putting them down to the Devil was a new idea of some comfort.

. . . and from Winsford a big field saw a stag found in the Quarme valley, near Wheddon Cross, which went by Hawkridge to West Molland and was taken at Garliford, near Bish Mill— a twelve and a half mile point.

As Carlo began to try the desk drawers, he had a picture of the stag and the hounds at the kill. Death and burial services. Killing was not difficult given a good reason, but to kill for sport was something he knew he could never do. All the drawers were locked, but he knew they would give no trouble when he wanted to open them. There was nothing else of much interest in the place; a glass-fronted bookcase filled mostly with sporting books and bound volumes of *Punch*, some framed photographs of father, mother, relatives, he guessed, but none of the woman of the portrait in the hall, a hunting picture over the fireplace, and two leather armchairs and a settee, all well worn as was the carpet on the floor.

As he was going out of the room Vera came in, almost bumping into him. She carried a duster in one hand and a long bamboo pole, feather-topped for ceiling dust and

67

cobwebs in the other. On the spur of the moment, without reason except maybe because of the high-spirited mood he was caught in, Carlo pressed her quickly back against the study wall, holding her to it by his spread hands on her large breasts which he moulded and worked briefly as though he were kneading plasticine. Before she could protest or move he was gone, closing the door behind him, chuckling to himself.

*   *   *

When Grace had been asked by John Kingsford if she would like to go to London with him her first instinct had been to excuse herself simply on the grounds—which she could not of course reveal—that, apart from having only recently arrived at Darlock House from London, the thought of being confined in a car with him for hours made no appeal to her. In the interval of reflection as he was making the offer, knowing that she could not be truthful and lacking any immediate excuse, she had been struck by the idea, springing from something almost distantly pleading in his manner, that he wished to escape from his own company during the long hours of the drive. So, purely from half-risen sympathy and a natural kindness, she had said she would be delighted. And then, in the refuge of her own room, she had wondered why the devil she had done so. She had nothing to offer him, was indeed a little irritated by him, and critical of the grief he stubbornly nursed. The uselessness of over-nurturing this indulgence was only too well known in her own personal experience. *You'll be as bored as hell having to make conversation with him.* Carlo's words. And her own thinking. Bored as hell. Awkward silences. Getting into the car with him, she had mentally braced herself for the ordeal, cursing herself for being trapped.

But—almost as though leaving Darlock House behind had liberated him—he had surprised her by his changed manner. He made conversation easily, and demanded little of her. The intervals when there were silences, long or short, between them held no embarrassment, no sense of the other searching agonizingly for some fresh comment or issue to kill the void. He could tell a good story and he had many to tell and quite a few of them were about parliamentary and Government figures and people in London Society. She found herself laughing and sometimes pressing for more details. Being little more than solitary herself she enjoyed gossip about others, and liked, however vicariously, to be drawn into coteries and scenes which her nature would have made her, given the chance, probably eschew. John Kingsford of Darlock was one man; the John Kingsford who had been a Member of Parliament for many years was another. And one capable of surprising her further.

Just before they reached London, he had said, and she liked the deliberate, slightly old-fashioned courtesy of his manner, 'I'd be guilty of accepting a favour without grace if I didn't say how much I appreciate your company. I was appalled at myself when I asked you. You must have groaned at the thought of five or more hours stuck with me. I was quite prepared for you to make some excuse. That you didn't was a relief. I've had far too much of my own company lately. Been the complete brooder. I don't have to tell you why. But I do have to say thank you.'

'What made you decide to come out from under the shadow?'

'I don't know. Time, perhaps. Or just the resurgence of common sense. I suppose some people take longer than others. The last time I did this drive was with my wife. I was a coward to the extent that I felt I needed company to face it again. It's odd really, but I think if you and Carlo

69

hadn't come to Darlock I might—as you said—still be under the shadow.'

'Well, you've said your thank-you very nicely. And I can tell you that I've enjoyed myself.'

'Good. What are you going to do with yourself while you're in town?'

'I've got some old friends to look up, and various things to do.'

'I think I'll have to be up three nights. Perhaps I can phone your hotel and you'd have dinner with me on one of them?'

They had dinner together on the third night. He took her first of all to have some drinks with old friends of his at a flat in Knightsbridge, and after that to Quaglino's where they ate and danced. Lying in bed that night Grace had the wry, slightly amused feeling, familiar to her from the early days when Graber and her sister, Margaret, had come to her rescue, carrying her off into a new world, that she had been cosseted and steered gently through a new experience; the kindness she had met from everyone marking, rather than disguising, their clear recognition that she did not belong to their world. At the Knightsbridge house the people and the talk had all been political. Every other man seemed to be, or have been, a Member of Parliament. There were two Cabinet members and various junior ministers, a couple of well known political journalists, and a Frenchman who was from the Common Market Commission who, seeing her adrift at one stage, had come and made up to her with a look in his eyes which she instantly recognized and for the time being welcomed because it gave her a little oasis of known ground as shelter in the desert of Westminster and constituency talk. The women, two of whom were also Members of Parliament, had a bright, overfriendly hardness and glitter of looks or speech which made her even more of an alien. When they discovered that she was not even so much as an M.P.'s wife they shifted the focus of their talk with friendly ease and then soon drifted away. To her surprise (even after knowing the easy way John Kingsford had talked in the car) she saw that he moved through this milieu with the same chameleon shifts of demeanour as the rest. There was, she realized, more to him than the man she knew at Darlock House.

Over coffee and brandy after dinner, she said to him, 'Do you want to go back into the political world?'

He eyed her for a moment and then smiled. 'You weren't very comfortable with that lot? I apologize. I didn't know it was going to be that kind of crush.'

'Oh, no. I enjoyed it. You know, a different set of tribal rites. Not that I would want to be a member of the tribe. They all seemed . . . well, like the way jockeys ride round before going in the starting gate, colourful, tensed and anxious, their minds full of strategies and calculations. Winning is everything. But I suppose that's the major part of political life, isn't it—ambition?'

He laughed. 'You don't miss much. Yes, ambition figures large for most of them. But that's not the full story. Men and women are none the worse for ambition, so long as they don't lose sight of the real reason which took them into politics.'

'To do some good? To build Jerusalem in England's green and pleasant land? Idealism didn't show much in Knightsbridge, or am I wrong?'

Pleasantly, he said, 'I think you're wrong and wrongly cynical. The idealism has to be tempered by common sense. If a horse runs away with the jockey it doesn't win. Power is the first principle. Get that—then you have the weapon in your hands, the authority to do something about your ideals. Never as much as you would like, of course. It would be wrong of me, though, not to admit that some of them are just after the power and the position—but that applies all down the line, bank managers, managing directors, generals, admirals, bishops—even my Very Reverend brother wouldn't dispute that—and so on. The interesting thing about power and position though is, once men get it, they often can't help using it for good. Power imposes a sort of morality of its own . . .' He trailed off. 'Sorry, I didn't mean to make a speech.'

'Why not. It brings us back to my original question. Do you want to go back?'

He lit a cigar, taking his time, watching her. Then he said, 'There was a time recently when I thought not. I thought the whole scene would be too full of memories which I wouldn't want kept alive. But now I'm not so sure. I've got to do something. Darlock and the work on the various properties isn't enough. Our agent really runs it. I just get in his way now, trying to be busy. Also it's something that——'

He reached for his brandy and drank and Grace knew that for a moment the move was to mask his face.

She said quietly, 'Your wife would have wanted it, wouldn't she?'

He lowered his glass, eyed her for a moment, firm lipped, considering, she knew well, the propriety of the remark. Then he said easily, 'Yes, she would.'

For a moment or two Grace thought that whatever he would say next would be deliberately designed to move the talk away from all memory of his wife; an easy, well-mannered change without any shade of rebuke or feeling towards her for raising it. To her surprise—and now she was becoming accustomed to being surprised by him—he said, 'You say things which a little while ago would have . . . well, been unwelcome.' He smiled. 'But not now. Yes, she would have wanted it. When I lost my seat, she took it for no more than it need be, a setback. She was already tackling that when . . . the accident happened. She was coming back from a visit to her brother-in-law in Norfolk when it happened. Sir Charles Read, apart from being what he is, is also the uncrowned king at Central Office. He could have fixed me the nomination for the first safe by-election that came up. Or rather Elizabeth was determined to twist his arm until he did. Probably had done. I never asked.' He began to rise. 'But don't let's talk any more about politics. Would you care to dance? Though I must warn you, the Kingsfords have never been renowned for ballroom grace.'

Lying in bed now, thinking over the evening, Grace's thoughts were far less with John Kingsford than his wife Elizabeth. It had been a surprise to her to learn that her brother-in-law had been Sir Charles Read. The Right Honourable Sir Charles Read, Secretary of State for Foreign and Commonwealth Affairs. Well, that fitted. She could see the woman whose portrait hung in the hall at Darlock moving easily among the people she had met that night. Behind many of the men there stood women like Elizabeth Kingsford. Often they were the truly ambitious ones, the drivers, the managers and the manipulators. Although she had never known the woman she knew she would have disliked her. Did that come from envy? A wish, perhaps, that in her own life there had been some compulsion to serve and deploy skills in the service of a man? Elizabeth Kingsford had been harder, infinitely more single-minded in ambition, than John Kingsford. And it would happen of course that her brother-in-law was the Foreign Secretary. Out of memory from a thousand newspaper and television images came the tall, lean hand-some figure. That carelessly swept back once fair hair now magisterially whitening, the easy style with which he carried his clothes, the deep-marked face, grave in crisis, smiling, almost boyish in triumph. Eton, Balliol and the

Guards, bearing senatorially the burdens of State and the world's grim problems. How could she have married unambitious John Kingsford, basically a solid, undistinguished country squire? Disappointment had to lurk there. But then he had probably shown early promise in political life. Yes . . . that was probably it. Elizabeth had picked him, hitched her star to his, and when his star had waned, had compounded her mistake and gone on still driving him forward ruthlessly . . . until her car had hit an icy patch on the Thetford road and had spun her off into oblivion.

*　　　　*　　　　*

While Grace and John Kingsford were away, Carlo had been enjoying himself. On the first day he had walked the first leg of the Kingsford Run. This was the side of the triangle running roughly north-west from the starting point where Landacre bridge on the Exford road crossed the river Barle. It was a seven-mile or more stretch of country that ran first of all up the Barle to the junction with Sherndon Water. Now, places that had been names on the map became real. The high rounded slope of Ferny Ball towered to his right hand across the Sherndon Water, dying away into softer, easier slopes past the derelict farmhouse of Lower Sherndon. He caught glimpses of Darlock House as he turned northwards where the Kingsford Water came twisting down the valley below Long Holcombe and Hangley Cleave. Following the water up, he had come to the end of the first leg at an old mine and a quarry alongside the ridge road, not far from the spot where he had first set eyes on John Kingsford. He did the walk a second time on the next day, familiar with it now and spending more time surveying the possible routes. The rules of the Run were that you started at Landacre bridge and touched no recognizable road until you reached (to cross) the ridge road at the old mine. The easier route was to stick to the river and water valleys, but this was by no means the more direct. A hard line up the flanks of Ferny Ball and over the top of the hill would bring him out well up the Kingsford Water valley. He sat in the car at Landacre bridge for a long time considering this. It was a route that called for strong legs and good wind.

For a moment he wondered why he was bothering with the idea of the Run at all and then, at this sign of weakness, became angry with himself. He was going to do it and he would beat John Kingsford's time. Tomorrow morning he would be out in track suit and running shoes at six o'clock getting into condition along the ridge road above Darlock House. He went into Barnstaple that afternoon and kitted himself out.

The next morning he began his training, taking no pleasure in it except the strengthening of his determination to do the Run and beat John Kingsford's time. Pleasure could wait on that moment. As he ran, to take his mind off the self-imposed labour, he kept his eyes open. He was beginning to learn many things which were new to him about this country and the people and creatures which inhabited it. He knew now that the bird at which he had shot had not been a rook, but a crow. From his bird book he had learned the difference between ravens and crows, knew that the birds he had seen flirting about the water courses were grey wagtails, and had brought a look of surprise into Birdie's eyes when she had come with him to Barnstaple and he had told her that while he was at Landacre bridge he had seen a big fish jump and wondered what it was.

' 'Twas a salmon, Carlo. They're running now, all the way up from the sea, right up to the small streams to

75

spawn. The old big-jawed cocks and the hens all on the way back to where they were born.'

'You mean salmon are born in rivers?'

She laughed. 'Don't be daft, Carlo. You knew that. You're pulling my leg.'

But he was not, and because he acquired knowledge easily and was proud of it, he felt cheated by this simple gap in his learning. He went to Barnstaple by himself the next day and bought more books, one of them a history of Exmoor.

He filled his days easily and in parts strenuously. But during the evenings, he really came into his own. The house was his to possess this side of the staff quarters with all the freedom he could wish for after he had had his dinner. In two nights there were few places he had not explored and no drawer or cupboard which excited his curiosity which he had not opened. The locked steel cabinet in the gun room had opened easily with one of the keys from his skeleton bunch. He smiled as he saw the pair of Purdeys and the Holland and Hollands. John Kingsford would never let him handle one of those. The only other gun in the cabinet, he noticed, was a rifle with telescopic sights, a nice looking weapon, just the thing for deer-stalking in Scotland. . . . Every Kingsford would do that, of course—pheasant, grouse, deer and, not too far in the past, tiger, elephant and rhino; they loved killing things.

He went through every drawer in John Kingsford's desk and read all his papers and letters, though they revealed little more of the man than he had already known or guessed. The only place in the study which was still closed to him was the wall safe to one side of the large mullioned windows. It was an old-fashioned safe, one which called for a much larger key than John Kingsford was likely to carry about his person. Somewhere—and reasonably handy—Carlo knew that the key would be hidden but so far—and he gave the man tribute for his cleverness—he had not been able to find the safe key. He promised himself he would. To use one of his skeleton keys would be too easy. What one Kingsford could hide another could find.

But, more important, while there had never been any doubt in his mind of the truth of his mother's tipsy words, he now found incontrovertible proof of it from a quite unexpected source.

Each evening after his explorations he rounded off his day by reading Parson John's diary. These were periods when his hand itched sometimes to move to the ritual of lighting a cigarette. He ached sometimes for the feel of a glass, smooth under his fingers. Palate and sweet habit gently plagued him. But he resisted: picturing the steep slopes of Ferny Ball, the long, tummocky stretches of marsh and stony gullies of the Kingsford Water to be taken without let, blood and bellows pumping, legs thrusting, and two hours thirty-eight minutes to be beaten. Not to prove he was a Kingsford. But because all Kingsford youths had done it, and his turn was due and, no matter what comfortably lodged contempt for senseless family traditions he harboured, this happened to be his family and the stupidity of their tradition belonged to him and was not to be resisted. If birth marked you—then you had to accept it. And he had been marked as a Kingsford more surely than any words of his mother had done. Parson John told him that. It was a moment he knew he would never forget: a page of John Kingsford's neat italianate script transcribed the entry for the 20th March, 1872.

3 Sunday in Lent, 20 March
Started in darkness for Dulverton where I was to take the service. There was ice on the tracks and the mare was none too happy. When the sun came up I could see yesterday's snow still capping the top of Dunkery Beacon. Coming down from Hawk-

ridge by Great Birchwood Cleave a peregrine falcon stooped at a black cock which had unwisely got up from the heather. The cock did a head over heels tumble back to safety and the falcon passed so closely that I could feel the wind of her going against my face. I have never been so close to one of these birds alive before. They do much damage to the stock of the pigeon breeders in Barnstaple.

Took breakfast at the Lamb and was served by the landlord's wife, a pretty, full-bodied woman whose growing plumpness, I fancy, will call for the baptizing of another Dulverton citizen before the year is much older. Having time still to spare, I called for paper and wrote to William. (His younger brother, married and with a medical practice in Plymouth, J.K.) *It is just over a year since he was wed to Sarah Campion, the youngest daughter of Admiral Campion at the Plymouth station and last week their first child, a boy, was born. William is much pleased that the boy carries the Kingsford mark on his right hip, the same mole-coloured pear-shaped blemish which I bear myself and which over the generations has been common amongst many Kingsford males.* (I have such a mark. J.K.) *I remember my grandfather telling me that there was a family legend that some male of the family would always carry this mark as a sign and reminder of a great sin done by one of our distant ancestors. Whether this is true or not I do not know. What is more to the point, if from human transgression it did spring, is the curious pride all Kingsford men so touched have taken in this mark. The boy is to be named Henry William and is to be baptized by the Naval Chaplain under the Admiral's command.*

Preached on Acts 7:48. Howbeit the most High dwelleth not in temples made by hands. *Did this with much vigour and, I hope, with some profit to the good Dulverton people.*

Dropping the diary on the desk Carlo sat and stared into space. He bore exactly the same mark on his right hip, a mark so long familiar that he scarcely thought about it. From what sin in the distant past did the mark come? Pure nonsense, of course. But how like the Kingsfords to believe it, and to take a pride in it.

On the following two evenings when he sat at the desk to go on with his reading of the diary, he always turned back to that entry at some time and read it through.

When he finished reading the diary on his third evening, he felt that Parson John had become for him a far more vivid and lively figure than John Kingsford. He could picture him, this still young, virile man, riding and preaching around the countryside, and then at night adopting a literary style which made him sound miles older than he was. This was probably deliberate, Carlo thought. Anticipating a persona that Parson John knew would come to him over the years, the character which he deemed suitable for his diaries—but everywhere the young, vigorous manhood showed through. Just as his eyes never missed the passage of a bird or failed to take delight in the hares' mad March capers, so his eyes lingered on any pretty face or well-turned ankle peeping from under a long skirt at a vicarage party or soirée at Castle Hill with the gentry. It was clear to him, too, that Parson John had been very much taken with his Hannah Darch. More, he was certain, had happened between them than was confided to his diary. He wondered if John Kingsford had felt this when transcribing? He would have to be an uptight dolt not to pick it up. Probably was. *Honi soit qui mal y pense*, but not surely in a passage which read—

. . . came back across country from Sherracombe Cross, much pleased with my business done at Whitefield Farm over this vexing matter of agister and grazing rights. Crossing the ford at Deercombe corner discovered Hannah Darch under the old oak on the high bank above the stream. She was gathering dillies and greeted me with her arms full of these golden blooms, the soft

*Spring zephyrs making free with her raven hair, and a wel-
coming lustre kindling in her eyes as she came to me. Dis-
mounted and walked with her as far as the old linhay at Beatley
where I tied the mare and we went inside to see the new lambs
which she has taken in charge since old Darch's sickness. A
sudden shower prolonged my visit and so conspired to a greater
acquaintanceship between us. She is a fine creature of surprising
sensibility and has a ready wit and a frolicksome manner which
pleased me very much. Of higher birth she could have taken her
place in the best drawing rooms in the land with a grace and
distinction to match her beauty.*

What exactly, Carlo wondered, had happened in the
linhay? He had a feeling that the frolicking had not been
confined to the lambs, and that that night the Devil—
though Parson John did not record it—had invaded his
dreams once more.

*   *   *

That night, after leaving Grace Lindsay at her hotel, John
Kingsford sat in the drawing-room of the Sloane Street
flat, drinking a nightcap. He had made arrangements for
an agent to let the flat, and also for certain pieces of
furniture—now marked with red labels—to be sent down
to Darlock House.

This was, he acknowledged, the end of a period. Now, he
could face his future calmly, plan and begin to organize. It
was a decision, too, which he felt Elizabeth would have
approved. Forthright and direct (ambitious, yes, if one
were frank) she had no time for the licking of wounds or
self-commiseration in defeat. She had died, he was certain
of this now, coming back from a mission directed entirely
towards providing him with a new start.

As he thought this, his eyes fell on the small Spanish

bureau which so many years before had been bought by Parson John to be presented—when the lady appeared on the scene—to his wife. He smiled to himself. As it had happened the parson had had only eighteen months to wait. Thinking this, he remembered too, the parson's comment about the secret drawer. He finished his whisky and went across to the bureau. It had been a favourite piece of Elizabeth's and she had insisted on having it in the flat. He had a picture of her now, sitting at it, fair head bowed, working at constituency correspondence, shaking her head over bills and sometimes turning to him to question some invitation. Only now, he realized, could he appreciate how much she had done for him and how much she had been behind him. He must, he supposed, have been somewhat of a disappointment to her, though no criticism was ever spoken, no shadow of her private thoughts ever allowed to cloud their love.

He squatted down before the piece and began to search along the ornamental gilded metal edge at the bottom of the bureau for the rosette of which Parson John had spoken. He found it and gave the raised boss of the flower a half turn clockwise. Part of the ivory inlaid panelling between the top drawers sprang out, the edge of the small door striking his face lightly. He stood up, rubbing his cheek, and then bent to look into the cavity.

Inside were two very thick piles of letters, still in their cut envelopes. Each bundle was tied together with a length of red ribbon. He pulled the letters out and looked at the inscription on the top envelope of one of the bundles. The letter had been addressed to his wife. He flipped through the two bundles and saw that all the letters were to her, some directed to the flat address and some to Darlock House.

He carried them back to his chair and poured himself another whisky. How like Elizabeth, he thought, to have

81

found the drawer (or, perhaps, was it a female Kingsford secret, passed long ago to his mother and then from her to Elizabeth?) and said nothing to him. She had liked to have her little secrets, acknowledged their existence openly sometimes to tease him. He wondered momentarily whether even now he had the right to invade that secrecy and read her correspondence. He decided that he had, and slipped the top letter from its bundle.

He read it. It was as though he had picked up a favourite book to read only to find that the casual page chosen was written in a foreign language. As he might have done with the book, half-closing it to verify the name on the cover, he took the envelope to verify the inscription. There was no doubt that it had been addressed to his wife.

He read the letter again, and this time there was no place for incomprehension, only a shocked bewilderment, a numbness so absolute that it gave no hold either to dismay or anger.

As a man in a dream might comport himself through a fantasy touched vividly with horrors, and yet himself remain untouched, he read through six or seven letters and then, at this point, pain flared into life through his numbness.

He threw the letters from him across the room, though even in that moment when his mind was one violent rage of savage anger, he knew that later he would retrieve them and read them all. He stood up and with a careless hand lifted his whisky glass and drank clumsily, the spirit running loose across his chin, searching for some action to release the fury that mounted in his mind. He drained the glass and threw it across the room where it shattered against the front of the bureau.

The noise of the breaking glass and the bite of raw spirit against his throat stilled him. After a moment or two he picked up the nearest bundle of letters and sat down. Somewhere at the back of his mind a John Kingsford, unknown to him until now, was saying evenly, 'Sit down and read them. There is no escape. These are letters from another man to your wife.'

He read all the letters. The bitter taste of treachery and unfaithfulness was undulled, but in his mind and emotions were locked in icy suspension. Knowledge that it had happened, and had been happening for almost all the years of his happiness with Elizabeth, was the only wound. The frank dwelling on love-making past and hopefully to come, the bawdiness followed by the gaucheries of sentimental passages, the references to himself now derisive, now critical to the point of pity, touched him only with a deepening of pain from his wound. Although only the man spoke in these pages, he knew that the letters which Elizabeth had written must have matched them.

He finished them, tidied the envelopes with their returned pages, bundled them and with steady hands knotted the faded red ribbons around them. The room was still, and there was a deeper stillness in himself and he was grateful for it. He knew the printed address at the head of the letters, knew the man who had signed them . . . and he knew, too, that he was going to kill the man; that this was the sole ambition he could now harbour. Until it was done, nothing else could hold importance in his mind.

*　　　　*　　　　*

That night Carlo found the key to the big, old-fashioned wall safe. He found it, not through any cleverness of his own, but by accident. Though—pondering on it—he had to admit it was an accident caused by Birdie.

Wandering around the study before going to bed he paused in front of the big glass-fronted bookcase and his eye was caught by a title in a row of brown-coloured volumes of The Badminton Library—*Fishing—Salmon & Trout. H. Cholmondeley-Pennell*. Remembering Birdie's surprise that he had not known anything about the life history of salmon he took the volume out and idly opened it. As he did so, a large key fell from its middle.

Chapter Five

THERE WAS a westerly gale blowing as Carlo did his morning training run. It had been roaring around the house, slashing sudden bursts of rain at the windows when he had been awakened by his alarm clock to a morning of sepia gloom. The effort to get out of bed and honour his schedule had been a test of his resolution. But now he was out, although his track suit was already soaking and giving him extra weight to carry, he was, to his surprise, enjoying himself with a perverse pleasure.

This, he told himself, was not Carlo Graber running. This was a creation of Carlo Graber's, still in the making, but coming along nicely. And even more surprising, he was aware now that he was far more conscious of the world around him than he ever remembered being. In the cities and towns, the playgrounds and rich society centres in which he had passed his time before, not only his, but other people's eyes were half shut. There was no need to look because one knew what was there and had seen it all before.

Now, though his body ached and his legs felt like lead, he found that he had a freedom of vision and spirit which was exhilarating. He watched a pair of pigeons go down the moor like meteors with the wind, and for a moment their speed and fine control were elements which he knew in his own flesh and blood. The wind, dead in his face from the not far distant sea, palmed its boisterous strength against him, slowed him, and now and then tipped his balance awry with a sudden blow from an unexpected quarter.

He liked, too, the angry, dark scud of the low flying clouds, streaming like a grey-blue flood across the sky. Ten yards ahead of him a weasel slipped from the grass verge to cross the road, saw him, and turned back into the cover of the dead bracken. Was it a weasel or a stoat? He didn't know. One or the other. On the high ridge not long before he reached his turning point he saw the white buildings of Emmett's Grange away near the top of Kingsford Water suddenly shrouded in a swaying curtain of rain and knew that in a few moments it would be swinging into his face. This, he thought, was the country of the Kingsford men. In an impulsive spurt of derision, he shouted aloud into the gale, 'Ra! Ra!' Mocking his own thoughts, mocking his own mockery of the Kingsford traditions. Parson John had ridden this road on the brown mare, and Parson John's son at seventeen had been the first to come panting up the long valley below Emmett's Grange and Wintershead Farm on the Kingsford Run. . . .

Exhilaration of body and spirit burst in Carlo, possessing him with a fury he had no desire to understand or deny. He only knew that never in his life before had there been anything—neither drink, nor woman, nor drugs—which had given him this lift. He did what he mocked, he was moved to a love of all he despised, and his eyes were delighted with the wildness around him and the men and creatures it harboured though there was no wish in him to claim open place or kinship with any part or person here. His mother had bedded with John Kingsford, no doubt in a snatched half-hour of tipsy lust or bravado, and he, Carlo Graber, bore the mark on his right hip as testimony and indelible witness to that clumsy and hasty coupling, a copulation without ceremony or love. In sudden anger he spat into the wind and the wind flung his spittle back into his face, and he began to giggle with the power of the unnamable delight within him.

When he turned back along the ridge road, the wind came with him, lifting him, giving a new speed to his feet so that he felt he had need only to flap his arms and he would take off, go swinging upwards to join the pair of buzzards that wheeled and spiralled in gale-play over the flat shoulder of Long Holcombe.

Half an hour later, served breakfast by Mrs Hurrell because it was Vera's day off, he ate eggs and bacon and toast and Darlock damson jam as though he had not seen food for a week.

When it was done, he killed the desire for a cigarette, and sat with his coffee and decided that it would be at least two months before he would be really fit to make the run, and that he would need a day of hard frost to do it. Days of hard frost if possible to harden the soggy marsh ground and the spongy sheep-bitten pastures . . . some time, he thought, in late December. He would have to be nice to Grace to keep her going here until then . . . dear Grace, for whom he had nothing but respect and love. One day, when he had worked through this Kingsford business, washed it from his mind, he must concentrate on her, find something, someone for her, give her back something of the patience and indulgence she had given—and had to go on giving for a while yet—to him. He grinned to himself. He really would take her in hand. Ah . . . so much to do, so much of pleasure! Kingsford and his stupid run, Kingsford to whom he would one day name the truth; and Birdie, sweet, sometimes stupid, but always unpredictable Birdie, maybe he would marry her and make her eyes pop with all he could offer, and then Grace, and then . . . and then. . . . He sighed and stretched arms and legs against the fierce sensation all the pleasures the future promised.

That afternoon Carlo left his car on the ridge road

beyond Two Barrows and walked the second leg of the run. It was the easiest of the legs, running downhill from Fyldon Common to the head of a small combe where a stream rose that eventually flowed into the river Mole some miles farther south. It was an easy walk down but a long slog back to the ridge road to regain his car. But it held one point of interest for him. The stream which ran down the combe—he had seen from his map—was cut not far from its source by the ford at Deercombe corner. The valley here was steep, and grown wild with fir growths and bracken and bramble beds. A strong head of flood run-off from the recent rains had put the ford under two feet of water. Below the ford the water course was steep banked and the bed strewn with rocks and boulders.

To his surprise he saw that the old oak which Parson John had mentioned on his meeting with Hannah Darch was still there, the top riven out by age or a lightning strike. Of the daffodils which grew on the sharp fall below the oak there was no sign, though it was easy for him to recreate them in fancy . . . Parson John splashing through the ford on his mare, and Hannah Darch poised on the steep bank, her arms full of blooms, her eyes—he was sure—watching the approaching horseman with far more than casual interest. The world was full of Hannah Darches. He wondered whether Parson John had thanked the good Lord for that when he had been marooned in the linhay with her? It pleased him, too, to note that a little way to the east, along the old road to Buttery Farm that Beatley linhay was marked on the map. For a moment or two he was tempted to make a diversion, and then decided against it. A possible romance, long dead, could only be of sentimental interest. The Run was his real business.

When he got back to Darlock House, with the light going fast, it was to find that Grace and John Kingsford had arrived from London.

88

He found Grace in their sitting-room, kissed and greeted her and asked, 'Well, did you enjoy yourself?'

'Very much, yes.'

'And the drive up and down? Did he bore the pants off you?'

'Surprisingly, no. You'll be interested to know that he was very good company. Also he took me out to dinner last night—and I enjoyed that. You must be pleased that your aunt had a very good time.'

Carlo grinned. 'Delighted.'

'And what have you been doing? Are you still non-smoking and non-drinking? Or was that just a flash in the pan?'

'Decidedly not. I also now take a training run early every morning.'

'You what?' Grace laughed. 'Oh, no. I don't believe it.'

'There are moments when I can't either. But it's true. I only mention it because you might hear me stumbling around in the early morning.'

'But what on earth for? Come on, Carlo—what *are* you up to?'

Carlo smiled. 'It's very simple. I'm going through my Spartan period. Mens sana in corpore sano.'

'Rubbish.'

'Not while it lasts. I'm very serious about it and don't wish to be teased about it, or to have it publicized. In addition I've bought myself a motor-cycle. It's being delivered from Barnstaple tomorrow.'

'What on earth do you want one of those filthy machines for?'

'To ride, of course, when I can't have your car. And it's not a filthy machine. In fact, it's quite beautiful. A handsome, growling beast, full of power. To ride it is to be master of the winds and lord of the road.'

Grace laughed. 'Such poetry without the benefit of

drink? Why on earth didn't you buy a car? You could still be master of the winds and lord of the road—God help us.'

'Because I didn't choose to. I meant to—but I saw this, standing there in the showroom, arrogant, gleaming, beauty masking its strength and demanding a master. I bought it.'

'You bought a race-horse once. That lasted six months.'

'Naturally. That's the limit, the extreme limit, of any of my passions—except for you.'

Grace shook her head. 'Buzz off—and don't come back until you can talk sensibly. I'm going to take a bath.'

'Good. Shall I come and scrub your back?'

Grace was silent for a moment, eyeing him. He was pressed down and brimming over with high spirits. Full of rhodomontade which meant that whatever mischief he was planning exhilarated him. And not for the first time she told herself that at an early age he had forsaken the ordinary because he was determined that one day he would be famous or infamous—and probably didn't care which. The touch of mad spirit in him had to be served whichever way it led.

She said, 'What would you say if I said—"Yes, I'd like that"?'

'I'd run a mile.'

'Then start now.' She went by him to leave the room and pulled his ear and for the first time she noticed that he was looking better, firmer and healthier than for a long time, the slack pudginess was going from him, taking lazy youthfulness with it, and the solid, hard lines of manhood were beginning to shape.

While John was in his study after dinner Mrs Hurrell came in to ask him if there was anything else he wanted that night.

John said, 'No, thank you, Mrs Hurrell. I meant to tell

you that the furniture from the London flat will be down next week some time. We can decide later on where it is to go.'

'Yes, sir.'

Knowing what her immediate thoughts would be and not wishing them to find even a remote expression in words, he said, 'How have things been while I was away? No problems?'

'No, sir . . .'

'I hope young Carlo's been behaving himself.'

Mrs Hurrell beamed. 'Oh, he's a nice young man, sir, is Mister Carlo. We all like him—though he's a bit cheeky with Vera sometimes.'

'I don't suppose Vera minds that.'

'Well, maybe not, sir. But she should. Not that 'tisn't all in fun though on Mister Carlo's part. Hurrell says he seen him the other morning, very early on, running along the top road . . . training or something. All dressed up in one of those sort of battledress outfit things.'

'Track suit?'

'Yes, sir.'

'Well, he could do to lose some weight. Sensible chap.'

'Yes, sir. He's eating well too. Always down to breakfast.'

When she was gone John slowly prepared himself a cigar and lit it. He poured himself a very stiff whisky—not because he needed it, but because he fancied it. He locked his study door, then took the key from the Badminton Library volume and opened the safe. He took out the two bundles of letters which he had put there and carried them to his desk. There was no longer any high emotion in him. Everything that had happened, and was going to happen, he felt, belonged in the life of another man. It was a curious sensation, and one for which he was mildly grateful since it left him utterly and emotionally free to follow his own courses, to plan and finally to act as though by proxy for this other man, this other John Kingsford.

This take-over by an *alter ego* had started not on the previous night after he had read the letters, but this morning when he had gone round to her hotel to pick up Grace Lindsay. He had dreaded that moment, and dreaded more the prospect of the long drive and the effort he would have to make to act normally.

There had been no need for effort. From the moment she had greeted him and stepped into the car this other John Kingsford—much to his relief—had taken over. He had been as easy and entertaining as he had been on the drive up. He was certain that she could never have guessed that anything unusual had happened to him. And that was as it should be. Not just for her. But with everyone with whom he would now come into contact. He was, when the time fell due, going to kill a man, and not one shadow of a movement, not one false note in a word, or even the faintest prick of an intuition must be able to be traced to him. He meant to kill, and to live the rest of his life without fear.

He began to read the letters, this time without passion. The new John Kingsford, alert and responsive to the world of memories they roused, was also full of an understanding of the origins and meanings of the treachery which had been practised against him. Killing meant planning, but before that must come understanding. When the moment of execution came he would destroy the letters, and draw the shutters on memory. But for the moment he could calmly give memory and comprehension all the liberty they demanded without being touched.

As he read the letters through, the picture of his betrayal was filled out. It had begun five years before Elizabeth's death—just before he had been made Parliamentary Private Secretary in a junior ministry. He realized now that he had been so elevated by the man who had been her lover right up to her death. In fact she had probably died—he could frame the phrase without emotion—almost still warm from his bed where no doubt she had put on her best performance because she had come seeking another favour. Performance was perhaps an inexact word. Her lover—since in his letters he dwelt at length and in detail on this—had clearly been in no doubt of her bodily honesty even though he must have known, having granted them in the past, that this passion was only the prelude to some favour to be begged in its aftermath. That last time, yes, a safe constituency at the first by-election. Well, one thing was certain. When he, John Kingsford, had killed Sir Charles Read, there would be no question of his wanting to go back into politics. Elizabeth should have been, was in a way, the politician, the place seeker, sublimating her ambitions by fostering his poor successes in another man's bed.

Reading, he could admire her shrewdness and cleverness. That she should have kept the letters was no surprise to him. Their value would never diminish. She had become the mistress of a Foreign Secretary, and more, a man who was well set to become Prime Minister one day. The disadvantages of an accidental discovery by a husband were far outweighed by the advantages for quiet blackmail on behalf of that husband in the perhaps not so distant future; her body on offer still to gild the threat. She might even—would have surely—looked so far ahead as the days when, old and untouchable, she could have included some of them in her memoirs. Like the good manager she was with money and about the house, in picking friends and using them without their real knowledge, infallibly rejecting or accepting the right invitations, she would never have done anything so stupid as throwing them away.

He sat back for a moment. Had it not been for Parson John, he could well possibly have lived the rest of his life never knowing that he had been a wooden puppet dancing and bowing under invisible strings. Parson John was now to become an accomplice in murder. He wondered what the old man of the portrait in the hall would have thought of that.

It was no surprise to him that their adultery respected neither time nor place. They had made love at Darlock, in the London flat, at Read's Norfolk home—his semi-invalid wife (her sister) either complaisant or ignorant—and at Read's mother's home, Pitt Wood House, not ten miles from Darlock, and had also snatched it in other and far more dangerous places. They were both people of large appetites and quick impulses; a thing he had always known about Read and now could blandly acknowledge in his wife. Thank God, he told himself evenly, Elizabeth had not left him with children. There could have been no smooth calmness in him then, wondering whether there was nothing of Kingsford in them. Elizabeth had obviously thought of that. Children until she was ready were out. While she clung to him in bed, opening her body against his desire, sharing with him in words the wish for a child, she was already safely—as her lover knew—taking the pill. And where, he wondered, did she hide those? Had no need to—for she knew he was the kind who strictly honoured another's privacy. When you were a Kingsford and loved your wife and knew she loved you there was no cause for idle or prurient curiosity. He would no more have thought of looking in her medicine cupboard or in her handbag or her desk drawers at any time than he would have considered shooting a sitting bird or hitting a man when he was down.

He read the letters right through, tidied them and put them back in the safe. Then he refilled his whisky glass and sat in the worn leather armchair whose seat had sagged under so many Kingsford bottoms, and calmly considered how he should kill Sir Charles Read. Not once since the resolution had set firmly in his mind had it occurred to him that there was any special significance or overwhelming difficulty to face because the man was also Her Majesty's Secretary of State for Foreign and Commonwealth Affairs. For John Kingsford he was just a man who had betrayed him by fornicating with his wife. Willingness on her part was unimportant, could claim no shade of consideration or leniency. A married man could—if a woman were willing and unattached—make love to her if the mettle of his character permitted him the licence. But to take another man's wife, out of lust, for the return of a few favours (political in his case and schemed for by Elizabeth) was not done. And, if his attitude was old-fashioned he didn't care a damn. That was how he felt. That was why he was going to kill Read. Elusive he might be by reason of his constant travelling and protection, but no matter what variations shaped a man's life there were always constants which had to be observed, moments of unprotected privacy.

He knew already exactly when and where he would kill, and how it was to be done. But there was a lot to be arranged, and time enough to play with before that moment came. And for this he was glad. Quite coldly and brutally he wanted revenge but also a period in which to relish, as the aroma of fine brandy orbiting in the swung glass slowly invades the senses, the coming moment of perfect satisfaction.

As he went up to bed that night he stopped for a moment in front of his wife's portrait. She had given him love as she knew it and with his own love for her a seeming completeness had been formed which he had cherished. The knowledge of betrayal had no power to alter what had been until betrayal's moment had come. It had once existed, this love. Almost as though she stood in flesh before him he silently thanked her for all that had been, and then passed on, carrying with him a calm and inflexible new passion.

At the top of the stairs he met Carlo coming along the gallery.

He stopped and said affably, 'Hullo, Carlo. Nice to see you again, I hear you're taking some weight off with a little road work.'

'Yes, I am, sir. But how did you know?'

John chuckled. 'Carlo, night or day up on the moor, no matter what you do you'd be surprised how many eyes are watching. Sometimes when I was your age I used to think even the sheep passed the word around. Actually, old Hurrell saw you, and it came along the grape vine through Mrs Hurrell. Do you mind?'

'Not at all. I like to take off a bit of weight once or twice a year and since there's no sauna bath around for miles . . . well I just have to run. Oh, by the way, sir, I read Parson John's diary. I really enjoyed it.'

'Thank you for saying so. As soon as I've done another batch you can read that.'

John went along to his room and, for a moment or two as he got ready for bed, he wondered whether Parson John in mentioning the bureau had done him any favour, and without hesitation decided that he had. There was no undervaluing truth because it was the foundation of every man's destiny.

The next morning, after breakfast, John Kingsford got out his car and drove towards Withypool, He parked the car in a layby near the top of the moor and then walked eastwards between Withypool Hill and Worth Hill. The deep saddle between the two hills took him across marshy ground where in late summer sundews and bog asphodels grew, and finally across the road running south from Withypool to Hawkridge. He knew the ground well. He kept away from farms and recognized footpaths, following sheep and pony tracks which he had known since a boy.

He crossed the road below Worth farm and struck an old cart-track which led down the steep valley side to the river Barle. The valley side dropped sharply nearly three hundred feet to the river. A pair of derelict farm cottages lay back in the hillside, stone walls crumbling, slate and thatch gone from the roofs, and the once well-kept cottage gardens now reclaimed by the original wilderness. Just beyond the cottages was an old well, deep, and still holding ten or fifteen feet of water. The top was half covered with a rusty sheet of corrugated iron.

A little way below the cottages the track swung to the right and ran out on to a small bluff which commanded a great oxbow curve of the Barle. John sat down on a boulder near the well, beneath a leafless, lichen- and moss-infested oak tree, and surveyed the scene below.

The track ran down to an old river ford, long disused. On the inner side of the great oxbow, the river was flanked by green meadows which at either end of the curve were lost in the rising ground of hedged moor pasture and thick woods. In the middle of the oxbow the meadows ran back to a low hill which rose through a semi-parkland of tall firs and occasional oaks to a plateau on which sat the white walled bulk of Pitt Wood House; the west country seat of Sir Charles Read, and lived in now principally by his eighty-year-old, widowed mother.

John knew the house well because he had visited it often enough as a boy and young man, and less often after his marriage. And on those occasions, he knew now, the relationship between Read and his wife was already established. It was more than likely—though there had been no mention of it in the letters—that there had been times when Elizabeth could have come riding across the southern slopes of Withypool Hill to this spot. Maybe had stood beside her tethered horse under this tree and had waited for Sir Charles to ride down from Pitt Wood House and splash across the old ford to meet her. God knows, since lust was grateful for any shelter, they could have made love among the bracken cover by the well or, in bad weather, have gone up to the old cottages. Pictures of their imaginary congress moved clearly across his mind. He had no power to stop them. But he was unmoved by them.

There were times when Sir Charles made fleeting, unexpected visits to his mother. Such chance visits were of no use to him. But always, it was well known (and how many dinner parties had he not gone to with Elizabeth in the white house over the river at that time?) Sir Charles came down for Christmas or the New Year. And each morning while he was down, in rain or shine, the man rode out from Pitt Wood House, across the meadow to the river, and then downstream along its bank and returned in a great circle over the Winsford Hill moors. A private detective always came down with him, but did not always ride with him. Sir Charles Read was obstinate, self-willed and—he gave him his due—often heedless of his own safety when it was most necessary. Well, when he came down this Christmas season if someone rode with him, it would make no difference.

He sat now watching the country and the river spread out below him and his trained eye told him that the range to the footpath on the other side of the river was no more than two hundred yards from this spot. There was a gate across the path where Sir Charles would have to stop and open it. The riverside shrubs and trees were low and there were long gaps cut in them to make bank fishing easier. At the gate Sir Charles would be in full view and give him all the time he needed to shoot. All a man had to do then was to move back from the well, out of sight, and go up the hill past the old cottages and be lost on the moor the other side of the road in ten minutes, and there were boggy, miry patches where a rifle could be thrust two and three feet deep into the black ooze and never see the light of day again, nor leave trace of its going.

He turned away and began to walk back. He was calm and cold beyond his own comprehension. Only one thought hung unemotionally in his mind. The man had wronged him. The man must die. He walked back to his car without hurry, a stiff south-westerly wind thrusting down the slopes against him. When the man was dead, he would put the whole thing from his mind. He was young comparatively. He would find some fulfilling work to do and he could marry again and hopefully wait for children . . . there was time and enough for Kingsford boys and girls, his sons and daughters to raise hell and laughter and wake Darlock House into life again. But whoever the woman might be he knew that the quality of trust in him had been marred for good.

When he got back to Darlock House, he went to the gun room and, with the key on his ring which he always carried with him, he unlocked the steel cabinet which held his Purdeys and Holland and Hollands. Racked with them was a Cogswell and Harrison .257 rifle which his father had used for deer stalking in Scotland and which he, years since, had used on these moors when invited to help in the culling of deer. It was a Mauser pattern with a light magazine that held four rounds and with one cartridge in the chamber gave him five rounds. One would almost certainly be enough, two positively so. On the rifle were telescopic sights which his father had had fitted. He would have to find a place where he could fire a few rounds and check the zeroing. More important—he knew that his father, who had bought it from an Indian army officer friend now long dead, had never licensed or registered it. With it was an unopened box of waterproof ammunition,

.275 belted, rimless magnum nitro express, 160 grains. With a muzzle velocity of 2,675 feet per second and an energy delivery of 2,550 lbs on impact, one shot anywhere above the neck would be enough to send Sir Charles Read on his way.

He took the rifle and ammunition up to his bedroom and locked them away in the bottom drawer of the big wardrobe which had once been used by his father. Not once did it cogently occur to him that this would be no ordinary death and would unleash forces of political and security activity far beyond any that would ever mark the going of almost any other man in the country. For him there was only one consideration. The man had betrayed him. That he had used his wife, who was willing to be so used, was unimportant.

Whistling gently to himself, safely in the grip of his cold passion, he went down to his study to attend to his day's correspondence.

*   *   *

That morning Carlo walked the third leg of the Run. It was all uphill following the upper reaches of the river Mole to its source on Darlock Moor only a few yards away from the ridge road and not far from the entrance to Darlock House. To save himself a double walk he had arranged with Birdie to come with him in the car to the beginning of the walk and then to drive back to the ridge road and wait for him there. Once he knew the whole course he could begin to train in earnest on each section and work out his timings. His morning runs were beginning to harden him up and to improve his wind, and he had already lost eight pounds in weight since starting his training.

As he walked, making mental notes of the route and

stopping now and then to consider the possibility of alternative lines, part of his mind was with Birdie, waiting for him up on the ridge.

Almost every day he had been seeing her now, if it were only for a quick hour after darkness, and he had been learning from her. She knew the moor inside out, knew each cottage and farm and the occupants and their history. She was not well educated or well read, but she knew all the creatures of the moor, the places where the badgers had their sets and the wild high plateaux where the curlews nested in the Spring, and the pools and runs in all the waters where the salmon and trout spawned. She knew the call of a young heifer coming into first heat, had helped her father with the birth of calves and lambs, felt no squeamishness at the sight of honest muck and blood, and, although she had a natural tenderness with all animals, would twist the neck of hen or rabbit for the pot without compunction. Once, in a playful tussle, she had held his wrists, laughing, with a grip which it was all he could do to shake off. She knew Barnstaple, Exeter and Taunton, but the farthest she had been afield was Plymouth. London was another world away and all countries outside the British Isles existed in a limbo. She fascinated him because she was unlike any other girl he had ever met. She was completely and honestly herself. What she felt about him—apart from the slow-moving sexual attraction and easy friendship which had quickly grown between them—he found it hard to guess. Maybe, he thought often, he was like some well-fashioned, intriguing visitor from another world who, more than any other emotion, stirred her curiosity but never so strongly that she felt forced to ask him pointed questions about his life and his past. There were many times when he thought it would have been nice in truth to have been an acknowledged Kingsford, a real son at Darlock House whose world was similar to her own and in which they could have moved and joined together with unquestioned naturalness. That it wasn't like that, he knew, was a challenge to achieve something he was not ready to name since it was only the shadow of a desire whose real form he was not competent to grasp. Maybe one day he would meet that challenge and prove himself. Meanwhile there were other things to prove.

When he got to the car Birdie was listening to the radio and painting her nails. He sat and waited until she had finished and then said, 'I'll drive you to Dulverton and we can have a drink and sandwiches in a pub. I'm starving.'

As he drove off, Birdie said, 'That first time we went out, you smoked and you drank—hard stuff, I mean. Now you don't. And you've lost weight and are fitter. Why are you bothering?'

'Bothering? About what?'

Birdie laughed and let the tip of her tongue slide along her upper lip.

'You know what. Why can't you ever say a thing straight out? Or is it really a secret?'

'It's a secret.'

'That's what you think. Training hard every morning. Walking the Sherndon and Kingsford Water, and then down Fyldon to Tinker's Ford. And today, me dropping you at Barham bridge, and you slogging all the way up to Darlock Moor top. You think that only the birds see you?'

Carlo smiled. 'Who does?'

'Lots of people. You don't know this little old moor and the people round these parts. If the wind blows your skirts up on the top of Worth Hill somebody'll see whether you're wearing knickers or not. It's no desert, you know. There's always a workman, shepherd, postman doing his rounds, or some bloke sitting up thatching or roofing. If Bob Gurney has a few pints too many in the Sportsman's Inn at dinner time, his missus knows it in Simonsbath before he gets home.'

'Bob Gurney sounds a good sort.'

'So he is mostly. But I'm not interested in him. What I want to know is—why you fancy doing the Kingsford Run? Has that Mr John put you up to it?'

Carlo said, 'Do things really get around like that?'

'Course they do. Folk put two and two together. You think half this country doesn't know we go out together? I tell you, Carlo love, they do. Knowing and talking about knowing is meat and drink to them. So it is to me. So what about this Run business? 'Tis that, isn't it?'

'Sort of.'

'Why?'

'Because I heard about it and thought it might be fun to do.'

She looked at him for a moment, then shook her head and said, 'All right. I'll mind my own business.' She leaned forward and kissed him on the cheek as he drove, and added, 'They'll get to know about it—and they'll be laying bets on your time. My father made ten pounds when he bet Mr John would never beat Mr Robert's time. Which reminds me that mother said I was to ask if you'd like to come back to supper with us tonight?'

'Would you like me to?'

'Yes, of course. But not if you don't want to.'

'I'd like it very much.' And as he said it he realized that he almost meant it.

When he got back at eleven o'clock that night there was a light showing under Grace's bedroom door. He knocked, waited for her call, and went in.

Grace, sitting up in bed, reading, gave him a raised eyebrow and said, 'The wanderer returns and waits to be

103

called after knocking. It was nice, too, to telephone and say you wouldn't be back to dinner——'

'I'm sorry. I meant to, but——'

'It slipped your mind. Don't worry: I made it all right with Mrs Hurrell. By the way, your motor-cycle thing arrived this afternoon with a lot of gear. Hurrell put it in the stable block.'

'Oh, good.'

'Do you think she'll like it?'

'Who?'

'The girl, of course. The one who was sitting in my car when I walked along the ridge road this morning. I must say she looked healthier and more wholesome than some I've seen you with in the past.'

Watching him, Grace recognized the sudden tightening of his mouth and a momentary fast blinking of his eyelids. Carlo's anger signals.

He said stiffly, 'I'm sorry. I don't wish to talk about her.' He moved to the bed and leaned forward and kissed her cheek and then moved back to the door. Then, with his fingers on the door handle, he was suddenly and helplessly taken with a quick storm of anger. "Why do you always have to be so interested in me and my girls! I should think it was healthier for you to stop living vicariously!' He slammed out of the room.

There was no surprise in Grace. It was the first occasion for some time now on which Carlo had treated her to such an outburst. To some extent she probably deserved it. She knew him so well, and he knew it. And the one thing Carlo did not like was being known, being questioned, particularly when he was under tension, and that tight-lipped, eyelid flickering face was always the mark of tension in him, the prelude to an irrational anger. She had known the same quick storms in his mother, and she knew that, even with some blame due to her, the aftermath was common to them both. Carlo would come, either before he slept or first thing in the morning, to apologize freely and genuinely.

*   *   *

Slumped back in the armchair in his bedroom Carlo felt the anger go from him and regretted it had ever arisen. But he knew why it had. It was nothing to do with Birdie directly. Yet it was all to do with the life which surrounded Birdie and which had made Birdie. And that ambience and family warmth was something which he would have liked to have had for himself.

Standing in front of Grace with the memory of it fresh in him, it had seemed a treasure, newly found, which he wished to keep secret to himself, to hoard and guard and never share or spend. Birdie was part of that richness, so much so that he had almost lost her in it. Birdie's personality, and her person itself—which he guessed needed only a positive move from him to trip off the charge of their physical, if no deeper, emotion for one another—had that evening lost identity, had been spun off into the bright nebulae which had seemed to enclose everyone and everything that made part of the long, low-raftered farm kitchen.

He had expected to be bored, to have to shroud his embarrassment and, long before politeness called time, to have had him itching to leave the place. Instead, from a quiet welcome he had been enchanted into a new accord with himself, and had found himself wanted and liked. Not simply because this was clearly Birdie's wish, but because her father, mother and her brother, two years older than Birdie, had taken him in as though they had known him for years and that he was well accustomed to their way of life. When he had refused cider or any stronger drink and Birdie had openly teased him before them, saying that he was in training because he fancied doing the Kingsford Run, they just took it as though it were the most natural thing in the world. 'Wait for a hard frost and a north-easterly wind. Frost'll make goin' firm and wind'll help you on the first two legs,' was Mr Carter's advice.

They had eaten at the long kitchen table with Mrs Carter and Birdie serving from pots and pans and dishes held hot and ready in the range which filled the old open fireplace. For the first time in his life Carlo had eaten, laughed, talked and joked as one of a family. Nobody had asked him any direct questions about his own life and when they spoke of their own affairs one or other of them had given him some quick explanation which stopped him from feeling excluded from the conversation. He realized, too, that the Carter family had the same feeling for Great Cotters Farm as John Kingsford had for Darlock House. The family had been there since the untouched moor was broken and tamed in the first days of the reclamation of the forest, generations of them being born to work the land and raise their cattle and sheep and to pass away leaving other Carters to carry on.

But more than anything else Carlo had been touched by the natural respect they had for the private affairs of others. He was a friend of Birdie's and their relationship was no matter for any open curiosity or even veiled inquiry. Whatever they were to one another was their business. They could not know him, but they knew Birdie and that was enough for them.

She had walked across the yard with him to his car and had kissed him good night, and it might have been something they had been doing for months. He drove off wishing—devoid of any sophisticated mockery of his own emotions—that he could have been born into the honesty and plain pattern of such a family, his feet on a flagged floor worn by the tread of his own kin for generations. In a way, secretly, he could claim something of that with the Kingsfords. But it was far from enough. And, because of this, he knew that with the Kingsfords his emotions must always fluctuate between love and contempt, between pride in his own solitary state and anguish because there was no true place for him which he could openly claim.

The stir of his feelings had made him turn on Grace angrily. But that was gone now. He got slowly to his feet and began to go along to her bedroom. One of the comfortable things about Grace was that she never made it difficult for him to apologize. Even in her anger or cynicism there was always an underlying warmth and understanding.

*   *   *

That night John Kingsford came to the end of the note-book diary he was decoding. The last entry in the book was dated 21 June, 1872. He picked up the next notebook in the sequence—Parson John had numbered them all with little blue-rimmed white labels stuck on the covers—and glancing at the date of the first coded entry saw that it was headed 10 September, 1872. Nearly a three-month gap, which was unusual. Sometimes the parson had missed a couple of days, once or twice a week, but never three months. He smiled to himself. There was good reason for this gap. During this time the parson would have had much on his mind to keep him away from his diary. Maybe, too, the gap could have been deliberate for he had met his wife-to-be in May, 1872, and possibly did not want to entrust his feelings to the diary. He had married in the July and, clearly, when his life had settled down to its marital state, had come back to the diary.

Interested to see whether the parson would have made

any reference to the gap, John decoded the first paragraph. It read——

Stayed abed all day with a bad chest cold which came from my ducking in the Taw two days since when I was taken a full quarter of a mile downstream following a salmon hooked below the bridge at Umberleigh and which I landed in Chichester's water below the Hawkridge brook. A fine, fresh run cock fish of 30 pounds, and a gallant fighter.

In the evening my beloved Jessica came and read to me from Mr Blackmore's Lorna Doone *of which, though I had not the heart to tell her, I think but little, finding the style prolix and the descriptions of the West Country heightened well beyond their true nature. Mr Blackmore was at Blundells some years before me.*

Tomorrow, if my cold allows, we go to a croquet and archery party at Swimbridge. Buttery Farm is to be sold this autumn old Tom Darch having lost all heart for the place following his recent bereavement. Jessica asked if I would buy it to run with the Darlock land and put in a tenant, but I told her that it was not in my mind to do so.

Before retiring, Jessica brought me a glass of mulled port with a few drops of laudanum and I slept fully and without dreams.

There was nothing there, he thought, to mark any reason for the gap other than the advent of the parson's marriage which had kept him too busy and too happy to bother with a diary for a while. It had been a long and happy marriage, fruitful and calm, the open grain of its nature running right through its length, true and un-warped. A very different affair from his own.

Chapter Six

THE FOLLOWING WEEKS until late November were wet and wild with westerly after westerly winds wreathing the tops of the moor with cloud mists and long, driving curtains of rain.

The spongy bogs and plateaux filled and overflowed, turning each small gulley and combe stream into peat-coloured torrents and filling the rivers bank-high, and in their lower reaches flooding out over the meadows and pastures. Flocks of redwings and fieldfares covered the leeward slopes behind Darlock House, and the garden trees and shrubs became a haven for refugees from the high tops and the flooded lower valleys. Crows roosted in the firs, and the shrubs and rhododendron clumps held nuthatches, marsh tits, meadow pipits, wrens and corn buntings.

Carlo, ignoring the weather, kept on with his training and also increased his knowledge of the countryside and its creatures. He knew the kingfishers and dippers on the high Mole reaches, knew the ravens that family-flocked still over the valley woods and the herons and occasional cormorants—refugees from the distant estuary—that fished the flood waters of the low southern combes and valleys. On his Norton, crash-helmeted and weather-proofed, he had the long moor roads, since no one drove them now for pleasure, almost to himself. Following his mood he drove like a madman along the straight ridge roads, and loved the heel and swing of the great machine as he swayed and swung through corners, or, mood changing, he would idle along, rain and wind beating at him, lost in a slow reverie, relishing with his body more than his mind the power beneath him and the delight of his control over the machine which moved and lived at his bidding.

Sometimes when the weather eased he would take Birdie out on the back of the machine, and once a week he went to Great Cotters Farm for supper. But he seldom now saw Birdie through the day because she had found herself a job in a Farmers' Co-operative store in South Molton. He liked having the day to himself, but two or three times a week he would take his aunt's car and meet her after work, bundling her scooter into the back, and driving her home. It was dark now by five o'clock in the afternoon and on the way home they would sometimes stop in the layby at Portford Bridge and sit talking and sometimes kissing or fondling one another.

There was a naturalness between them that made obliqueness or amorous guile unnecessary. Neither of them talked of love or of the future. They were two creatures, attracted to each other, and following without haste some pattern of courtship which they both instinctively respected.

Late one afternoon, on the way home, while they were parked, Birdie lay back on the long front bench seat and Carlo made love to her. There was no rush or short-lived excitement, they took each other and enjoyed each other lingeringly as though they had long been lovers, their individual passions, almost until the last, charged with the desire of giving more than of receiving. Lying on top of her afterwards Carlo held her face and kissed her lips gently. There had never been a moment for him like this before, but he had no need to say it because what he had known was also in her eyes. That she had not been a virgin meant nothing and he had no jealous wish to question her about it.

Three days later they made love more comfortably in the back of the car, the scooter standing in the rain outside, themselves cushioned on the rugs which he had provided. Afterwards, Birdie, shivering a moment against her almost total nakedness, sat up and reached for her clothes and said—less to him than perhaps to herself, because it was a simple act of shriving—'I only did it once before. Some London bloke it was what camped up the back of the farm. He was nice enough in himself. But there was nothing in it . . . not for me, like. It was as though I wasn't there.' She laughed. 'Like some old ram to a ewe in the field. Any ewe. I remember thinking . . . well, if that's all 'tis, they can keep it.' She reached down and put her hand on his mouth and Carlo ran his tongue over her warm palm. 'He was gone the next morning.'

Carlo sat up and said, 'I'm not surprised. To be right you've got to belong, not just to each other, but to something else. I don't know what that something else is, but I know you've got to have it. Otherwise a chap's like an old ram with a blue dubby bag tied on his belly to mark the ewes he does.'

Birdie laughed. 'Now you'm talking like some old farmer. Is that what you'd like to be?'

'I don't know. But I do know this—' His face tightened and there was a momentary, angry flicker of his eyelids, '—I'd like to belong to some place—and then,' his anger went abruptly and he smiled, putting out his hand and touching her, 'to have you with me.'

At breakfast some mornings later John said to Carlo, 'I had a policeman out here from South Molton yesterday. He told me you were in some trouble at Barnstaple a few nights ago.'

Carlo nodded. 'Yes, I was.'

'You beat up one of the town lads, I understand.'

'That's right, sir. One of these Hell's Angels types. Has he complained?'

'His parents have.'

'They're the ones originally at fault. They should have taught him manners.'

Momentarily a little annoyed by Carlo's indifferent manner, John said curtly, 'Just tell me what happened.'

'I went to a dance with a girl. This chap was looking for trouble all the evening. When we went to get my Norton to go home he followed us and said something I didn't like.'

'What?'

'Something about the girl I was with. So I went for him.'

'I gather you were pretty drastic.'

Carlo shrugged his shoulders. 'I meant to be—after what he'd said. He thought I would be easy and he found he was wrong.'

'Who was the girl—Birdie Carter?'

'Yes, sir. You'd have done the same in my place, I'm sure. Do the police want to see me?'

'I don't think that's necessary. I'll have a word with them. They know me. However, I'd advise you to steer clear of Barnstaple for a while. That kind of thug doesn't forget.'

'Yes, sir. But I can look after myself.'

'So it seems.'

Carlo, spreading marmalade on his toast, said, 'You have to these days. Somebody could be kicking you to death and other people just cross the street. They don't want to know.'

'Maybe so.'

To John's surprise Carlo gave a chuckle and said, 'The nice thing is—when you see their surprise. You have to watch yourself then otherwise you can't help overdoing it. Really putting the boot in.'

'Which is what you did?'

'A little. Not too much. But he deserved it.'

John stood up. 'Well, we won't go on about it. Just stay away from Barnstaple for a bit.'

'Yes, sir.'

As John left the room, Carlo ran on to himself, 'Yes, sir. No, sir. Three bags full, sir. . . .' If Birdie hadn't come shouting and pulling at him he'd have kicked the filthy bastard to pieces. Well, there was no need to worry. John Kingsford would deal with the police. Probably played golf with the Chief Constable, had known him all his life.

* * *

Two days later on his training run, when Carlo reached the turning point by the old mine, to make a change he left the road and went out on to the top slopes of Hangley Cleave. He swung right-handed to follow the slope across the saddle to the top of Long Holcombe on a cross country line which would take him back to Darlock House. A faint rain was falling on a wind which had swung round into the north-east overnight.

As he began to breast the rise to Long Holcombe the sound of a shot away to his left front was carried to him on the wind. Almost immediately came another shot, then a long pause which was followed by another shot. His curiosity roused, Carlo swung away to his left, jogging through heather patches and picking his way from hummock to hummock on the soggy ground. Over his curiosity he told himself that nothing would make him attempt the Kingsford Run in this kind of weather. Hard frost and a north-easter Mr Carter had said, and he was right.

Another two shots came from the valley to his left. Carlo

worked his way out on to the left shoulder of the hill and looked down. A few yards from him was a small stream that ran down to join the Kingsford water in the valley. Two hundred yards away a man wearing a shooting jacket and a cap was lying on the near slope of the combe, his head turned away from Carlo. The man was holding a rifle.

As Carlo watched, the man fired a single shot across the combe and Carlo saw that he was aiming at a large boulder on the opposite side. A puff of rock chips and stone dust flew up from the head of the boulder. Recognizing the man, Carlo squatted low on the ground.

Why on earth, he wondered, should John Kingsford choose to be abroad so early on such a bad morning to do a little rifle practice?—for rifle it was; no double-barrelled shotgun. Curiosity flowed through him, a familiar itch, the well-known and welcomed challenge that a locked drawer or door always presented.

John Kingsford fired one more shot and then got up and walked down the combe and up the other side to the boulder. Carlo watched him as he examined the top of the boulder and then began to search around the stone, bending now and then to pick something from the ground. That he was picking up smashed and shattered bullets was obvious. After a few minutes John Kingsford went away up over the combe ridge and out of sight, clearly on his way back to Darlock.

Carlo gave him a few minutes' grace and then worked his way down to the firing point. The damp grass and heather was flattened where John Kingsford had been lying. But it had the look also, Carlo thought, of having been flattened more than once before this. He searched around in the heather hoping to find a spent cartridge case, but he could find none.

Puzzled, he went down into the combe and up to the

boulder. It stood about five feet high and narrowed at the top to a stubby waisted head about the size of a football. The top half of the head was chipped and scarred with bullet marks, all of them grouped within the size of a man's hand. One look at the marks and the jagged star fissures which ran from some of them in the rock face told him that John Kingsford had not been practising with the Walther .22 rifle. There was only one weapon in the gun room which could have made the marks.

Carlo said nothing to John that morning at breakfast. A sure instinct warned him that this man would not have gone out so early on a bad morning just for the sake of a little rifle practice. Curiosity about the man and this house which had run strong in him in the weeks following his arrival and then had dropped away when he had made the house his own, and ebbed farther still before the growing importance to him of making the Kingsford Run, was revived.

Later that morning John went off to Barnstaple on business and Grace went with him. Watching them go, Carlo made a little grimace to himself. Quite often now Grace went off with John, either to Taunton or one of the neighbouring towns where he might have business; and twice he had taken her out to dinner. Carlo had the sudden, chiding thought, that he had been slipping in his natural awareness and curiosity about people and the life around him. The Kingsford Run and Birdie had over-occupied his mind. Grace might be accepting these drives and invitations out of some kindness, or she might be starting to have some feeling for the man. After all he was a widower, free, and she was an attractive woman with a need for passion and some attachment, if only temporary, in her life. With a spurt of self-censure, he realized that he might be missing something which was right under his nose. If he went on like this he might wake up one morning to find that his natural father had become his legitimate uncle. The thought so amused him that he went off into a giggling chuckle. Maybe, for God's sake, they were already sleeping together! He slept himself so soundly now at night that an army of men could have thundered down the passageway past his door to Grace's room and he would not have been awakened.

He fetched his keys from the locked case in his bedroom and went along to the gun room. He opened the steel cabinet which held the Purdeys, the Holland and Hollands and the rifle. The rifle was not there. Why not? John Kingsford would never have left a gun uncleaned. He would either do it himself or leave it out for Hurrell to do. Either way it should have been in this room where all the cleaning materials lived.

Carlo locked the cabinet and went into the study. The rifle was not to be seen. It was too big to go into the safe or any drawer in the desk. If it was not here, there was only one other place for it unless John had decided to keep it outside the house somewhere. But that was unlikely. The man's code would not let him keep it anywhere that would allow damp or rust to attack it. A rifle was like a wife, to be kept warm and dry and always ready for use.

Warm with the delight of this diversion, he went upstairs, knowing that Vera and Mrs Hurrell had long done their cleaning and were safely below, and went into John's bedroom. One look round took him to the wardrobe. The long doors of the top section were unlocked. No rifle was hidden behind the hanging clothes. The deep drawer below the hanging section was locked. He fiddled with a few of his keys and found one that unlocked it.

The rifle was lying on a folded blanket. With it was a pull-through and cleaning rags and oil, and also a large, opened box of ammunition. Carlo picked up the box. He guessed that about a dozen of the cartridges were missing.

116

He went along to his own bedroom, dropped into the armchair and gave himself over to a pleasing, tantalizing mood of speculation. For the first time for weeks his hand itched to hold a cigarette and his palate longed for the bite of liquor. They were all within easy reach, but he chased the desire away. After the Kingsford Run, yes. Now, no. Why was John Kingsford hiding the rifle in his room? Why? Why? He didn't know, and he couldn't guess. But he would find out.

That night before he went to bed, he went along to Grace's room to say goodnight. After kissing her he sat down in a chair, looked at her for a while as she lay in bed, and then said, 'John Kingsford.'

Grace, one hand resting on the cover of her bedtime book, said nothing for a while. She knew exactly what he meant. It was not a question. Not even a ball thrown idly into the air with the obvious invitation for her to play. It was Carlo unsure of himself, driven either by boredom or plain devilment into a moment's provocation wondering what would come from the bald initiative.

For a moment or two she was tempted to get rid of him, to tell him she was tired or wanted to read her book, and then decided that this would only provoke him. She knew his mood, knew this posture of a night which so often went with it, elbows on his knees, his hands cupped round his face, a face that usually showed puffier than ever under the pressure but was now—and she gave him merit for this—fined down and weather-brown, the weather of wind and rain, not the oil-trapped tan from a Bermuda sun.

She said, 'I'm not in love with him. I haven't slept with him. You can lie in your bed without an ear cocked for a creaking floor board. But I like him more than at first sight I imagined I would. All right?'

Carlo smiled. 'I like him in a way. There are things about him I envy.'

'I don't think you envy anyone.'

'Oh, yes I do. I envy old Hurrell. Just for the way he is with horses. I envy the Carters. They're solid all through . . . they're so bloody real and themselves all the time. And that's what John Kingsford is. He's himself all the time. You're not like that, and I'm not like that.' He stood up. 'Tough, isn't it?'

'No.'

'Of course it is, Grace. You and I are just floating. I don't know what started you floating, and I don't want to know. Our kind always have to have a part they keep to themselves. I think we're floaters because we won't come to terms with what's happened to us. I wasn't Graber's son —did you know that?'

Grace nodded. 'Yes, I did, Carlo.'

'Was she sober when she told you?'

'Yes, she was. But she didn't tell me who it was. She wouldn't—though I tried to make her.'

Carlo grunted, a twisted laugh. He lied easily, 'She'd have told me if she hadn't been so drunk. The next morning I couldn't ask her because I knew it had been the drink speaking. She never meant me to know. Why have you never said anything to me about knowing?'

'Because I saw no point in putting more on you than you already had to carry. But if at any time before this you'd asked me the question I would have told you. Just as I have done now.'

'Well, it makes no odds. I could have gone on all my life thinking I was Graber's son—but I would still have been me.'

Grace shook her head. 'You've got it all wrong, Carlo. Nothing's fixed for ever.'

'Oh, yes it is. The snake can slough its skin, but it's still a snake.' He grinned. 'I'm learning a lot about natural history these days.'

Grace smiled. 'One always learns fast from a good teacher.'

Thinking about him after he had left the room, Grace wondered what it was that could have sparked off the direct question of his legitimacy. Her sister, Margaret, had always been a poor handler of her own affairs. It would have been far better if she had told Carlo the truth while she was sober, but how like her to let it slip while she was drunk. Carlo was the type who would have preferred that kind of truth to come to him with at least some wrapping of decency. Poor Margaret, she had always messed things up. Maybe it was something about her helplessness which had drawn Graber to her . . . a pretty bird trailing a broken wing. Like so many hard men of business, there had been a broad streak of sentiment in him. In a way Carlo was like that; one side hard, selfish, knowledgeable and competent, and then the other curiously sentimental, day-dreaming, working himself into so many different postures and dilemmas as though in them he would find some escape . . . or maybe the real truth about himself. Maybe it wasn't so odd. Maybe that was what everyone was doing—always trying to break through to something they felt was the real person, the true character.

Something of that was now apparent in John Kingsford. Since their visit to London he had begun to change, slowly, but positively. He had pushed London and politics behind him, the flat there had been taken off his hands, and the loss of his wife, she sensed, was now rapidly dropping away from him as a constant memory. There had to come soon a moment of pause when he gathered himself together and said 'What now?' And, while the question hung unanswered, he was obliged, largely for immediate comfort, to turn to whatever came to hand most readily. That that something in human terms had been her she accepted as an accident of proximity.

Forthright in her assessments of other people, even if she could not apply the same honesty always to herself, Grace saw that at the commonest level people's bodily needs were usually the first to surface. From small, tentative beginnings John Kingsford had taken to driving her around and now and then inviting her out to dinner. At no time, during all this, did he reach for any form of intimacy. Company, yes. The presence of a woman, yes. His masculinity, long denied a familiar female usage, pushed him so far and he had no reason to resist. Had he made any further move, she knew she would not have resisted because the combinations were right. She, too, had her hungers which were nothing to do with the mind or the spirit. The body was a frank, powerful master with no need to rely on subtleties. If by one word or touch he had shown that he wanted to sleep with her, reaching for a simple comfort, she would have made no resistance against the giving and taking of a natural charity. There would have been no betrayal on either side. She had no memories which demanded loyalty and he, clearly, must have made an equable composition with his own memories. There was no place for love on his side or hers, but there was every need for the honest satisfaction of common needs. Plenty of marriages existed happily at that level. The rare intangibles of true bliss and love were the exception not the rule. This was no cause for weeping—not for her; she had done all the weeping she would ever do.

Nevertheless—she smiled to herself as she picked up her book—the sooner she saw the back of this moor the better. To become the mistress of Darlock House held no charms. Pavements suited her feet better than any plough or pasture land. The sooner Carlo tired of this place, the better pleased she would be.

* * *

Carlo had now run all three stages of the Kingsford Run. He did them each separately four or five times. On the first leg he had timed himself on the different routes and had decided that the fastest line was to go up the river Barle as far as the junction with the Sherndon Water and then, leaving the valley, to strike uphill across Great Ferny Ball and come down the other side well up the Kingsford Water. He took his best times on each leg and made an adjustment for the fact that he had done them separately, therefore faster. Making a rough estimate for the overall run on a day of hard frost and a good north-easterly wind, he found that he was a good ten minutes outside John Kingsford's time. Given more training he was confident that he could knock at least five minutes off this time. The other five minutes he felt he could pull from himself on the actual day because he would be running against John Kingsford and not against the clock. The best time had to come on the day. The first time that he made the whole run in practice he was well outside the time. Hard frost and the right wind would cut that down, and constant training cut it further. So far as he was concerned now he was determined to stay on at Darlock until he got the right weather conditions. He had decided now that only if he equalled or beat John Kingsford's time would he have earned the right to reveal that he was a Kingsford. There were moments when he could admit to himself that it was a pretty pointless exercise, anyway. But the ones which seized his imagination usually were—and he knew better now than to deny himself them because others equally silly —or dangerous—immediately filled the vacuum. This at least was an innocent family game—bastard son against a bastard of a father.

In early December, Grace told Carlo that John was taking her to a Hunt Ball which was being held at a country house near Exeter.

Carlo made no comment, except to say that he hoped she would have a good time.

On the night of the ball, Carlo drove over on his Norton to have supper with the Carters. He got back about eleven. He let himself in with his front door key. The servants were all in bed. That morning Carlo had asked John if there was any more of the diary he could read, and John had promised to leave it out on his desk.

Carlo went into the study and sat down at the desk to read. But somehow this evening Parson John failed to hold him with the same interest. Carlo put his feet up on the desk and tipped back in his chair. The house was still and silent.

He looked around at the room. It had remained like this, practically unchanged, since Parson John had started to write his diaries. Had been like this when he, Carlo, had been conceived under this roof. His thoughts moving idly, he wondered why—he had to be honest about it—his feelings for John Kingsford were so ambivalent. There were things about him he admired, and yet basically he had an abiding contempt and mockery for the man and his ways. A love-hate relationship some would say. And 'some' would be wide of the mark. It wasn't as simple as that. It was more the feeling of being shut out of a place you really had no wish to enter—and being illogically angry and upset about it. Deprived of something you didn't want. Which was all bloody nonsense. The world was full of nonsense anyway. . . . What, for instance, was all this early morning nonsense practising with a rifle?

Why do that? And why also keep the rifle in his bedroom? If originally the rifle had been kept openly on a rack in the gun room where he, Carlo, must certainly have noticed it, would John still have taken it and hidden it? He might have, of course. And to any question have said that it had gone for repair or that he had sold it. But John

122

did not know that he had ever seen the rifle. So, there was no need for any story, any excuse.

The itch of curiosity was strong in Carlo. Anyone who broke the rules of common habits and substituted a furtive behaviour must have a good reason. Or—even more stimulating—perhaps not a good reason. Yet—more stimulating still—that fell down because John was clearly a man who by nature was an open book, a man of principle, of integrity, a firm believer in law and order. Unless—no matter how noble a man's character—some point had been reached, or some unexpected slew of events had occurred, which suddenly distorted long, accepted morality and forced him to adopt a new set of ethics. Too fanciful? Maybe, but interesting, Carlo told himself. Not only interesting, but irritating to him. He could sense something in the air. He wanted to know its nature.

He pushed his chair back, got up and began to wander round the room. He was a jackdaw ready to be tempted by a new wall crevice, a magpie to be attracted by the momentary glitter of something in the bushes—and by the odd fact that John Kingsford kept a rifle and ammunition hidden in his bedroom. Fear of burglars, thieves? No—there was an old Service revolver in the gun room which would have answered far better.

He paused in front of the bookcase, saw the Badminton Library volume and thought about the safe. He cocked his head towards it. A thrush, he thought to himself this time, enjoying his own ornithological analogies, listening for the faint sound of the turn of a worm in the turf. Yes, it might be. If there were anything to explain John's behaviour, anything material, it could be in the safe. He had only ever looked in it once, weeks ago. A safe in this house was sacred and the ultimate in security. S for secrets and S for safe . . . he giggled a little to himself, feeling excitement begin to run fast in him.

He reached for the Badminton Library volume. It fell open in his hands at the pages which normally enfolded the safe key. The faint imprint of the key marked both pages. But there was no key. Excitement leaped to a higher level in him. In the moment of its high surge his mind registered two of the printed lines that ran across the recto page indentation. *When fishing private water the angler can choose his own time for beginning operations, and will have the satisfaction.* . . . Calmly under his fever of curiosity he acknowledged the encouragement of the *sortes*. All the omens were right. Nothing would ever normally have made John change a perfectly good hiding place. There was no doubt in his mind that there must now be something in the safe so important to John Kingsford that the man had gone right out of character and decided to find a new hiding place for the key.

Carlo put the book back and went up to his room. When he had first poked around the study he had not tried any of his skeleton keys on the safe because he preferred the challenge of discovering the hiding place of the real key. He wanted to see what there might be new in the safe which was of so much importance to John Kingsford.

He went back to the study with his keys: the souvenir of an exploit many years before, which—despite the trouble he had so narrowly escaped, thanks to the influence of his father's friends and Grace—was still a memory he cherished. Within a few moments he had opened the old-fashioned safe. He recognized the two bundles of ribbon-wrapped letters as new additions.

He looked at his watch. It was almost midnight. Grace and John would not be back until three o'clock or later. If by any chance they had decided to return early he would hear the car coming down the drive, and have time to slip away.

He sat down and began to read the letters.

He realized at once that he was indeed fishing private waters. He read the letters through twice and then put them back in the safe. He went up to bed and lay thinking about them. For quite a long time before her death John Kingsford's wife had been having an affair with a man who signed himself Charles. And the man's letters were headed—when not written on blank paper—with two addresses. One in Norfolk and the other, more intriguingly, from a Pitt Wood House, Dulverton—not many miles away. While reading them he had been sorry for John Kingsford, not because he had been betrayed but because of the references to him which were belittling enough to reach almost a form of contempt. The woman was a bitch who happily gave herself for the preferment (which he, Carlo, was damned sure would never have come to anything) of her husband in his political career; and the man, this Charles (obviously someone pretty high-up) struck him as a satyr. If he had been John Kingsford—and there was no doubt in his mind now of the man's intentions—he, too, would have reached for a rifle. But to reach for a rifle was one thing. To use it was another. He lay considering whether John Kingsford was really the kind of man who would go through with murder. That was the high point of curiosity. In the first flush of anger and bitterness a man could be certain of his intentions. But time could warp and soften them. What were the odds, he wondered, that John Kingsford would keep the rifle in his wardrobe, nourishing the thought of using it, and then never do so? Murder called for special talents if the killer wished to go unsuspected and unmasked. Given the right provocation Carlo was sure he could do it, would do it—but not, he felt, John Kingsford. The man had made his gesture already, and there it would stop . . . far, far short of action.

*   *   *

When Grace and John Kingsford returned from the Hunt Ball they went into the study to have a nightcap before retiring to bed. Grace dropped into the large, worn leather armchair by the safe and lay back as John fixed them whisky and soda. She had had plenty to drink already and had enjoyed herself. If John had had as much as she or more it would have been hard to tell. He was one of those men who carried his drink well. (He would be, she could hear Carlo saying, if she ever remarked on this.) He also, she realized, was the kind of man, too, no matter how late or vigorously he danced—and some of the later Highland reel stuff had been pretty boisterous—never seemed to get untidy or ruffled. (Maybe that was a characteristic which Carlo would approve, because Carlo hated untidiness.) Why Carlo was in her mind so much at this moment she had no idea. Maybe, perhaps, because she had had enough to drink to liberate her thoughts to the point of not being entirely in control of them. . . . No, that wasn't true. Carlo was there because as they had driven down the drive the thought had come to her that Carlo—always avidly interested in the development of any human relationship—would probably be lying in bed awake, awaiting their return and have his ears cocked to find out whether she went to her bedroom alone or with company. Dear Carlo, prurient and unpredictable. . . .

John handed her a glass of whisky and then sat down in the chair at his desk. He raised his drink and nodded to her, saying, 'Well, I thoroughly enjoyed all that. I hope you did?'

'Very much. And thank you. Though I think I had a little too much to drink.'

'So what? Now and again it does us all good to let go.' He put his glass down and was silent for a moment or two and ran his fingers idly over the cover of the diary looseleaf which rested on the desk. Then he looked across at her and smiled, and went on, 'Getting to know people is hard, isn't it? At least, for me it is. That's why I was never really cut out to be a politician. You have to be born with the knack of wading in right away and making yourself . . . well, wide open and available to all sorts. I was never good at that. Not even after I'd known people for a long time. And it seems now—particularly after this evening—that I've known you a long time. Yet I feel tongue-tied.'

Grace laughed. 'That's a pretty good speech for a tongue-tied man.'

John grinned. 'Oh, I'm all right at speeches. I suppose I've just made one. Which, of course, is the last thing I wanted to do. Is that whisky the way you like it?'

'I'm beyond telling. And anyway, you haven't known me for a long time. But if it helps I'm ready to pretend that you have, that we've known one another for years. Old friends . . . who speak frankly. Would you like me to start the ball rolling?'

She watched the hesitation and surprise in him come through, marked by a sudden nervous little tattoo of his fingers on the looseleaf cover. Drink and a pleasant evening, and pleasure in his company, she acknowledged, had liberated her—the only decision she had to make was how she used that freedom. She could be kind and honest with him, or—and God knows the temptation was great when she considered some of the things which had happened to her in the past—she could be quietly wounding. She shied away from a decision. Take it as it comes, play it as it strikes you, she thought.

Quietly, he said, 'Yes, why don't you?'

'All right. Mind you I'm going to have to do a lot of guessing. I suppose you'd like to know why I've never married?'

With a quick, almost angry jerk of his head, John said, 'Good Lord, no. I'd never ask that.'

'Why?'

'Well, it's no business of mine.'

'Oh go on—have a guess. Right or wrong, I shan't mind. Neither of us is in the mood for a fight.'

He smiled. 'You're in some kind of mood. Anyway, if you want my guess you can have it. I suppose it's as simple as somewhere along the line someone you loved and you thought loved you . . . well, let you down.'

Grace drained her glass and made her choice.

'That's quite true. But not once. Twice. The second time I had a child. But he never knew. And when the child, a girl, was three she died of meningitis.'

'Good God, what a terrible thing for you. What a bastard he must have been.'

She shook her head. 'No he wasn't. He was quite a nice man, but he just happened to have no conventional morals. And you don't have to get angry on my behalf. I got over that some years ago. It's a common enough story. It happens to lots of girls and still doesn't put them off marriage. It just so happened with me that it did. I've had affairs with men since, naturally, but I decided never to trust myself to marriage or to the promise of marriage. That's all really there is to know about me. Shall I do some guessing about you?'

He stood up and crossed to her and held out his hand for her glass. For a moment she hesitated, and then handed it to him. With his back to her as he went to the whisky decanter, he said, 'If you want to.'

'Why not? When a man and a woman get to know one another, have a good time together, and they're free to do what they choose without harming anyone else in the world, there's a natural progression. Sooner or later they think of getting into bed with one another. Don't tell me that you haven't thought about that.'

John turned. 'I'd be a liar to deny it. And I must say,'

he smiled faintly, 'you really are something when you start going, aren't you?'

'You've got it wrong. You are. I'm speaking on your behalf, remember?'

He laughed then, and brought the glass back to her, and said, 'That's the last you get. I don't want you waking up in the morning and wondering whether to leave quickly or stay and brazen it out.'

'Don't worry. I'm staying. I have to. Wild horses wouldn't pull Carlo away from here yet—though don't ask me why.'

Welcoming the change of subject, John asked, 'Why did he want to come so much?'

'Who can tell with Carlo? He says that his mother talked often of her visit here. He wanted to see the place. Frankly I don't believe that. What Carlo says often bears little relation to what he is thinking. Do you remember Margaret—his mother?'

John squatted on the edge of the desk, and nodded.

'Yes, I do—very clearly. She scared the wits out of me.'

Grace laughed. 'You mean she made a pass at you?'

'Yes. I was about eighteen, I think, at the time and very raw where women were concerned. She came into my bedroom one night. When I woke up she grinned at me and slipped off her dressing gown. She was naked underneath. It was the first time in my life I'd ever seen a naked woman. Then she just plonked into bed alongside me and grabbed me.'

'What happened?'

'Nothing. I mean nothing serious. I was much too impatient and uncontrolled and she was giggling and laughing all the time—and rather drunk! I'm pretty sure she was in no condition perhaps even to remember what had happened. I can remember hoping that she would come again, but she never did.'

Grace stood up. 'Some opportunities only come once. We either make a mess of them—or things click.' She moved to him, put her glass on the desk, and then bent down and kissed him briefly on the cheek. She moved to the door and then turned and said, 'You stay there and finish your drink. I'd like to go up alone.'

'All right, Grace. Good night, and sleep well.'

He dropped into his chair and suddenly felt tired and oppressed. There was never any guessing the way life would run. When you felt most secure, you could be on the edge of insecurity. Certainty in the morning was doubt in the evening. A young man's humiliation with one sister became the promise of needful ease with the other. As with Grace, an acceptance of emotion's new terms was the alternative. Nevertheless, he knew that he would not be going to her room. Even while she had talked and he had admired her frankness he had shied away from the complication. At the moment he had one purpose and it was paramount. Some superstitious stir imposed its own logic on him. Do this before that—or bad luck would strike. He was no stranger to the feeling, had known it since a boy, and had never ignored it. Yes, he wanted to sleep with her —but not until he had finished with Sir Charles Read.

He took a drink from his glass and then idly picked up the diary from his desk and opened it at random. What, he wondered, would the good Parson John have thought could he have known that here, in this room where most of it had been written, would one day sit a descendant, a great-grandson who would be calmly contemplating the murder of a Foreign Secretary? He would never have believed it. Murder was not part of the Kingsford make-up. A passage in the diary caught his eye and he read it.

To South Molton station with the carriage to meet Jessica's father who is to stay with us for a few days before he goes on to

Exeter. A pompous, but good-natured man who travelled much in his younger days and is full of good stories about those times —in which he features prominently. He told me that the great gale last week blew down three of the pinnacles of St Thomas's Church at Exeter. As we came down Darlock drive I showed him the three beeches which the same gale had uprooted.

After dinner Jessica played and sang for us. She has a thin, but sweet and pretty voice and listening to her I was suddenly near to tears at the blessings which have been showered on me in having such a wife. Her innocence and goodness so far exceeding mine make me aware how little we can divine the true nature of the Lord's designs for us wretched mortals who inhabit his world. A moment's unconsidered anger can alter the rest of a man's life for in such ireful moments the Devil is always present. . . .

John closed the diary. What small sin, he wondered, had the Parson committed which had made him uneasy? Nothing very great for sure. The Parson was always chiding himself for not coming up to scratch, particularly since his marriage. His great happiness in his marriage, he supposed, was making him over-emphasize his own small failings.

He stood up suddenly and put the diary away. The parson's world was long gone—though the old man had lived to see the early nineteen-twenties. His own world remained. This night he had danced and enjoyed himself, and drunk more than he normally did and all thought of what he had to do in the nearing weeks had been forgotten. Now the thought was back. He had no reason to wait for a moment's unconsidered anger or violence to alter his life. It had been altered the first time that Elizabeth had slept with Charles Read. The Lord's design had started then—unknown to him. Now he was part of it, had the power to shape it, and would do so. In far less than a year the John Kingsford he had known had changed. He could walk up now and move into Grace's bed. He had talked to her and said things, the things particularly about her sister, which wild horses could not have dragged from him before. He had shown a curiosity about Grace's life, too, which—no matter her willingness to satisfy it—would have been unthinkable before. And soon he was going to murder a man. Where had the old John Kingsford gone? He didn't know, and he didn't care a damn.

Chapter Seven

THERE WAS a bright, early evening moon floating high over Withypool Common with a thin fleece of cloud hanging high in the northern sky. A light hoar frost lay over the roadside grasses and the bronze bracken clumps. On the wet road coming down to the Portford Bridge layby there had been occasional patches of brittle, crackling ice. The wind was in the north-east, weak but strengthening.

Sitting with Birdie in the front of the car, Carlo said, 'You're the country girl. Are we going to get the weather I want?'

'Could be. You still stuck on that?'

'Why not? When I set my mind on something I don't give up.'

Birdie, close against him, looked into his face and smiled.

'There's more to it than that, though, isn't there?'

'Than what?'

'Just doing the Run. You've got to have a reason for wanting to do it.'

Carlo paused for a moment or two, considering this, and then said, surprising himself, 'That's true. Maybe I'll tell you some day.'

Birdie laughed. 'You needn't bother. I know already.'

'You couldn't possibly. Not even a witch like you.'

'I could you know. At least, a fair guess. You don't fool me. Carlo. Not now. You did at first, before I learned how to read you. When I first took you for a fancy stranger with an eye on me because what else around here was there to have an eye on except maybe Vera Thorn. No, when someone starts to talk about someone a lot it means they either fancy them or they don't. You know how much you talk about John Kingsford?'

'No.'

'Too much.'

'And why should I do that?'

'Well, I'm not sure about this . . . but I think it's because you'd like to be like him. I see it in my brother lots of times. If Dad says he's not up to something or not old enough for something—he'll damn near rupture himself to show he is. That's because he thinks Dad's the best there is and he wants to be like him. Fact is the more you like someone you even get to wanting to show you can do things better than they can.'

'That's a backhanded compliment.'

'So it may be. You want to do that Kingsford Run, yes. But also you want to beat Mr John's time.'

'Think I can do it?'

'Dad does. But he never bets on form much. Just on fancy. He likes you so he wouldn't dream of not backing you.'

'That's nice. What about you?'

Birdie moved away from him and looked at him in silence for a while. Then she said, 'I don't know whether you can or not. Win or lose, it makes no difference to me. But if it's important to you, then I hope you can beat his time. You think you can?'

'I don't know. That's why I'm going to have a try. If I knew I could I wouldn't bother.'

Birdie laughed. 'You'll twist yourself in knots one of these days.'

'Then you can untie me and smooth me out.'

Taking Birdie back home he deliberately made a long

detour down the river Barle and came back along the Dulverton road to Great Cotters Farm. Some way before the entrance to the farm they passed the white gates of the drive entrance to Pitt Wood House. Carlo had already found the house marked on the map. Knowing, even more so now, how quick she was to guess at the truth or the shade of some significance behind a casual remark, he said with a jerk of his head at the white gates as they passed, 'Posh sort of place. Who lives there?'

'That's Sir Charles Read's house. He's not around much though.'

'Why not?'

'He's some nob in the government. You know, a cabinet minister and all that. His old mother lives there. It's a lovely place.'

'Someday I'll buy a lovely place, marry you and take you there.'

'Chance is a fine thing.'

'You don't believe me?'

'Ask me in five years' time.'

'I will.'

'Sure you will—if you haven't forgotten my name by then.' She leaned forward and switched on the radio.

Just for a moment there was a tight twist to Carlo's mouth and his eyelids flickered. Although he hadn't shown it before somehow Birdie was gently getting under his skin tonight, largely he realized because the Kingsford Run and anything to do with him and John Kingsford was his affair. On the point of saying something sharp, he was stopped by Birdie resting her hand lightly on the back of his neck as he drove.

She said, 'Mum and the rest of them are going to Taunton Sunday afternoon to see some relatives. I'll be on my own at the farm from lunchtime on.'

'So . . .?' a shade of his anger still lingered.

'A nice big comfortable bed is better than the back of a car. And I'll cook you supper.'

Carlo laughed. 'All right. We'll celebrate.'

'What?'

'The Run. If this weather lasts I'll do it on Saturday.'

The next afternoon when he drove into South Molton to pick Birdie up from work he arrived early and went into the public library and looked at a copy of *Who's Who* and found Sir Charles Read. Not being a great reader of newspapers he was surprised to find that Sir Charles Read really was some 'nod in the government'. Foreign Secretary!

Suddenly he began to shake with silent laughter and he felt his skin prickle over his cheeks. Then, with equal suddenness, the muscles of his whole body tightened, the physical reaction hitting him before the mental one followed close on its heels. If what he imagined John Kingsford was going to do was true then the man was out of his mind! You couldn't go around shooting Foreign Secretaries! Not even if they had slept with your wife. That was asking for trouble. But why not? My God, you had to give it to him. This *really* was John Kingsford. John Kingsford of Darlock. Of course, he wouldn't care a damn who or what the man was who had played around with his wife. The man deserved a bullet and was going to get it. And there would be no knocking him off in a hasty, ill-considered rush. Oh, no. He'd have worked it all out. He could bide his time. A fragment of breakfast conversation came back to him: John telling how years ago he had sat up five nights in a row to shoot a stray dog that had been marauding sheep. Sir Charles Read didn't know it, but he was dead already.

For the first time since he had met him Carlo freely acknowledged his admiration for the man, and the acknowledgment was given proudly because the man was his father. If it had happened to him, Carlo, he would have done the same. If it had been that he really was the acknowledged son at Darlock and John Kingsford, say, blind or crippled, had handed him the rifle and said what was to be done that he could not perform himself, then he would have taken the gun and done it for him. His father's blood was his blood. . . . He became aware that a man lower down the row of reference books was looking curiously at him, and hoisted the *Who's Who* back into place.

He went out to his car and drove off, back towards the moor. He had not told Birdie that he was going to pick her up. She had her scooter. He wanted to be by himself.

Had Sir Charles Read been just one of the undistinguished gentry around, or a wealthy farmer, there would have been risk—but nothing like the risk of wiping out a Foreign Secretary. The echo of the shot which wiped him out would go round the world. And, by God, there wouldn't be a stone or a leaf left unturned. John Kingsford wasn't crazy, and he was damned sure he had no intention of throwing his life away. Admiration for him was one thing—but was he clever enough to kill and keep himself safe?

He drove slowly, thinking about it. If he could he had to find out how John Kingsford was going to do it. The best way to do that was to put himself in his . . . yes, his father's place and see what he would have done. Every track would have to be covered. The letters in the safe, the rifle, the time and the place, and an alibi for the moment of murder which couldn't be shaken. For the first time in many weeks Carlo's hand itched hard for the feel of a cigarette.

*   *   *

Two mornings later at breakfast with John Kingsford, Carlo said, 'Sir, would you be free on Saturday morning?'

'Why?'

'I was thinking that if this weather held till then . . . I might have a go at the Kingsford Run.'

John sat back and studied Carlo. There had been so much on his own mind lately that he had come to accept Carlo about the place without really being particularly aware of him. As his eyes went over him, he saw that the youth had changed quite a bit since his arrival. Pudgy, slack and self-indulgent had been his verdict then. But not now. Carlo's training runs and his days on and about the moors had changed him. There was no fat on him. If anything his face looked a little too lean and drawn. But he was fit and hard. He smiled. 'So that's what all the morning training has been about?'

'Yes, sir.'

'Why do you want to do it?'

Carlo shrugged his shoulders. 'Not to have my name on the board. I know that's for family. But plenty of outsiders have had a crack, haven't they?'

'That's true.'

'I'd like a go. Just for fun. You know, like people climb mountains because they are there. That's if you could spare the time to be watchkeeper.'

'Why not? I'd be delighted. The weather's right at the moment, if it lasts. Let's hope it does.' John leaned back and lit a cigarette, then with a broad, friendly grin, he went on, 'Don't take this wrong—but you're a funny chap, Carlo. It's the last thing I would have expected from you.'

Carlo nodded. 'I agree, sir. But I just get a bee in my bonnet occasionally. It's something to do, something I've had to get ready for.'

'How old are you?'

'Nearly eighteen, sir.'

'Well, I'm all for the Run—but that's a pretty limited challenge. It's none of my business, of course, but don't you fancy you ought to be thinking of your future in more serious terms than, say, any passing challenge that comes along?'

Not long before this, Carlo knew that he would have resented, even secretly mocked at the rather pompous line Kingsford was taking. Life was real and life was earnest, and time was slipping by. But now he could feel no stir of resentment or contempt. He wasn't faced with a stuffed shirt, dyed-in-the-wool public school, university, Guards Brigade, Member of Parliament (though ex-) representative of an old, ancestor-worshipping family. This was John Kingsford who was his father and was going to revenge the family honour by shooting a Foreign Secretary. That made him primitive, understandable.

'I have been thinking about it,' said Carlo. Though the truth was that it had only just occurred to him and he gave it off the cuff not knowing whether he meant it or not, anxious only for some unformed reason to give this man pleasure. 'I've an idea I'd like to farm. I could go to some agricultural college first to learn the ropes, and then buy a place of my own. Luckily money's no problem.'

'I think that's a damned good idea. If you want any help or advice I'll be glad to give it.'

'Thank you, sir. Then it's all right for Saturday?'

'If the weather holds.' John smiled. 'You've done your homework on the right conditions.' He paused and then went on, 'Why were you so keen, Carlo, to come down here—particularly at the worst time of the year?'

Carlo said without hesitation, 'I think I must have been getting fed up with myself and the kind of life I was leading. All soft and purposeless. Just floating around and being bored. I didn't work it out too clearly to myself, but I suppose I wanted a complete change. Then I remembered my mother, who'd been down here once in the summer, saying some time or the other that in winter it must be absolute hell. . . .' He laughed, but watched John's face for any shade of reaction at the mention of his mother. Seeing none, he went on smoothly, 'I just thought absolute hell would be a change from absolute luxury. Anyway, she was wrong. I like it here. I like the hardness and the bareness of the country.'

Sitting at his desk in the study a little later, John, not for the first time recently, acknowledged how easy it was to be wrong about people; Elizabeth, Sir Charles Read, and himself—and now Carlo. Perhaps most people were only blurred reflections which hid truth.

He reached for the telephone, called Pitt Wood House and spoke to Dorothy Read—Sir Charles's mother—to ask if Charles would be down over Christmas and would like some shooting. The use of the phrase 'some shooting' touched him only ironically, distantly. The man now possessed no humanity for him. He was just something that had to be removed. Sir Charles he learned would—if nothing unexpected cropped up on the international political scene—be down for Christmas and stay through to the New Year as usual. John was invited to the New Year's Eve party as usual and—since Dorothy Read, eighty, kept well abreast of all local news—was welcome to bring any guests he might have staying. They chatted for a while, he without any feeling of embarrassment or guilt or pity.

He dealt with his correspondence and then cleared his desk, an ingrained act of tidiness. As he put away the diary notebook he had been working on the previous night he saw that there were only two more notebooks left. It would be a nice thing he thought if he could finish decoding the lot before the New Year because Robert usually came down then and he would, he knew, like to take away the transcript and read the complete diary. Then he sat back and began to think about the protection he must devise for himself to cover the few hours before and after shooting Sir Charles Read.

That evening he had dinner with Grace in the tower wing dining-room, and afterwards as they were taking coffee in the sitting-room he told her about Carlo and the Kingsford Run, and that Carlo was considering the idea of taking up farming.

John said, 'I really think he's serious about the farming thing.'

'Well, I hope so. But you can never tell with Carlo. He's lived and acted too long on the spur of the moment. That's led him into trouble . . . bad trouble once.'

'Am I allowed to ask what?'

Grace laughed. 'Why not? I don't think Carlo would mind. He doesn't broadcast it, but he's quite proud of it. He calls it his "Raffles period".'

'Raffles?'

'You know. The Robin Hood, gentleman-burglar scene. Stealing from the rich to help the poor.'

'Oh, yes, of course.'

'With a couple of young people of his own type—one of them a girl—the idea was cooked up that they should steal jewellery, mostly from people they knew and who were wealthy, and then offer to return it for a ransom. The money they got was sent to various charities.'

'What a crazy idea! Good Lord!'

'There was nothing crazy about the way they did it. It was highly professional and everything worked out to the last detail. They had everything. Rings of skeleton keys, safe-blowing equipment . . . the whole lot. Although they did give the money to charity, they were really doing it for the excitement. They were caught, but the whole thing was hushed up. Fortunately they'd only robbed four or five people, and they were all friends of the various families involved. One way and another the whole affair was settled without any publicity.'

'Well, let's hope it was a lesson to him. There's nothing worse for young people than to have too much time and money on their hands——'

'Or too much time and no money?'

'That too. Well, I can only hope that he's serious about this farming thing. It's just what he needs at his age. Some definite aim in life.'

Carlo, Grace thought, could have predicted John's sentiments and normally would have been contemptuous of them. But perhaps not now. Perhaps he really was changing. Something was happening to him here at Darlock. It would be heartening to think that it was something for the good, but as far as Carlo was concerned she knew him too well to be too optimistic. Still, he was young and it would be uncharitable not to give him the benefit of the doubt.

*   *   *

The hard weather and the north-east wind held right through to Saturday. Carlo had a light breakfast and afterwards John and he drove down to Landacre bridge on the river Barle. There were ice patches on the roads and a white frost feathered each blade and stalk of the moor grasses and rushes. Sitting in the car with an overcoat over his running kit Carlo was nervous and anxious to begin.

He asked, 'It's all right if I wear a watch to check my going?'

'Yes, of course. There are no rules except that you can cross a recognized road but you mustn't run along one. You can use farm and moor tracks. I shall check you at the old mine on the ridge road, and again at Barham Bridge.

You know the finishing point—the big old stone on the top of Darlock Moor.'

'Yes, sir.'

'I'll be there to time you in. It's a few minutes to ten. I should strip off and warm up outside the car. I'll blow the horn for the off at ten.' John gave him a smile. 'I almost wish I was back at your age and about to do it. But I don't mind telling you I had a tummy full of butterflies.'

Carlo grinned. 'So have I. If I had any sense I'd call it off.'

John shook his head. 'No you wouldn't. You're doing it because it's there. Sometimes challenges creep up on you and you've got to accept them. Right—out you get.'

Carlo got out of the car, stripped off his coat and began to pad around the car, loosening up.

The car horn suddenly blew and John called, 'Off you go and good luck!'

Carlo glanced at his watch. It was ten o'clock. He went across the road and on to the rough pasture at the side of the river. Close to the bank the marshy ground had only a thin crust over the sodden, waterlogged soil below. He kept off this, veering up the slope away from the river where the ground was firmer. It would be the easiest thing in the world to go through the hard marsh top into a foot of soft ground and twist an ankle. He ran at a steady pace, picking his route by marks already established . . . the slab of a boulder ahead in the hill turf, the rusty brown growth of dead bracken clumps, the iron grey, sheep-and-pony-printed line of a track and far away, at the top of the river where the Sherndon Water joined it, the steep green slopes of the narrow combe that ran up between Ferny Ball and Sherndon Hill. This first leg was the longest of the three and he knew that if it were forced at too great a pace he could be left with too little reserve to make the most of the fast downhill stretch to Bardham Bridge. As he ran he saw, not only the quick flight of a dipper up the Barle, the sudden starting away of black-faced sheep as he topped a small rise and the slow, ragged winging of a pair of ravens which had made the sides of the valley their territory, but also the mahogany board in the gun room with its list of names, and the name of John Kingsford with his time set out in gold figures—*2 hours 38 minutes*. He was going to beat or equal that time. There was no point in what he was doing, yet he had to do it; the strong compulsion in him completely unsusceptible to logic.

As Carlo disappeared up the river, John turned the car and drove back up the hill. Towards the top of the hill, just beyond the cattle grid that marked the beginning of the open moor, he stopped and took out his field glasses.

From the roadside he had a view down the Sherndon valley to the junction of the Barle. He was in time to pick up Carlo as he splashed across the stream above the junction pool and began to head up the lower slopes of Great Ferny Ball on an angled line which would take him up the combe past the ruins of Ferny Ball farm. He smiled to himself, remembering arguments with his brother. Robert had taken that line, a shorter but harder one, while he had favoured the longer and easier detour following Sherndon Water and then passing on to the Kingsford Water. The Very Reverend had been right . . . but then Bob had had, in those days, lungs of leather and legs that never tired.

He got back in the car after watching Carlo disappear into the first of the trees on the combe side.

Going over the long slope fall on the north-west slope of Sherndon Hill, the Kingsford Water far below him, Carlo checked his going on his watch. He was a minute slower than he had laid down for himself. With the wind behind him, and stronger now up on this high point, he put on speed, racing down to the twisting valley below. Away to his left he could see the smooth shoulder of Long Holcombe and the trees around Darlock House. He had seen the field glasses in the car and he knew that John Kingsford would be watching him from time to time. John Kingsford who as calmly as kiss your hand was going—he was certain —to shoot the Foreign Secretary. My God, that was something. Not like the comparatively kid stuff of robbing a few jewel boxes and ropy old safes which had set the blood pounding in his ears and the adrenalin pumping away. No, that had been a false excitement right from the start because all of them had had the security of family, and family wealth and influence behind them.

He jumped across Kingsford Water, the stream fringes laced with little fans of ice. A snipe got up from a patch of low gorse ahead, the dead blooms of the heather were blossoming again with pale hoar frost, silver and white bells. This little stretch of shallow valley had been a favourite place of Parson John's for shooting, he knew, from the diary. He liked to walk up here after woodcock and snipe with his dog Skip. Donkey's years ago. And not so long back, John Kingsford had been on the hill just above . . . getting ready . . . probably zeroing his rifle . . . to knock off the Foreign Secretary. Good luck to him. That would be something to watch.

As he came up the side of the valley, threading his way around the humps of the old mine workings just below the ridge road, he glanced at his watch. He was a shade outside the time he had set himself still, but not enough to worry him. He was going well and the worst leg was behind him.

As he crossed the ridge road he saw John standing by his car. The man raised a hand to him. He slid through the wire fence and began to pound fast now down the long pasture slope, going caterwise to hit the lower road and cross that into the top of the little fold running down to

Deercombe corner and on to the long drop down the stream to the bottom of Fyldon Hill and Tinker's Ford. For a time the strong wind was on his left flank, but he lost it as he dropped into the valley. In a few minutes he was at the Deercombe corner ford. He ran up the track a few yards to gain the path that followed the hillslope down the water. For a moment or two Parson John was with him again. Hannah Darch picking daffodils under the old oak . . . sometime he must get John to let him read more of the transcript. He tripped suddenly, a half-buried root catching his foot. He fell sideways and crashed a couple of yards down the bank. A sapling slashed his face. For a moment, the temptation suddenly surprising him, he felt that he wanted to lie there, winded, and give the whole stupid business up, but almost before the thought could live he was up and running again. He put his fingers to his cheek. They came away covered in blood. So what? But he kept his eyes now watchfully on the twisting awkward track.

When Carlo came up on to the road at Barham Bridge John was waiting. Carlo crossed the road with hardly a glance in his direction and dropped over the parapet into the tangle of underbrush and low trees by the stream. John saw the cut on Carlo's cheek and the dark stain of drying blood. A tumble somewhere. Well, both he and Robert had suffered that. You had to keep your eyes open on the run down Fyldon. He looked at his watch. He was not surprised now to see that Carlo was doing well. That had been clear upon the ridge road. Surprise he had known there, though on reflection he should have known better from all that Grace had told him about Carlo. If the lad set his mind to something he tolerated no half measures. The trouble lay in the things he set his mind on. But maybe those days were gone. Maybe a new Carlo was emerging. He hoped so. As he watched Carlo slogging away across the hard meadow towards the river Mole, the green plantations of Long Wood rising behind it, he had a sudden pang of wishful thinking. How good it would have been if this morning it were his son he was timing, a Robert, Henry or William Kingsford, running to take a place on the board in the gun room. Elizabeth could have given him a child long ago . . . cold anger filled him at the thought. All her talk, and all her false longing for it to happen when all the time she must have been keeping herself immune from conception so that she . . .

He turned to his car, seized with a swift bitterness. Far better if Carlo were his son. Far better if that stupid, futile fumbling and the shame of over-excitement with Margaret Lindsay had found him, instead, experienced. If she had had a child by him he would have married her. No less would have been acceptable to him, though he would have been landed with a drunkard for a wife. But he would have had a son: a young man, running now on a bitter, hard morning, slogging his guts out to beat father and uncle, and that father and uncle the first to rejoice at their defeats. Well . . . it was not too late. There might not be love, but there were other women, women who, no more than he, would demand love. Grace, for instance. There was no love between them. But they liked each other. Last night, after their dinner together, he could have gone to her bed or she to his. He would have brought it about, knew she must wonder why he had not, were it not for the firmly growing idea, almost a superstition, in him that there was no place for it until the death of Charles Read finally freed him from Elizabeth.

With the Mole to his right, Carlo headed up the long valley towards Shortacombe and the top of Darlock Moor. This was the stretch he liked best and, maybe because he did, he felt himself going freely and faster. He had walked down here once or twice with Birdie and she had shown him the places where the salmon and seatrout spawned and they had stood and watched one afternoon, quietly and still at the side of a crystal clear pool, a large hen fish cutting her redd, her body twisting and arching as she scoured and fanned the gravel away into a grove while the old cock hung poised alongside her, waiting for the egg-shedding curve of her body and the white gape of her mouth to signal him to cover the falling eggs with his milt. Here, too, he had met a badger head on along one of the rides in Long Wood and the old boar had sniffed and turned aside like some solitary old gent resenting company. Now as he ran a sparrow-hawk came round a lichen- and moss-covered oak and threw up high into the air at the sudden sight of him. The sight of the predator hanging high and exposed sent a flock of fieldfares foraging upstream into broken panic flight.

Carlo glanced at his watch, saw that the downhill leg from the ridge road had gained him all the time he had reckoned on. He pressed himself hard now to the rising valley slope. He knew every hedge gap, every curve and recurve of the river and where to splash across or stick to the bank. He was going dead into the north-east wind now and its coldness took the heat from his sweaty chest and lay there like a clammy hand. He was now two minutes ahead of the time he had calculated might have been John Kingsford's time to the valley below Shortacombe Farm. He caught a glimpse of the farm hanging on the shoulder of moor high above him. Below the farm the river forked. The right-hand and main stream swung round a little and followed a longer but easier course up on to the moor and the bogs and springs which gave it birth. Carlo veered away to the left, following the minor stream through oak and beech trees and occasional stands of firs. The course was steep and narrow but by following the stream he could swing off right-handed after about four hundred yards and take the sharp, hard rise to the top of the moor. He was going now, he thought, like some old hound dog, fixed on the scent-line . . . thump, thump, thump with his feet, eyes on the ground, picking up the marks he knew, his throat and lungs singing with the icy bite of indrawn breath. Here I come, he thought, Carlo on the road to Athens from Marathon: Carlo the victory-bearer . . . but no bloody crown of laurels, no golden inscription . . . just bloody stupid Carlo flogging his guts out for damn-all. . . . Up on the moor top, a few hundred yards away from the flattening out of the final rise, was the old grey boulder that marked the end of the run, a boulder that stood no more than a hundred yards from the ridge road and the entrance to the Darlock House drive. John Kingsford would be there now . . . waiting. And not in the wildest stretch of imagination, a commodity he considered limited enough in Kingsford, would the man know that he waited there to time his own son to the end of the Run. If he had known that here came his own bastard, would he consider even for a moment that in all justice the name Carlo Graber (no matter what time he made, and he was making far better than Kingsford's time now) deserved a place on the gun room board? Not on your life. No bastards admitted. But Parson John might have . . . Parson John with his Hannah Darch was that kind of man.

He jumped a boulder down to the stream side to cross and attack the steep slope up to the moor and slipped again. This time he fell heavily, face down into the shallows, winding himself and taking the skin off his right palm against a rock. Breath sobbing, he pulled himself up and, anguished from the fall, breasted the rise, forcing himself to it, slowly feeling his breath easing and power coming back to him, and forced himself harder, knowing the fall had lost him time. Two hours and thirty-eight minutes. No less. No less. The blood from his hand dripped across his running vest and spotted his shorts. He wanted to look at his watch to see what time he had lost but he held back the temptation, waiting to reach the top. He would look at the time there and know what he had to do across the bare, dun expanse of moor to make his time.

Up on the moor, standing by the boulder, John waited for Carlo. For a time he had watched the main valley of the Mole running up to its source but had quickly realized, when Carlo had not appeared, that he must be taking the left-hand stream, the shorter but much harder route. He swung round, holding his glasses on the spot away to the west where Carlo would appear. He had done this too on the day that Robert had made his run. Robert and Carlo, neither of them having any truck with an easy route, going baldheaded along their own course, taking the gamble of a fall in harder country that could twist an ankle, break a bone. . . . Robert running as he always rode, hell-bent from point to point. He would never have thought that Carlo would be the same. All that was required of him was that he should do the run in decent time. There was no family pride involved, no brotherly rivalry. Well, that was everything to his credit. To do something to the utmost when there was nothing to gain, no long-standing family challenge or rivalry to spur him on, showed he had a deep pride just in himself. Maybe, in a way, that was more worthy. To do something which pride in yourself alone dictated . . . to do it because it was there to be done.

Carlo came up over the skyline. The flat dome of the moortop spread before him, the stronger blast of the north-easter assaulting his body. He could see John in the distance by the boulder, and behind him the pale, cold blue sweep of the sky and the distant top of Dunkery Hill clear and sharp in the smoothly ranging silhouette of hills and highlands. He glanced at his watch, and elation coursed through him like the first bite of alcohol, obliterating the ache and fatigue of his body. He had all the time in hand he wanted to beat John Kingsford. He could make it in two hours thirty-six minutes easily. He could beat this man who raised such different emotions in him. He ran on easily. A meadow pipit flirted away from a dwarfed furze bush. He was John in the distance lower his field glasses and look at his watch. He could do it, he could do it; the knowledge pounded exhilaratingly in him as vividly as blood and breath. And then suddenly, trapped completely by a raw emotion which took him imperatively and illogically, he knew that he did not want to do it. To know he could was enough. Nobody could rob him of that. He was a Kingsford and had proved it. But the proof held no value for him, unless this man waiting for him also knew and acknowledged it. Deliberately, realizing he must make it look authentic, he pretended to trip and fell. He lay flat on his stomach, body heaving, and looked at his watch, looked and waited and while he did so he heard a distant, encouraging shout from John. Past questioning himself now and enjoying his own acting he made a show of trying to raise himself and then dropped to the turf once more, giggling quietly to himself. Distantly he heard John shout again. He looked at his watch and then rose to his feet and plugged on, exaggerating his distress.

He came breath-sobbing, half-plodding, half-running up to John Kingsford and collapsed at his feet and as the man bent to help him up heard him cry, 'Two-thirty-eight exactly! Well done, Carlo!'

Carlo got slowly to his feet, grinned and said, 'Pity I fell back there, sir. Lost me quite a bit.' Just the right tone, he thought: decent sort of chap, Carlo. Always puts up a good show. . . .

John put the overcoat he had brought from the car round Carlo's shoulders. 'Come on—what you want is a hot bath and someone to look at those cuts.'

'What I want,' said Carlo, wondering what this man's reaction would be, 'is a damned good drink and a cigarette.'

Laughing, John put his arm round Carlo's shoulder and began to lead him away. 'And why not? You bloody well deserve it. I can tell you that the Very Reverend had to be carried to bed from a surfeit of port on the night of his run.'

'And you, sir?'

'I just managed to get to bed under my own steam. And please, Carlo, I'd like it if you cut out this "sir" business. My name's John.'

'Yes, of course . . . John.' Not the final accolade, Carlo thought, but a nice one. No name on the gun room board, but the next best thing, admittance to the order of the good chaps, the decent sorts who knew the rules and the right and proper moments when training could be broken. And why in God's name had he faked his time . . . why, why, why? He must have gone crazy. . . . No, crazier than ever, because he had been crazy in the first place to want to do this stupid run.

*   *   *

They lay in bed together, naked under the covers. He had his arm around Birdie and she was sleeping, her cheek pressed against his bare shoulder, her body warm and familiar against his. Carlo stared at the floral wallpaper touched by a shaft of sunlight through the window. He liked this room. Not just because it was Birdie's, but because it had always been some Carter child's room since the house had been built. A velvet-framed photograph over the ducknest-grate fireplace showed a faded, sepia-coloured group of Carter men and women and neighbours posed in stiff best clothes outside a church porch. One of the women held a long-clothed swaddled infant . . . some christening ceremony, probably at Simonsbath. He had joked about buying a fine place and marrying Birdie. Now he wondered whether it was a joke. Deep purpose could grow from idle fantasy. He could marry Birdie, learn to farm, buy a place and start to put down roots. There always had to be a beginning. The first Carter had come here when the forest was reclaimed, a butcher's son coming from Dorset with three wagons and horses driven by his men, and himself and his new wife in a gig, to break the land and build a house while they quartered themselves at Withypool until the homestead should be ready. That first Carter had sent down the first roots. And sometime or other there had been a first Kingsford, not at Darlock, but at the old house near North Molton. Someone had to be first, somebody had to sweat things out at the beginning and leave others to go on after he had gone. . . . Maybe that was what he had to do. He had come from nothing, unwanted, unplanned, the fruit of unloving copulation. So what? Who cared about love? Certainly not Nature. Love was man's invention. Old Mother Nature just said 'Get on with the coupling or the system will break down.' He chuckled gently to himself and fingered the dry cut on his face. The Kingsford Run was done, and God knows why he had forced himself to it. There was no point in trying to rationalize it, no point in wondering just what had compelled him to hold back from breaking John's time. *My name's John . . . Call me John.* A crumb from the rich man's table. *My name's Carlo . . . Call me Carlo Kingsford. Call me son. . . .* Birdie stirred in her light sleep. Lovely Birdie, tucked safely under his wing, uncomplicated, generous Birdie. He would marry her, find himself a place . . . walk his ground, watch the ewes with their lambs, the cows with their calves, and worry about the hay crop, the hedging and ditching and warble fly and sheep fluke . . . father children and teach the boys to be men and the girls to behave themselves, and if any man tried to touch Birdie take a rifle to him—calmly and surely, like John was going to do.

It fascinated him to know that John was going to do it. Men's faces and behaviour masked their secrets easily when the purpose behind those secrets was born of character and inflexible codes. Last night they had all had dinner together, a celebration, marked with claret for the pheasant and port with the nuts, and laughter and jokes and easiness. Almost a family group. And Grace with her eyes on John, which meant that Grace was relaxed, looking for some divertissement . . . or perhaps she had already found and taken it. Lucky John—first one sister and then the other. . . .

Birdie's eyelashes flickered against his skin and she said, 'What are you giggling about?'

'Life.'

'Oh, I thought it might be something funny.'

'It is.'

'You're too deep for me—almost.'

'Almost what?'

'Almost always. Except when you think you've gone real deep and you haven't at all.'

'You'd better go back to sleep. You're not making sense.'

'Oh, yes I am.' She rolled herself half on top of him and laughingly teased his lips with the nipples of her small breasts. 'You timed yourself, didn't you? Because otherwise it would have been too much a freak of chance. You could have beaten him—but you wouldn't. You just wanted to get the same time exactly. What you do that for, Carlo?'

'You tell me.'

'Why bother? There's better things to do.' She rolled

right on top of him. 'Except there's got to be a reason somewhere.' She put her lips against his and held them there cool and unmoving.

He moved his hands over her, felt his own and her body begin to stir, and thought for the first time that people looked too much for reasons, himself included. Some things were done without reason. Body and brain moving with their own, undiscoverable purpose.

Later he acknowledged it again when Birdie told him that she didn't want him around while she was preparing their supper dish, for without deliberate purpose he found himself moving down the hill below the farm to the river, taking the path that followed its curves downstream until he was in the broad, tree-pocked meadow below Pitt Wood House. He went up through the trees to the crest of the mound on which the house, ringed by shrubberies and gardens, stood. It was a long, low white house with stables and outyards, the whole property and grounds immaculately kept and ordered. There were lights showing in the lower windows as the late afternoon began to darken.

He turned away, drifting, down to the river to take the path back. Across the river was a high bluff, its crown of trees cut by a rough track that sloped to the Barle and ended at the waterside. A man with a rifle; a rifle with a two to three hundred yards effective range in the right hands. . . . That must mean that John was going to kill from a good, safe distance. But where and when? He could guess the when, for he knew now from talking to Birdie that Sir Charles Read always came down to visit his mother at Christmas or the New Year. John would hunt in the country he knew. He'd be a fool not to—and John was no fool. He moved up the bank, the light going fast, and watched a high flying scatter of wood pigeons homing to the trees around Pitt Wood House to roost. To kill a man you had to know his movements and to choose a time and a place, surely, when the man was alone and predictably vulnerable because his own habits innocently compelled it. One shot, two at the most, and the light had to be good, and following death there had to be time for the killer to move away fast, to put ground between himself and the victim. He bit at a thumbnail, trying to picture the scene, trying to put himself in John's place.

He wanted to watch, to see it happen. And the strength of that desire, he could admit to himself, was no more than the detached compulsion of a vicarious voyeur. To see people as they were when they considered themselves unobserved, to probe their desks and their private correspondence, to know something about them which they could never know you knew, there was a pulse-raising pleasure in that. And to do that with John would establish, too, a new dimension in their esoteric relationship. He was John's son—and John didn't know it. And John would be a murderer—and would never know that he, Carlo, knew it. Secret knowledge was the magical basis of power, even if the power were never to be used, the possession of the arcane an end in itself. John Kingsford was going to shoot Charles Read—the opportunities for that were strictly limited by his position. The proper study, Carlo saw as he walked back to the farm, was not John, but Sir Charles. There was no need to watch John. He had to find out all he could about Sir Charles's habits down here, and that must lead him to the moment of Sir Charles's death which he was determined to witness. He smiled to himself, rubbing his hands, not only against the cold of the wind that was strengthening down the valley, but gloating over the richness of life's strange bounties. The Run was over. Carlo's occupation was gone. But now Carlo had another occupation.

Birdie and he ate alone in the kitchen; the labourer

returned, his wife greeting him with comfort and victuals. One day, he thought, yes, truly, one day he would sit in his own home with Birdie and it would all be as simple as that. He'd sit wolfing steak and kidney pie with creamed potatoes and brussels sprouts and, with mouth half-full, detail the doings of the day; the market prices, the lamb count as the ewes dropped, the ordering of a new tractor or harvest combine. Rich acres, fine bed-worthy wife, a quiver full of children and his own gun room with a board there to mark some test, some run, some challenge which all the boys would have to face or feel the smack of his boot against their backsides. Yes, it was time to think about putting down a tap root and the moment Sir Charles had his head blown off would mark the beginning because one secret cancelled out another and the slate would be clean. He began to chuckle and ended up by half-choking from the food in his mouth so that Birdie came round and smacked him heartily on the back, bringing tears to his eyes.

He drove back to Darlock late, long after the Carters had returned from Taunton, and he knew more then than he had when he had gone to the farm that day. Mr Carter and Mrs Carter liked talking, liked gossip, knew all their neighbours. And how easy it was to steer one's innocently veiled questions.

He could hear Mr Carter saying of Sir Charles, 'For all his position he's a terrible wilful man. There's a regular detective sort of chap that comes down wi' un—but he spends most of his time in servants' quarters. Most mornings when he's down I see Sir Charles riding along the river by hisself. Set your watch by him, you could. Good seat on a horse and not a gate or stone wall round these parts to stop un when he gets goin'.'

Chapter Eight

OVER A WEEK before Christmas, John filled the rifle magazine with ammunition, wiping the rifle first and then using gloves during the loading. He wrapped the rifle in two towels which he had bought in an Exeter multiple store, and then made the package waterproof with an outer covering of an old blue fertilizer sack which he had picked up in a hedge on the roadside thirty miles away some days before. He fastened the parcel with a length of binder twine which he had found at the foot of a hayrick not far from the place where he had picked up the fertilizer sack.

He was confident that if any of these items were ever found they could not be traced back to him.

Late in the afternoon with only an hour's daylight left he took the parcel and drove over the moor on the back road to Dulverton and parked his car in a layby some miles from Worth Farm. Away to the right the ground dropped through old oak woods and steep cliff to the river Barle. He had often used the layby when he came pigeon shooting in the woods, which belonged to an old friend of his. Any local seeing the car would take little notice of it.

He went into the oak woods and worked his way along narrow, little-used paths until he came to the end of the trees. Two fields away was the ruined cottage, sitting at the top of the bluff which overlooked the river and the meadows of Pitt Wood House on the other side of the Barle. He crossed the fields in the lee of the hedges.

He went into one of the broken-down cottages, all the floors heaped with broken rubble and some of the rooms open to the sky where the roof had gone. Moss covered the rubble heaps, ferns grew between the stones and here and there lean elderberry growths had rooted in the walls. In the kitchen the old range had partly tipped away from its fixing in the large open fireplace, leaving a gap between it and the back wall. He dropped the rifle down the gap and then piled loose bricks and stones across the short length of the gap so that its existence was hidden. Then he walked back in the growing dusk to his car. There was no emotion in him. Nobody knew what he was going to do. His only concern now was not to raise any curiosity about his movements before the shooting which might linger suspiciously or with idle curiosity in anyone's memory.

Back at Darlock that evening, he locked himself in his study after dinner, opened the safe and, without even glancing at any of them, burnt all the letters from Charles Read to his wife on the log fire, stirring the white ashes until no trace of them was left. Then he poured himself a large whisky and sat at his desk to go on with his transcribing of Parson John's diary. There was a calmness in him which he had not known for a long time as though this first positive step towards action had assured the promise of future real contentment.

*   *   *

Carlo saw him. Carlo now had long been watching John, unobtrusively, distantly. He had made it his business to mark the man's movements all through the day as much as he could. The surveillance, always casually masked, was a quickly acquired habit. From his bedroom he could overlook the yard at the rear of the house where John's car so often stood on the cobbles. From their sitting room he could watch the front of the house and the car if it were parked there. Sometimes, at night, when he knew John was safely in the house, he would lie in his chair in his bedroom, feet up, smoking an occasional cigarette, though from choice he now used them much less and only rarely felt the need for a whisky or a glass of sherry, and think about John, and put himself in his place. He lived in the man's mind and—since the thought of murder was an excitement in him, the peak of all hazards—he found little difficulty in the surrogate exercise of being John. That John had already picked a spot from which to kill he felt must be certain. Felt, too, that the choice for that spot was self-limiting since Sir Charles had to be killed from a distance and at some place where—on a limited visit to Pitt Wood House—his presence could be predicted by the habit of a routine which would leave him alone and unprotected. Knowing what he did now, from his first and then further unobtrusive probings at the Carters' place, the conviction had grown with him that the killing would be done—to make the getaway safe—from the far side of the river, from the bluff overlooking the meadows. One . . . two shots at the most and then John Kingsford had to put ground fast between himself and the meadow. In fifteen minutes on foot he could be away and up on the wide, desolate spaces of the Worth or Withypool moor.

There were moments when Carlo lay thinking, hugging himself with excitement. He wanted to see the killing. The need for that was a fever in him. When that moment came their individual secrets would be properly balanced. Knowledge that was never to be used, simply treasured as a magpie treasures a bright milk bottle top, was more precious than any gold.

It was no surprise to him when at half-past three in the afternoon he saw John go to his car in the driveway carrying a long, blue parcel and put it in the boot of the car. It had been what he had expected to happen some time. You could walk the moor with a shotgun and a dog, but not with a rifle. There was not a countryman, a moor hand, within thirty miles who could not tell the difference between the two at a hundred yards. So, the weapon had to be hidden in place long before the act.

From the window he watched John drive away. There was no hurry in him to follow. Whatever he did had to be done in isolation, divorced in time and place from John's movements. The abiding imperative in his mind was that John should never suspect his interest in him. He waited half an hour and then went down and got his motor-cycle. The rifle must be hidden on or very close to the chosen murder spot. And John's car would have to be parked somewhere within a mile or two of that spot, parked casually, innocently so that no nagging lift of memory would ever linger in any casual observer's mind.

He drove down the Withypool road but just outside the village turned back hard right along the road running south to Dulverton. A few miles along the road he saw John's car parked in a layby. He drove by without stopping and went on as far as Worth Farm on the right. Not far from the farm on the left-hand side of the road an old track ran away to the east and—as he knew from his map which he had studied assiduously now for many days—went down the hill towards the old ford across the river by the Pitt Wood House meadows. He rode on and turned back hard right after a few miles to take the road westwards across Hawkridge plain and Twitchen Barrows, and so complete a great circle which brought him finally to Darlock House.

He was at his bedroom window when John drove his car into the yard at the back. John left his car on the hard standing and—clear in the yard lights—went empty-handed into the kitchen. There was no doubt in Carlo's mind that the rifle would no longer be in the car.

Carlo turned away from the window, poured himself a whisky from his travelling bar, and lit a cigarette. He lay back in his chair and stared into space, lost in the sequence of pictures which crowded his mind . . . Sir Charles Read riding in the bright winter morning sunshine. . . . No mist or rain, or wild wind blowing because the conditions for shooting had to be perfect. The deceived husband up on the bluff, the unsuspecting adulterer moving to the gait of his horse and the passage from life to death to be marked by the slow contraction of a trigger finger. A flush of rare pleasure streamed through his body, shaking him with a moment or two of giddiness. He put his hand to his forehead and it came away damp with sweat.

*   *   *

In his study that night John Kingsford gathered together the loose pages of the transcriptions he had made from the diary. While decoding he seldom took in the run of the parson's comments. It was only when he had finished a spell that he liked to read the pages through leisurely, enjoying for the first time the old man's words.

Although the parson had written his lines well over a hundred years ago, and wrote simply and straightforwardly of events and personalities, John often found it difficult to be conscious of the gap in time which separated them, for the words had been penned in this study and at this desk. Parson John was always present speaking not through the written word but as though he sat in the armchair by the fire, legs sprawling, detailing the doings of his day.

Came back with Jessica on the Irish packet to Bristol where we stayed the night with the Harringways. The next morning

162

Doctor Harringway took me round his gardens and nursery houses and when we left presented me with a sapling of the Chile pine, araucaria imbrecata, for Darlock. I doubt that it will do well there for the moor takes unkindly to exotics yet is sometimes capricious enough to show unexpected tenderness to alien growths. I shall plant it on the west side of the drive in the lee of the beeches above the yard.

John smiled to himself. The moor had taken kindly to the monkey-puzzle tree where it had grown tall over the years until a gale had toppled it when he was twelve years old. Many a time he and Robert had tried to climb it without success. It had been planted in March, 1873, a month before Jessica Kingsford had given birth to her first child, a son, William Kingsford.

The record of the birth was in the transcriptions he had made that night:

Sunday, 27 April, 1873

At an hour after midnight Jessica was delivered of a boy, a full week in advance of her expected time. Wilson took me in to see her after a while. Jessica lay pale, happy and proud and her dear eyes were shining with a bliss which matched my own joy and contentment at her safe delivery. I asked Wilson and the nurse to leave the room for a few moments and then knelt at the bedside and said a prayer of thanksgiving for mother and child. When Jessica asked me did I not think it was the most beautiful creature, I heartily agreed though to be honest I have yet to see any newborn child which could be designated beautiful, particularly boys. It had a thin thatch of black hair and a port wine face. But showed a goodly grip of the hand when I presented it with my finger to hold. Later, when I walked out of the house to compose my thoughts and emotions before retiring, it was to find that a light drift of late snow had fallen since darkness and the sky was clear with a fine moon shining. Near the drive I saw an old dog otter come up across the lawn from the Sherndon Water, making an overnight run for the Mole no doubt. Skip, who was with me, stood and watched it, making no move to harry the otter. Normally, no words of mine would have held him back from the chase. I took this for a sign of peace and accord fitting for this night.

Rode to Simonsbath later to take morning prayer, and Holy Communion, and then afterwards stayed alone in the church for a while to make my own private devotion and contrition, only too aware of my many failings.

The child is to be called William Morrison Kingsford. The Morrison for Jessica's father, and the William for my own.

For John it was easy to imagine the scene, the light, late drift of snow which often took the moor tops, and the otter tailmarking the white lawn as it climbed from the stream below to make the passage overland to the Mole. Many an otter he had seen move so at night from his own bedroom window.

He tidied the loose sheets and clipped them into place in the holder. As he took the original diary volume to put it back in its box with the others he flipped the pages over with his thumb. This was the last volume of the set of diaries, for the parson had given up keeping a diary towards the end of the year 1873. The idea had taken him recently that he would like to finish the transcription before he made his move against Charles Read. It was a quirkish, superstitious notion which had slowly grown with him, an irrational conception that to do so would be talismanic and ensure for himself complete success and future safety. It was not a strange notion to him. All his life he had now and then been seized with the idea that he had to do *this* first (something usually of no importance) in order to be free successfully to do *that*, something of real importance. He saw that he would have plenty of time to finish his work. A few more nights and the task would be finished. Suddenly, arising from this, a new pattern of superstition imposed itself, not to be resisted—he would reserve the last entry in the volume for the night before he went out to kill Charles Read.

*   *   *

Carlo found the rifle easily because he already knew roughly where it had to be. He rode over the next morning and left the Norton in a spinney well south of Worth Farm. Then he went down to the river and walked its westerly woods upstream to the ford and the overlooking bluff, coming to the cottages from the opposite direction to the one which John had taken. He went into the cottages and looked around, stepping carefully, eyeing the piles of stones and rubbish for any sign of disturbance. John would have well wrapped the rifle but, even so, would not leave it exposed to the weather if he could devise otherwise. So, it would not be under a pile of rubble where rain could seep through.

Pleased with himself, bubbling inwardly with pleasure, he played the part of John. Moving round the first of the pair of cottages he came to the only room that was partly sheltered by half a crazy roof and saw the kitchen range, the rusty doors gaping wide, and then the piled stones and rubble wedged along its back. Some of the stones and bricks were damp whereas the ceiling and chimney rubble lying across the top of the range was dry and dusty. He lifted a brick and exposed the blue of the wrapping around the parcel. He put the brick back and went out. He walked back down the river, lifted in spirit by his own prescience and a delicious surge of anticipation of things to come.

He rode back to Darlock slowly, savouring the thought

of the near future. Unseen, he would have a ringside seat. Already he had chosen his spot. There was an elation and nervous tension in him which had never been equalled at any moment when he and the others had played their robbery game. Always, because of their wealth and families, there had been almost certain safety behind them, a sanctuary easily at hand. But now—this was to be murder, the irredeemable act, and—without question, although no one would ever know it—he was an accessory to murder. He could save the life of Sir Charles Read, should save it— but would not. He was, he told himself, elation building higher suddenly, peaking in an arrogant potency of spirit and body, a god watching the play of mortals below, their futures wide open to him; only a few words from his mouth needed to alter or reshape them. But neither movement nor sound would come from him. Divine Carlo, watching from the gods. The joke was so good that he suddenly shouted aloud with laughter, twisted the throttle grip and sent the machine beneath him leaping forwards, wind flattening his cheeks, the rising roar of the exhausts a great paean to Carlo . . . Carlo . . . Carlo . . .

*　　　*　　　*

John's brother Robert, the Very Reverend, arrived unexpectedly the next morning to spend a couple of nights. He was on his way back from Truro where he had been staying with the Bishop, and was going from Darlock on to Winchester to spend Christmas there. The first evening John, Robert and Grace had dinner together. Carlo had gone out to have supper with the Carters. Robert was good and easy company with the art of unobtrusively keeping a conversation going, knowing the right moment for pause and change, never too long-winded himself, but—as Grace already knew—always happy to take a little more than his fair share of the talk. The contrast between the two brothers was very marked.

The likeness in build and colouring between them was evident, but in the place of John's lean hardness of physique Robert had acquired a pleasing and almost professional degree of plumpness making him seem more important, more worldly and profound than John. There was a comfortable ecclesiastical twinkle in his eyes and he practised a gallantry towards Grace which she enjoyed—and had never known from John—and which, she guessed, Robert had long ago deliberately acquired for dealing with the ladies of cathedral circles and church wives and spinsters. A diocesan politician and an ambitious, skilful promoter of his own career, Grace sensed, but also a man with a great goodness of heart.

Over coffee when John had been called away to his study to take a telephone call, Robert said to her, 'I am glad that you and Carlo came down here for this visit, Grace.'

Grace smiled. She could not remember at which point he had first called her Grace. It could have been here or at their London meeting, but it was entirely acceptable and natural. She said, 'Glad for whom?'

Robert chuckled and began to prepare a cigar.

'For everyone. Carlo is looking a thousand times fitter than when I first saw him. And I hear he's done the Run in magnificent time. That is something the moor can do to some people. Greek begins to speak to Greek. He's a well set up young man.'

'And myself? What has this wilderness done for me?'

'You really want to know?'

'Of course.'

'Well then, to a natural Grace—if you will pardon the pun—have been added, I sense, a growing lightness of spirit, but much more important the habit of laughter and

relaxation. You were very tense and withdrawn when ·
first met.' He lit his cigar and went on, 'I could say thir
to you now which I would not, could not, when we fi
met.'

'Are you going to say them?'

'No, Grace. There is no need.'

'You said you were glad for everyone that Carlo anc
came here. That must include John.'

'Clearly. You came at a bad point in his life. Time wou
have dealt with that. But Time is often a slow cure. D
you know that he writes to me once a week and I to hir
It is a practice of many years. When you and Carlo fi
came there was little mention of either of you in his lette
Now he writes often about you both, but . . .'

Grace, enjoying herself, caught the ball and returned

'But, more often of me than Carlo?'

'That is so. Without any attempt to put a fine edge on
I would like to see him marry again, and this house to ha
children. Confidentially, although I was very fond
Elizabeth, I never felt that she was the right woman f
him. And don't think I'm a meddling old matchmak·
The good Lord forbid. One can safely leave that to Natu·
All I mean is that having someone like you at Darlo·
could not help but give Time's slow pace a prod or tw
from behind. The power of a woman rests not in what s·
does or says or feels, but in just being a woman and preser
a visible reminder of the natural state which God h·
ordained for human beings.'

Grace laughed. 'My goodness, that sounds Ve·
Reverend.'

'I meant it. When I become a little embarrassed ·
having gone too far I escape into pomposity and the co·
fortable clichés of the preacher.'

'And do you mean to preach a similar sermon to John·

'No, my dear Grace. Between brothers all over the wor·

there are some lines of communication which are for ever closed. There . . . well, one just relies on time.'

'The time, the place and the loved one all together?'

'Now you tease me, and I deserve it.' He rose. 'Let me get you some more coffee. . . .'

Lying in bed later, her open novel face down on the sheet before her, Grace thought about the Very Reverend's essay in matchmaking. There had been no resentment in her; amusement, yes. But also recognition of a faint truth behind it all. If a man and woman were left alone on a desert island the odds were overwhelming that they would ultimately come together. Life was full of desert islands without water surrounding them. And there were degrees of coming together between men and women. The body was a world of its own, demanding food and fulfilment. That John had made no move to sleep with her was a mystery. Well, his restraint was his affair. Perhaps Time's slow cure was lagging more than the Very Reverend could guess. But—far more important to her—when the moment came and they passed into the comfort of knowing each other as man and woman, would she wish for more than that? She had a feeling that even the Very Reverend —who could, like most intelligent churchmen, be broader minded than most people—had not honestly advocated that. He would be content for them to get into bed with one another and leave the rest to them. An earthly act of union devoid of religious sanction. But then the Church had always known when the temporal licence was momentarily more important than any spiritual canon. But what did she think? Four legs in a bed, as dear Carlo would say, was a notion quite acceptable to her. But more than that? Marriage? Mistress of Darlock? Love, children —a few months ago she would never have put the question to herself. Now she could—but there was no response in her. She had no quick answer and, realizing this, she had to acknowledge that the Very Reverend was right only to a point.

Carlo came into the bedroom immediately after knocking on the door. Grace made no protest against this familiar lack of politeness. She was pleased to see him, to have her train of thought broken.

He came over and kissed her, picked up the book she was reading and said, 'Well, that's a change from the usual junk you read. What's happened to the tall dark handsome stranger who stops to help the heroine change a wheel on the Corniche? *Moment of Mountain Madness* I think the last one was called.'

'They're dead,' said Grace. 'A hit and run driver got them both as they were struggling with the wheel, or it may have been with one another. Did you have a good evening?'

'Yes, indeed. And I've got good news for you. I've signed an order for your release from captivity. I've definitely made up my mind to go to an agricultural training college in the New Year. There should be no trouble. I've got the qualifications. So, as far as I can see, we can leave here some time early in January. You can get a place in London, abroad, or wherever you want and I'll come to you out of term time. Kiss the gloomy moor good-bye Glad?'

Suddenly aware of a sharp, conflicting stir of emotions, unexpected and unsettling, Grace avoided an answer and said, 'And what about your great love affair with Birdie?'

'Oh, that's all fixed—but it's a secret between us you're welcome to know. The moment I'm qualified and have a farm we'll be married.'

'If you still feel like it.'

Carlo laughed. 'That would have made me cross once. But not now. Don't worry. I shall still feel like it and so will Birdie. Anyway . . . in a couple of weeks you'll be free of Darlock, free of the wind, the rain, the bogs, the dreary heather and the dumpy sheep.'

He kissed her again and went.

Grace lay back against her pillow, waiting for the confusion in her mind to resolve itself.

Chapter Nine

SIR CHARLES READ arrived at Pitt Wood House two days before Christmas in the late afternoon. Carlo learned of his arrival while he was sitting in the Carters' kitchen talking to Birdie's mother and waiting for Birdie to come down from changing in her room. He was taking her to a discothèque in Barnstaple in Grace's car which he had borrowed. Mr Carter came in with the last of the daylight long gone.

He greeted Carlo and then said to his wife, 'What's the matter with you, Mother—letting the lad sit there without a glass of something to drink?'

'It's been offered and refused. Carlo's taking Birdie out tonight and he's not the one—like some I could name—to start drinking before there's proper call for it and driving back to be done later.'

'Well, I'm not driving tonight.'

Mr Carter went off to the still room beyond the kitchen to get himself a glass of cider. Mrs Carter grinned at Carlo. Carlo had never heard Mr Carter call his wife anything but 'Mother' or she him anything but 'Father'. The usage pleased him. Lovers to begin with, then man and wife, but when children came mother and father—a true progression to the final and royal titles. For a moment or two of day-dreaming he saw himself as 'Father' and Birdie as 'Mother', and a kitchen like this theirs, a farm theirs with its sheep and fattening store cattle. A fixed love and a fixed place. Coming out of the dream he knew that there was only one desire of any truth in him. He and Birdie would create their own place. That Birdie was still sceptical though she had given her promise—but had imposed an embargo on any talk of it to her parents—worried him not at all. He knew his Birdie. The contract had been made and she would stay true to it as long as he did. If he failed or turned away from her, no one, not even he, would know whether she wept secretly or acknowledged calmly to herself what she had always known would happen. With a passion stronger than any he had known he was determined that it should not happen. Lovers they were, man and wife they would be, and finally father and mother. For the first time he was ready to concede to himself that this visit to Darlock, begun out of a bitter caprice born of a few minutes' drunken talk by his mother, was the best thing that had ever happened to him. Maybe there was a god somewhere who played spillikins with the destinies of human beings, or fixed the fall of dice to make the game more interesting to relieve divine boredom. Through the pleasure he was taking in his reverie, he heard Mr Carter say from the still room door——

'Met old Reeves top side of Pitt Wood lookin' for that old ewe of his what's always a-wanderin' away. Tells me Sir Charles come down today. Helicopter thing dropped him in the river meadow, all the way from London. Now there's a man don't have to think about drink before driving, which is lucky for him for he's able to put it back with the best. . . .'

Driving Birdie to Barnstaple, Carlo knew that from each morning onwards he would have to watch the weather if he were not to miss a ringside seat at the best Christmas pantomime ever on offer. At two hundred yards' range not even John Kingsford would risk firing in a gale of wind or a storm of rain.

John Kingsford learned of the arrival of Sir Charles

Read a little later that evening. The telephone rang and he recognized the voice on the other end at once.

'John?'

'Hullo, Charles. How are you? Nice to hear your voice.'

'And a long time, too long, since I heard yours. I'm well, and I trust you are. You should be—you've been rusticating long enough. I'm looking forward to seeing you on New Year's Eve. Bring any guests you may have . . .'

Sir Charles went on speaking, inquiring about local affairs and, as he did so, John wondered at the calmness in himself. He had known that the man might—would—ring. Anticipating that moment had left him wondering not how he would handle it—for he knew that it was imperative that he should sound normal—but at the emotions which might be stirred in him. To his surprise he felt nothing and took pleasure from it. All emotion had long gone from him. The man was a survivor from a bad past coloured by deceit and treachery. All that remained was to get rid of him so that the stage could be set and dressed again with new characters and scenery. Once the man was killed, he could wake from an unpleasant dream, forget it, and turn to new days.

He heard himself say, not from any design or need to verify habit or custom, but purely a repetition of similar words on past occasions, 'Maybe I'll ride over one morning and join you on your morning round.'

'Do that. Do that, John. We could have a good talk. There's a lot I want to say to you about your future. These are times when we need people like you.' He laughed. 'One lost election is no tragedy that can't be redressed. Bye-elections keep popping up. I'm sure we can arrange something. Still, we can talk about all that when we meet.' He ran on for a while, affable and easy; though, when he wished, he could cut a conversation dead in a few cold words. John remembered without a tremor of feeling a

174

phrase from one of this man's early letters to his wife. *I'm not at all surprised at what you say about his love-making. His speeches are the same, largely ineffectual, a half-hearted beating about the bush (!) and seldom coming to the point (!!).*

When the conversation was over, John went to the barometer in the hall. It had dropped a little since midday. He went out and stood on the front steps and looked at the night weather. The wind was westerly, strong and, he guessed, rising. Swathes of heavy rain exploded now and then through the darkness. He had a handful of days ahead of him and he needed a fine one, but the need was not imperative. If time began to run out before fine weather came he would have to close the range, go down the slope of the bluff to the river bank and shoot from the cover of the fringing alders. He would aim for the body and use the whole magazine of ammunition. He stood there for a moment or two with the thought in his mind, but no picture of the moment in his imagination. For him the man was already dead, the thing already done. Imagination had flowered and died weeks ago.

At six o'clock the next morning the sky was full of west wind and hard driving rain. Carlo checked it at first light and went back to bed. After breakfast he borrowed Grace's car and drove through the rain to a layby a few miles north of Worth Farm. Wearing a raincoat and cap he went across the fields to the river woods and then threaded his way through them, well above the Barle, until he was far enough downstream to be able to observe the Pitt Wood House meadows. He wanted to know whether Sir Charles Read was just a fair weather man. If he were, then John would have to have a fine morning. If he were not, then in the last resort John would have to ignore the weather—or content himself to wait for another visit from Sir Charles. And that contentment he guessed was not a likely quality to be found in John.

Sir Charles was not a fair weather man—as John already knew. At ten o'clock he came trotting down through the trees on the mound below the house well covered against the rain.

Carlo watched him ride across the field path to the riverside, open the fence gate and then turn downstream, the rain sleeking the quarters of the big chestnut mare he was riding.

Carlo watched the man through the field glasses he had brought with him. For a while he held him in side view, saw the long, ruddy complexioned face, the imperiously hooked nose and jutting chin. It was a face familiar to him now from newspaper photographs and television news items. In his mind he could recapture the voice coming from the screen in the tower sitting-room; precise, measured, never moving into a sentence without giving the feeling that the whole of what he wished to say was already lodged, firmly formed in his mind. He saw too the slight, almost disparaging smile which marked faintly the thin mouth when some awkward question was asked of him, the little display of vanity in his position and powers and the confidence he had in easily avoiding any trap, any suggestion of floundering for an answer. A man who walked surely in the world's chancelleries, who, when he rose to his feet in conference, immediately banished indifference or boredom from all listeners. Her Majesty's Secretary of State for Foreign Affairs, a country house here on Exmoor, another in Norfolk of grander acres and well-stocked pheasant coverts, a fishing lodge in Scotland, and a London house where kings, princes and dictators dined and wined and the quiet arrangements and bargains of power politics were smoothly consecrated . . . and, Carlo felt contempt at the thought, where more than once John Kingsford's wife must have lain naked, no more than a high-class whore giving service for any crumb of preferment Sir Charles might choose to throw her husband's way. She must have been a stupid, silly, easily guiled woman far from ever deserving a place among the great courtesans.

He watched the man ride out of sight and be lost where the river path entered the trees downstream. But when horse and rider were gone, he still sat and watched, combing the far moorside above and beyond the river. For all he knew the man might be in the habit of returning by the same route. John might take him either going or returning. Carlo's passion for precise knowledge held him there. Knowing all was the joy. He had to be John, sharing everything with him, the truth of every movement and every habit that belonged to Sir Charles. There was suddenly a vicarious, anguished longing in him for that split second which had to come, the heart-stopping sound of a shot punctuating the morning air, the whine of a bullet, lingering like the singing of a passing hornet, and the sight of the slow crumpling of a man in the saddle, collapsing over the chestnut mane of the horse or punched viciously sideways from the beast. What would it do? Stand quivering, immobile, frozen while the man fell, blood flecking the noble arch of its neck? Or panic, rear and gallop away across the meadow riderless or, his foot caught in a stirrup, drag Sir Charles like a bumping sack with it?

An hour later, through the glasses, he saw Sir Charles ride back to Pitt Wood House, coming from the east down the open slopes of Winsford Hill to thread his way through the growth of trees which marked the rise to the house a good half a mile away. He stood up, put his glasses away, the rain running from his clothes and turned back along his path. John would have to shoot as Sir Charles went out on his round. A few yards away from the bluff a grove of lichened, bare oaks grew to a narrow point. On the riverside there was a half-dead tree, stag-headed, and festooned

177

with a luxuriant growth of thick ivy at the top. Carlo climbed it and found that he could burrow himself into a small bower of the ivy tangle almost at the top of the tree. From here, through the screening evergreen leaves, he commanded a view down the bluff to the river and the meadow beyond. To his right he could see the ruined cottages and the well, and the ford track that ran down to the river.

Nature, he thought, could not have provided him with a more fitting front row seat.

* * *

On Christmas Eve the weather turned soft with a fine, almost windless drizzle. Over the moor the clouds dropped so that the land was blanketed in a thin mist which forced the few cars using the roads to need their lights all day. In the evening John took Grace to a party given by an old friend of his who lived on a farm well up the river Taw. Once they dropped off the moor southwards to North and South Molton they lost the cloud mist and motored through thin drizzle. It was a small, pleasant party and when they returned Grace and John went into the study for a goodnight drink. Sipping her nightcap with him Grace said, 'Carlo has decided to go to an agricultural training college in the New Year. When he's qualified he's going to buy a farm somewhere.'

John said, 'Why, that's splendid, Grace. It's the best thing that could happen to him.'

'We shall be leaving about the middle of January. I don't know where he will go, but I shall get a flat in London and—' she could not resist the mildly malicious turn, '—and kiss this dark and dreary moor good-bye.'

For a moment or two he looked at her and then said, 'Has it all been so dark and dreary?'

'Except for your kindness to me—frankly, yes. I'm not a country girl.'

To her surprise he laughed and said, 'You underrate yourself. You could be anything you wanted if the reason were strong enough.' He came over and took her glass. 'Enough—or another one?'

She stood up and shook her head. 'No, thank you.' She started to turn away, conscious of an almost adolescent disappointment. No polite phrase about missing her; must she go so soon? Stupid, of course, but she would like to have heard it nevertheless. Then his hand came out and took her shoulder gently, turned her and he put his arms around her and kissed her as he had done many times before. As he slowly released her, he said, 'London's not so far away and I think I may often be there, but even so I shall miss you. You may not be a country girl but you seem right at Darlock and you'll . . .' He broke off and she sensed the quick embarrassment in him at his own clumsiness.

'I'll what?' she asked, careless with a quick instinct to wound, 'Always be welcome here?'

Quietly he said, 'I'm sorry. I can be very clumsy sometimes. What I meant was——'

'No.' She stopped him, angry with herself now. 'I was bitchy. Let's forget it. You can see me home to the bottom of the great stairway.'

He put his arm round her shoulders and went out into the hall and kissed her good night at the bottom of the stairs. As she climbed them, turning once to look back at him, he was tempted suddenly to follow her, to take her arm and lead her along the gallery towards his own room. There would have been no protest. But he could not do it though his whole body was full of desire. Do *this* before *that*. Avoid the cracks in the pavement for the whole length of the street. Keep your fingers crossed until you see a white dog or underpassing the ladder will bring bad luck. She'd become part of every superstition he had grown up with. If you wanted something, wanted things to be right, you must keep on the side of the primitive gods. No matter how well you planned, how sure you felt, they could bitch you if you failed to give them their twisted homage and brittle dues.

He went to the front door and out into the night. The overhead portal light was haloed with moor mist and the air was full of the sound of water that dripped steadily from eaves and the thick foliage of the blanket of virginia creeper that covered the walls. There would be no shooting tomorrow.

Restless, reluctant for bed, he went back to the study and poured himself another drink. He had had enough already, but another would make him sleep and he knew the weather signs well enough to know that there would be no call for a steady hand and clear eyes tomorrow. He sat down at his desk and pulled the last volume of Parson John's diaries to him. He had only a few more entries to decode and sat wondering whether he should start on them at this late hour. He flipped through the pages. The last entry was almost three-quarters of the way through the book.

Through the run of errant thoughts in his mind he stared without concentration at the beginning of the last entry. A long time ago when he had started to decode the diaries and had looked through them before the code was familiar to him, he had noticed that the writing and the ink of the last entry were different from all the others. Time had not browned and faded the ink so much as with the others, and the writing had a less precise, less bold character than in the others. So familiar was he with the code now that he could with familiar words decode them by sight. Thinking of Grace, Carlo and his agricultural college, of a morning soon to come on the high bluff over the river, his eyes held the underlined coded date at the top of the entry. He realized slowly that the date heading read—*Ninth Sunday after Trinity. 1922.*

Surprise stirred curiosity. The entry had been made only a few months before the old man had died. He turned back to the preceding entry. It was nearly fifty years earlier. What, he wondered, had made the parson make this last entry so long after the other?

He reached for his pad and began to decode the entry. Half an hour later he had finished.

The entry read:

Ninth Sunday after Trinity. 1922.
It is now three years to the day that my beloved Jessica died and just such a beautiful mid August day as this. That my own time is not far away, no matter the assurances of my doctor, is becoming clear to me.

I write this, not in the hope of making peace or seeking forgiveness from my Maker. He has known my sin for many long years, heard my confession and my prayers and has already decreed the terms of my life hereafter. That I have lived so much of my life with a grieving heart yet putting on the appearance of happiness and well-being nobody on this earth knows. The Devil is ever ready to aid his own in dissembling the truth. Yet I would not want to leave this life without some few of my descendants in due time understanding the man I was and charitably to find it in their hearts possible to offer their prayers for me and for the young creature I so dreadfully wronged.

Some few months before my marriage I killed a young woman named Hannah Darch who lived, when not engaged away from home in service, at Buttery Farm. She was very personable as well as being agreeably spoken from her years in service at some of the best houses in these parts. Though I did not know it at first, she was most firmly set on improving her station by a good

181

marriage. As for myself, I was then a single man of vigour and often of too demanding an appetite for all the pleasures of life. Regrettably I was also of a quick temper and nourished a high and proud regard for my position and prospects as the Kingsford heir.

It would ill-fit me to recount the intimate details of our relationship other than to say that, despite my calling, from a mutual liking and friendship we secretly became lovers. Shortly after my betrothal to my beloved Jessica, Hannah met me under the old oak at Deercombe corner and gave me the news that she was some months pregnant with my child. Nothing, she said, would satisfy her but marriage. Failing that, she angrily threatened to bruit the news about the country. That this she would do and so ruin my good name and all my prospects which rested on a marriage already arranged, and truly founded on love, I knew full well.

I offered her a substantial sum to leave the county and gave a sworn promise to care for her and the child during their life-times. She refused and we quarrelled, and losing my temper the Devil put the will and the power into my hand to strike her.

She fell down the steep, rocky bank to the stream below the ford and in so doing her head violently hit a rock. Going down to her full of immediate remorse I found her lying in the water and already dead. In one hand she still held some of the sprays of sweet yellow broom which she had been gathering while awaiting my arrival.

Knowing that she was dead, confident that none knew of our present or past trystings and easily tempted by the ever-present counsellor of evil, I left her there. When she was found later that day it was readily assumed by all that, in gathering the broom sprigs, she had slipped and fallen to her death. Not a day or night has passed since then when at some time I have ever escaped the recall of the picture of poor Hannah lying at the stream's edge. May God forgive me.

I write this now that the truth may be known of it one day to

182

my descendants. They will make of it what they will, for I am beyond all pleading. I ask only for their prayers and would say only this for all to know.

It is easy for a man to reach out through sin to stiffen his pride and to ensure his place in comfort here below for the Devil will be promptly at his side, firing his grievances and strengthening his anger. But the Devil must ever be repaid.

A man should live to seek only for Heaven and to strive ceaselessly to acquire God's gift of true charity, true humbleness and that true and noble pride in himself which rejects violence against others and turns wrath into understanding and forgiveness.

John read the entry through twice and then with his desk scissors he cut the original entry from the diary and took it to the fire and burnt it, together with the transcription he had made. Towards the end of his life it was well known that Parson John had become rambling and often mixed up not only about the events of the past, but with the names and relationships of those who surrounded him. And all his life, as the diaries showed, he had been dream haunted by feelings of guilt for small or even imagined sins, for the rough and common failings which all men knew. The old man probably had made Hannah Darch pregnant. In those days that would have been no great matter. The sons of good families enjoyed a licence with servants and farm girls which was accepted. But Parson John, because of his cloth and his own nature, would have exaggerated the sin. Even in the entry he had made he had said that he had killed Hannah, not murdered her. The thing clearly had been an unfortunate accident. Hannah had been standing out for the big prize, marriage. In the event of a calm, inflexible refusal she would have come to terms. Unfortunately a moment of temper on the parson's part had brought tragedy and for the rest of his life he had magnified and brooded on the unfortunate incident, convincing himself that he had struck to kill when simple anger had moved his arm to repel the girl. To be guilty of murder the deliberate intent had to precede the act.

He was going to kill Sir Charles because the man had in full consciousness of his act secretly defiled his name, his wife and his house. Where the law gave no redress a man was entitled, at his own risk, to make his own judgment, announce his own sentence, and administer the final punishment. For himself he accepted that this reasoning was absolute and, because it was so, there was no power in this fortuitous call to him over the years from Parson John. Honour had to be served otherwise pride withered.

He put the diary away and went to bed and was asleep within minutes.

*   *   *

On Christmas morning the cloud was still low over the moor and the steady drizzle had set the ditches and feeder streams running high. Carlo came down to join John at breakfast carrying with him the present he had for him. They exchanged greetings and Carlo handed him the gift. It was a small water-colour which he had painted some weeks before and had had framed in South Molton, a view of the front of Darlock House from the far side of the combe near the old tree-stump target. It was a pleasing, very competent painting in washes of brown, green and blue.

John, touched by the unexpectedness of the gift, was delighted with it. Whatever he might have felt about Carlo originally he had now long come to expect the unexpected from him and to accept that the young man's character was one which could only be read with the help of time.

He said, 'It's splendid, Carlo. Thank you very much. I

shall hang it in the study. I had no idea you could do this kind of thing.'

'Well . . . it's just a knack.' Carlo grinned. 'There was a time when I thought I might go in for it properly, but I never seemed to get round to it. My mother wanted me to. She was really talented. . . .'

John smiled, the mention of his mother only dimly stirring memory, and said, 'Well, I can't match your originality, but I thought you might like this.' He handed over his present.

Carlo unwrapped it. It was a small, red morocco leather-bound travelling clock. On the lid was inset a narrow, silver plaque. Engraved on it was an inscription which read—*Carlo Graber. The Kingsford Run—2 hours 38 minutes*.

For a moment or two Carlo did not know what to say or what to feel. He hovered between being delighted and being angry, between acknowledging the good will and admiration for him which the inscription held and bitterness at the thought that the commemorating lines should rightly be set in gold-leaf on the mahogany board in the gun room. Then his pleasure overwhelmed him, and he was profuse, too profuse, he knew, in his thanks but unable to limit his words, and was glad when at that moment Mrs Hurrell came in with his breakfast.

When he went up to Grace in her bedroom after breakfast he presented her with his Christmas gift, a set of silver-backed hair brushes and hand mirror inscribed with her initials, and received from her a portable typewriter.

'You can begin writing your memoirs, Carlo. Or keep a diary like old Parson John Kingsford.'

'Well, I might at that. Look——'

He showed her the clock.

'Oh, Carlo—that's nice! And it was a nice thought. You deserve some memento of your Spartan period. When you're married and have children you can tell them all about it and extol the virtues of *mens sana, etcetera.*'

'I shall without question. The little brutes are going to have a hell of a time.' He chuckled suddenly. 'Now, let's have a little guess. What do you think John Kingsford of Darlock will give you?'

'No, I don't think I want to play that game.'

'All right. Then let me guess what you're going to give him. Or might even have given him already?'

'Nor that game—though I know it's one you love because of its dirty opportunities.'

Carlo shrugged his shoulders. 'Well, that's settled that. Shall I go and run your bath for you?'

'Yes, do that. And you can stay and scrub my back. I'm sure Birdie would like you to do that.'

Laughing, Carlo picked up his clock from the bed and retreated to the door.

Later that morning, Carlo drove over to Great Cotters Farm where he was to have lunch with Birdie and her family, having already committed himself to dinner with John and Grace. He was feeling pleased with himself and opened the throttle of the Norton as he passed the Sportsman's Inn. The cloud mist only gave him twenty or thirty yards vision, but he knew the road like the back of his hand and enjoyed the challenge of anticipating each curve and rise and dip in his mind, as though he were driving blindfold along the drizzle-slicked road. Enjoyment rose swiftly to exhilaration, to an utter indifference to all danger; to a plane of feeling where immunity from all peril reigned absolute. Goggles off because of the drizzle, the air stream one steady pulse against his face, he let a torrent of all his joys—no day this for bitterness or envy—spew out. Here came Carlo! Great Carlo! Peace on earth, good will to men . . . and God send a bright, fair morning soon. Here came Carlo. Artist. Master of locks and secrets.

Acknowledged never, but a true son of Darlock. A god racing on the wind. A god to look down one sunny morning soon and watch murder most foul and for ever after to hold the pearl of his knowledge in the ever closed oyster of his memory. Carlo! Wheeeee! Carlo . . . !

He swung into the first of the bends that curved like a snake around Portford Bridge, leaning to it a fraction of a second before the heathered, boulder-pocked bluff on his right came up through the mist. As he did so—godlike divination momentarily forsaking him—he saw the pale, grey-white smudge of a wet-fleeced sheep blocking the centre of the road. He swung away from it and touched the brake as he eased the throttle back. The rear wheel slewed sideways. The metal tip of his footrest scored the road, sending a shower of sparks cascading into the mist. The machine snaked and bucked under him as he fought to regain balance. He found and held it as the stone parapet of the bridge rose up out of the gloom. He went by, his left shoulder briefly brushing it, and so, steadying but not stopping, out into the straight beyond the bridge and the drop to the valley below. He rode on, taking the few moments' fear into the body of his ecstasy and swamping it. Carlo . . . Carlo . . . Carlo riding the whirlwind . . . !

On the bridge at Withypool he stopped. He was wet with sweat and across the black leather of the left shoulder of his motoring tunic were faint white scratches where it had barely touched the parapet stones. Suddenly his body began to shake uncontrollably. Sitting astride the saddle, his feet on the ground to support himself and the machine, he leant forward and rested his head on the handlebars until the black spasm passed. Then, calm at last, he rode slowly on to Great Cotters.

At the farm, one of the family now, and mother and father according him the liberties which arose from their love and understanding of Birdie, Carlo—on being told

187

that Birdie was in her room—went up to her, called after by Mrs Carter, 'Tell her to get a move on, Father and Tom'll be in soon and I could do with some help down here.'

Birdie wearing a blue and white striped dress had just finished making her bed. As she turned to him he knew that not only was she the most beautiful thing he had ever seen but that she was the most wanted thing he had ever wanted, and beyond that he had no time for words, no time for reason. She was Birdie. Her magic undefinable, its power irresistible. He put his arms around her and they kissed, and as their lips were together he knew, too, that everything had to be as he wished it to be. He would make it so. Agricultural college. A farm. Eventually an estate; for she would come to an acceptance of what his wealth could and would give her. Somewhere he would build another Darlock, and she with him would start to create their own legend to be handed on to their children. Darlock had spawned him casually and never marked his existence. But with Birdie he would be the first. Put down roots . . . deep, deep down and let the top growth soar, soar. . . .

Birdie broke away from him, laughing and gasping for air. 'For God's sake, Carlo—you don't have to eat me! There's a Christmas dinner coming up for that.'

Carlo, suddenly full of joy, said, 'I could kiss you until the moon turned green and on through the whole of eternity.'

'Well, that's nice. We'll try it some time. But just now if I don't get down to the kitchen to help Mum there'll be more cussin' than kissing.'

'One day when we're married I'll give you all the servants you want and then you can sit on a cushion and sew a fine seam. Just sit and look beautiful, and never stop loving me.'

'I don't mind the sitting, or the beautiful part. But sewing, no. I hate it.'

'I give up.'

She came close to him. 'No, don't do that. I like it. Here, try this. But no hanging on to see if the moon turns green.' She put her arms around him again and kissed him, holding herself hard to him.

Some time later that afternoon Mrs Carter came into the bedroom where Birdie was sitting by herself, looking into her mirror and admiring the little heart-shaped gold locket and chain which Carlo had given her as a Christmas present.

Her mother said, 'Father's snoring his head off by the fire. Tom's away to his girl-friend's place. And you, what are you doing, my lady?'

'I was thinking about Carlo.'

'And so was I. Let me see it.'

Birdie took off the locket and handed it to her mother who opened it. On the inside were engraved the words— *For Birdie for ever. Carlo.*

Mrs Carter handed it back.

She said, 'He's a nice young man. But for ever is a long time, Just don't build things up too much.'

'Don't worry, Mum. For ever is what he feels now. What I feel, too. So why think any more than that? Thinking too far ahead only spoils things.'

'Well, you know your own business. Father fusses sometimes, but then men always do about their daughters. But I know you've got a good head on your shoulders.'

When her mother had gone, Birdie sat, holding the locket in her hand. For Birdie for ever. She hoped so, really hoped so. But if she was wrong . . . well, it wouldn't be the end of the world.

Chapter Ten

DURING THE AFTERNOON of Boxing Day, the weather changed. The wind went round to the east, the sky cleared, and there was a bite in the breeze which promised frost during the night. When the sun set it went down in a flaming smoky red ball behind Fyldon Common.

Carlo watched it from his bedroom window. When an east wind set in over the moor he knew now that it usually lasted for a few days. John Kingsford would not have missed the weather change. When he went to bed Carlo set the alarm on his new travelling clock for three. When the bell woke him he saw from the window that the sky was clear, chipped with bright stars and there was a fine mantle of frost laid across the far slopes of the combe. He reset the alarm for six and was down to breakfast by half-past seven. He took it in the kitchen with Mrs Hurrell and Vera and let it be known that he was going over to the Carters' farm to take Birdie out for the day.

An hour later he opened a field gate on the road below Withypool and well above Worth Farm. It was a pasture field and free of any grazing sheep or bullocks which meant that no farm hands were likely to come into it. He left the motor-cycle against the hedge some way up from the gate where it could not be seen from the road. Keeping to the hedges, he went round the field and dropped down into the woods above the river.

He had plenty of time so he sat on a moss-covered fallen tree above the river and smoked a cigarette. The sun was well up now, the sky clear and only the suggestion of a breeze moving. Ideal conditions.

There was a deep, steady excitement in him which reamed his mouth with dryness, and now and again his body shook with an involuntary spasm of tension. How would he have been feeling and reacting if, instead of John, it was himself who in a little while would be going on to the firing post? Not like this, he hoped. To do what John was going to do, a man would long ago have had to shrive himself of all emotion. John would have let that run weeks ago, drained himself of all passion except the cold, steady flow, unmarked, unrippled, of set purpose. The prelude to action would be beyond touching him because in his mind he must have killed the man a hundred times before . . . imagination long ago having anaesthetized the nerves. Something like that had happened with him when with the others they had come to the actual point of robbery. Planning and arranging it days before had been the high peaks of intent . . . when you were in the darkened room you moved as though you had known it for years, facile in the gloom, the mind a blank except for the straightforward calm compulsion which governed you.

John Kingsford had his breakfast half an hour after Carlo. He then took the old shotgun and a handful of cartridges from the gun room, called Skip, and drove off in his car. In a way he was doing nothing unusual for there had been many times, first with Robert, sometimes with Elizabeth, but more often alone, when he had driven beyond the Sportsman's Inn and parked the car on a turfed pull-off at the edge of Hawkridge Common and worked across country between Withypool and Worth Hills watching the heather and bracken ahead for the sudden whirring flight of partridges.

Skirting the boggy patches, the light frost already melting, dewing the dry, dead heather blooms, he felt the growing strength of the sun begin to warm his face and hands. On the little saddle-backed plateau between the two hills, where a small valley began to break gently towards Worth Farm, Skip put up a pair of partridges. Automatically he took them with a left and right, the shot echoes whimpering and dying between the hills. He waited while Skip retrieved the birds. Needing to shoot no more he walked down the slope, the rivulet on his right beginning to strengthen and cascade over boulders and through gravelly pools. A hundred yards down the stream there was a large outcrop of rock, cut back at its base to form a shallow overhang. The ground was bare and hard trodden from the sheep and moor ponies that often sheltered there. He put the unloaded gun on the ground, dropped the partridges alongside it, and then told Skip to sit and stay. Skip sat, nuzzled the warm birds momentarily, and then whined gently as John went on. The dog would sit until he returned.

Half an hour later John was at the ruined cottage. He took the rifle from behind the old kitchen range and unwrapped it. Using the towelling scarf from around his neck, woollen mittens pulled on to his hands, he wiped the weapon, checked the magazine and the one round already in the chamber. Then he went down to the well-head and into the shelter of the near-by bramble and bracken thicket. He lay down, rolled on the briar and bracken growths to make himself a couch, then drew the rifle into position so that he covered the river below and the meadow beyond it. It was five minutes to ten.

Fifty yards away, in the ivy bower of the old oak, Carlo watched John take his place. Almost without knowing it he was shivering and quivering like a cold dog and biting absently his right thumb nail. This was the place, and the moment was nearing when this man—his father—would kill Sir Charles Read. John had created him heedlessly, unknowing. He, Carlo, could destroy his father if he wished and balance birth against death. But when the thing was done he would be satisfied. He would go away and say nothing to anyone ever. The scales would have been balanced. He would have a murderer for a father, and that father would never know that he had a son with the power to destroy him as casually as he himself had been created. It was a twisted fancy that made him laugh quietly to himself. It was a Carlo thing, a distorted, macabre joke which would never lose its flavour, never go stale. . . .

The sun was clear of the woods downstream. Its light silvered and burnished the surface of the river with rippling, broken gleams. Already the frost had gone from the meadow except in the long shadow of the middle hedgerow and in irregular patches under the trees that crested the mound before Pitt Wood House; the mound from which John seldom let his eyes wander. Standing under those trees he had shot pigeons with the man he was going to kill. He had fished this river with him, throwing a small pheasant-tail fly to the ring of a rising trout. He had ridden down from the house with him, following the hedge line to the river gate, talked and laughed and sometimes been grateful to listen as Sir Charles had passed to politics, to the promise that lay in Westminster for him, hinting more than affirming—for commitment was not his game— at the sponsorship he could expect, and had got in a very limited degree. Enough, he realized now, to keep Elizabeth content in the man's bed and ensure her continued place there by the shrewdly spaced doles of unimportant preferment. For weeks now he had lain awake at night living this morning. No whimsical religiosities from old Parson John could touch him. When the rat darted from under the lifted corn sack the raised stick fell because hand and arm had a life of their own. When Sir Charles reined in at the river gate and reached down to open it with his riding crop the cross wires would be steady on the man's head; his hands and arms would be steady, his sight unblurred by passion, and the slow draw of his finger would follow as though that finger had a life of its own needing no direction from him.

A black-and-white-headed coal tit flirted through the briars a couple of feet from the muzzle of the rifle, now and again hanging upside down, wings spread, under a dead leaf searching for wintering grubs. At Darlock these birds nested some years in the old virginia creeper on the house but were shy of the food table which Elizabeth had set up on the lawn. Beyond the bird he saw suddenly the sun-sheen on the neck of the chestnut mare as Sir Charles came out of the trees.

He flattened his cheek against the stock and watched man and horse through the sights, the well-groomed mare spuming her misty breath into the morning air, the rider, cloth-capped, tweed-jacketed with a coloured foulard at his throat, old riding breeches and riding boots whose brilliance and tan matched the shine and colour of the mare's coat. They came down the path by the hedge, head on and then the horse was reined in by the gate, playing up for a moment with the freshness in her and then settling docilely as the rider leaned forward to free the gate crook with his crop head.

John steadied the crosswires on the man's head and then raised them a shade, knowing this rifle now, adjusting for its throw and his elevation. The gate swung slowly open on its deliberately adjusted cant. Horse and rider stood immobile through ten seconds of time as the gate fell away, bounced back a foot from its stop and then returned to rest wide open. With the man's head in his sights, John held his breath and slowly brought his trigger finger back to rest on its waiting cold metal, brought it back knowing that the movement would follow through into the easy, deliberate pressure that would move the trigger and set the bright morning ringing with the echoes of the shot.

And in that moment, dominated by a power beyond his control, he turned from killer to victim, the victim of a rebellion in his own body against his will. No matter the deep desire in him to do as he had planned, he found that there was a power—greater than his own—in his right hand, in his trigger finger which he could not master. He would kill, but he could not; the true nature of his body defied and paralysed him. A sudden sweat began to blur his eyes and the rifle dropped from his hands. Two hundred yards away Sir Charles rode through the gate and set the mare to a gentle canter down the riverside. John lay on the ground, lost in the misery of humiliation and the sudden, angry knowledge of his own cowardice, for cowardice was the only answer he could find to explain his betrayal of himself.

From his hiding place, Carlo, strung tense with excitement with a wild longing for the moment of chaos, aching with a desire stronger than he had known for anything in his life—beyond Birdie, beyond risk, beyond any challenge—watched Sir Charles ride away and then looked back to John Kingsford.

The man was lying flat on his face, the rifle now slanted from under the clasped hands which supported his head. He raised his glasses and focused them on John. The man's shoulders were trembling and the tanned left cheek exposed by the tilt of his head was wet and polished with sweat. A wave of angry, bitter disappointment raced through Carlo. For a moment he half moved with the impulse to leave the tree, to race across to the man, shouting at and abusing him. Then he held himself back, shaking with anger, and the longing to loose himself in abuse at the man's weakness which had robbed him of the joy and power which this bright morning had promised. John Kingsford would never come here again. When it had come to the real sticking point he had found himself a coward, a gutless, stupid, bloody no-gooder. . . . If someone had done to Birdie what Read had done to this man's wife he would have ripped the life out of him—just as he had almost kicked the guts out of that oaf in Barnstaple. Careless almost of concealment he battered his fist against the hard trunk of the tree, and bit his lip hard to keep back the fury of his contempt for John, his rage at being cheated.

As his turmoil began to spend itself, Carlo saw John slowly stand up, holding the rifle in one hand, and work his way out of the cover in which he had been lying. When John came to the well-head he raised the rifle, looking at it as though it was some alien thing which had suddenly appeared in his hand. Then raising one corner of the corrugated sheet on the well opening, he let the rifle fall into the well. The iron sheet was dropped back, the noise echoing across to Carlo. John Kingsford turned away and began to walk uphill, past the ruined cottages, along the old road which would take him to Worth Farm and up on to the moor.

When John was out of sight, Carlo climbed down from the tree. He was calmer now, much calmer. He lit himself a cigarette and drew hard on it. He walked across the slope to the well and slid the sheet aside. John Kingsford of Darlock, his father, never wanted to see the rifle again. What man would, having spurred himself to the point of redeeming his honour only to find himself a coward when the moment for deliberate action came? He began to smile, a warm thought slowly invading his mind. Why not? He had been robbed of one entertainment, but that loss could open the way to another and even richer one. Grinning to himself, he could see the scene, every detail plain, every word to be spoken by him clear. . . . The day before he left Darlock, no, perhaps the day he left Darlock —leave it until the last moment—he would walk into the study. John sitting at his desk. He would lay the rifle in front of him. He could see the look on the man's face. And as he sat there wordless, he, Carlo, would speak. . . . He began to chuckle at the thought and his body trembled with so much nervous charge that he had to open his flies and relieve himself against the well-head. The words raced through his brain. . . . *I've brought it back. I know what happened between Sir Charles and your wife. I know what you couldn't do because you preferred cowardice to honour. Or did some soft Christian kick hit you at the last moment? Well, John Kingsford of Darlock, you could have asked your son. . . . Me, drunkenly spawned in this house. Your son, John Kingsford, who carries the Kingsford mark as you do.*

Banging his fists on the stones of the well-head, words and scene flowed through his imagination. *Yes, your son! I'd have done it for you, for my spineless father. But not now, not now. I never want to see or hear of Darlock again. I'm away and you've got your rifle back.* Now, almost beyond control, the words no longer in his mind, but cutting the air, free and clear, he shouted. *Hang it in the gun room for a souvenir. Stick it up by your stupid, bloody gold-inscribed Run board. And even at that I could have done better than you. Two hours thirty-eight minutes—and two of them I spent lying on my face, pretending to be whacked.* . . .

He turned away suddenly from the well and went back down the slope into the wood and took the path which would lead him to the field where he had left his motor-cycle. Quiet now, tight-lipped, his face set, he knew he would do it. There could be anything up to ten, probably more, feet of water in the old well. Nothing. One thing lazing with his mother in Bermuda and around the Mediterranean had given him was no fear of water. All he needed was a mask, and a torch and a length of good rope.

The details raced clearly through his mind. He could go down, leaning outwards, feet braced against the well wall and come up the same way, the rifle hanging across his back on its sling. Easy. And then just hang on to it until his last day. And, on that last day, walk into the study and say his good-bye, putting the rifle on the desk. Maybe he should say nothing. Just put it there, look at John and walk out. Perhaps. Perhaps not. Anyway there was time to settle that later. The first thing was to get the rifle from the well. Could do it tomorrow. He had a torch. Waterproof it with insulating tape. Want a big towel to dry himself. Water wouldn't be too cold. Yes, he'd do it. Make a grand, never-to-be-forgotten exit from Darlock when the time came. Pity, though, that the real thing hadn't come off. The rifle tableau with John was a once and for all thing. But a murdered Sir Charles, the secret only known to him, would have lasted all his life. God, who would have believed it? John Kingsford turning soft at the last moment. He should have blasted a hole right through the man's rotten head.

*   *   *

That night, entirely unpremeditated, John told Grace about it.

Carlo was away at Carters' farm for the evening and Grace had dinner alone with John. Over coffee in the main sitting room he told her. As he spoke he felt the beginning of a slow comfort, an assuagement of his lingering anger at his cowardice, inability to act, at the swift and undefinable grip of paralysis of mind and body which had so unexpectedly overtaken him. He told her the whole story; the sick rage when he had first read the letters from Sir Charles Read to his wife, and then the gradual lapse into the cold, implacable decision to kill the man, the planning,

198

and the acceptance—should any of his precautions have gone wrong—of taking the consequences.

'But I couldn't do it, Grace. God knows why. He was in the rifle sights and there wasn't a nerve in my body that wasn't steady . . . but I just couldn't will myself to make that small finger movement to kill him. I've been thinking about it all day. Trying to work it out. . . .'

Grace, surprise at this confession still confusing her, thrown from her usual calm, said, 'You should thank God you couldn't. You wouldn't just have destroyed him. You'd have destroyed yourself!'

John shook his head. 'That's what I've told myself. But it isn't true. I wanted him dead, and I still want him dead but I know now I could never touch him. The courage just isn't there in my hand to do it.'

'Then forget it. Wipe it out of your mind. I'm not surprised that you couldn't do it. You're not that kind of man. You thought you were, but you aren't. But I'm glad you told me all about it. That leaves me free to be frank with you. You should get away from Darlock for a time. You've sat here brooding, first over the loss of your wife, and then over this other business. You've been hit hard, and you were thrown right off balance. Get away. Go back into politics or business . . . anything.'

'Yes, I see that. But at the moment I still can't get over those few moments when I couldn't fire. Why couldn't I? I'm not a religious man in that way. Something just took over.'

Deliberately humouring him, knowing that less than an adult man she was facing momentarily a puzzled child, maybe even a disappointed adolescent whose fantasy of intention had crumpled around him, she said, 'All right, don't accept that God stayed your hand. But you were lucky. The Devil just didn't have any time at that moment for you.' She smiled. 'He was away on another case, perhaps. But one thing I want you to promise me. Don't ever think of trying again. You might find the Devil at your elbow. Promise?'

'I promise. I suppose there's some sense somewhere behind all these things that happen to one in life. Some design or pattern which we either in time get to know about—or don't.'

Grace stood up, moved to him and kissed him. Aware that he was ready to seize bodily comfort to compensate for his own still anger-touched bafflement, she said, 'Men and women are always failing themselves or one another. It happens so often you'd think we'd get used to it. The sun shines one day and it rains the next. We accept it.' They were easy words, she thought, and without any great meaning, an answer to correspondents' troubles placebo, but they had no need to be more. Some situations could only be met by comfort not sense. The frightened, uneasy child needed arms around it, soothing noises, not logic. . . . Well, that was a role all women could play without prompting. This man would never ask it from her, but he wanted it. And now that it was clear between them she knew, that if only from charity, she would find herself giving it.

Carlo returned from the Carters at eleven o'clock. The household had gone to bed and he let himself through the front door with the key which had been provided for him. He undressed, whistling gently to himself. He was in a good mood. He had enjoyed himself at the farm and had come back at high speed on the Norton under a star-bright sky. Coming up the hill to Hawkridge Common a hare had leaped into the road and, dazed by the headlight, had raced zigzagging ahead of him for fifty yards before leaping sideways into the heather. Soon now, he thought, he would be away to college. Get down to some real work. Build a future. Honest yeoman stuff to follow when he had his farm. Be like old man Carter, coming in whacked from barn and byre, flopping into a creaking old armchair before the fire and kicking off gumboots, every muscle stretched and Birdie waiting for him . . . Birdie, the blue bird of his paradise. He pulled on his dressing gown, chuckling to himself at the pictures that flickered through his mind. A small farm at first, with just a man, no, a couple of men to help. Then later, when Birdie grew to accept what he could do, what he had to offer, an estate. Parkland, arable, one of those elegant Georgian red-bricked houses, drive posts like white immaculate fingers. Staff, an estate manager, and himself at county shows . . . prize bulls and sheep red-and-blue rosetted. Carlo wipes the board again. And—before all this, before taking flight to paradise, the delicious contemptuous farewell to Darlock . . . laying the rifle before his father. The bastard's gift to the coward.

Elated, he went along to Grace's room, knocked briefly on the door and went in. The room was in darkness. He switched on the light not caring if it should wake her, and saw that she was not in the bed. But she had been. The cover was thrown back. One crumpled pillow atop another marked her reading position. The open book lay on the cover.

He went to the adjoining bathroom. The door was open and the place empty. He went back and sat on the bed. He could guess where she was, and although for many weeks he had expected it, he was surprised. What, at last, had made Grace go quietly along to John's room? He would have expected it to be the other way round, had many a time expected to find her bedroom door locked against his goodnight sortie for he seldom missed the ritual. He stood up, shrugged his shoulders, and went back to his room. What did it matter, anyway? It was Grace's affair. Now his precious, pusillanimous father was in bed with the other sister. First his mother, now his aunt. John Kingsford, master of mismanaged melodrama. Contempt for the man welled strong in him. He poured himself a stiff neat whisky and sat in his chair, sipping and brooding, and then was slowly drawn forward again to the moment when the rifle should be laid across the desk and John's face would turn to him as he began to speak.

*   *   *

At ten-fifteen the next morning, Carlo shot Sir Charles Read. He had recovered the rifle from the well, and was standing by it after dressing himself when he saw Sir Charles come riding down to the river. As the man reined in the mare to open the gate, Carlo raised the rifle and covered him through the sights. So, he thought, had done John Kingsford . . . his father, the round in the chamber still which cowardice had stopped him from firing. As Sir Charles sat back, waiting for the gate to swing open, Carlo held his breath, felt a bold, commanding excess of contempt smooth its way through him, and fired.

The first round struck the man in the neck and knocked him from the horse, free of the stirrups. The chestnut mare bolted, the thud of her hooves on the soft meadow ground taking up the dying echo of the shot. As Sir Charles lay on the ground he made a slow movement of his body, rolling over on to his back. Carlo fired two more rounds, one smashing through his left temple and the other, for the steadiness of his hands suddenly gave way to a fast muscle tremble, hitting the foot of the riverside gate post, sending weathered brown chips of wood into the air. By the time the chips hit the ground Sir Charles Read was dead.

Carlo hoisted the rifle over his shoulder by the wet sling and walked away. The tremble in his hands and arms passed and he was calm in mind and body, held by a potent euphoria. At the well-head he picked up his torch and put it in his pocket. He wrapped the damp towel about his neck, tucking the ends neatly inside the front of his riding jacket and then neatly looped the long length of knotted blue nylon rope and walked away swinging it in his hand. He felt good, knew strength and certainty, relishing the sureness and power which had held him at *the moment*.

He walked up the river through the woods and climbed the slope to the field where he had left his motor-cycle. He moved and thought with a caution and clearness that rode free of the steady pulse of exhilaration in him. His own safety was very much his concern. In a lower degree he had known it before . . . on the nights when he and the others had moved away separately from some robbery, mastering the quick lift of excitement, thinking and moving sensibly. But now the excitement stayed with him, steadying him, feeding him with confidence. At his motor-cycle he put the rifle, stock first, into the left-hand pannier over the rear wheel. He dropped the three loose cartridge cases in, then the rope and finally the towel from his neck, wrapping it round the section of the rifle barrel which extruded from the pannier when he fastened the flap down. He wheeled the machine out to the road and then went back and checked that it had left no tyre marks on the frost-hard ground.

Half an hour later he was in Barnstaple. He left his motor-cycle in the main car park and walked to the central post office. He consulted a London telephone directory and then made a long call from one of the booths. He was still calm, still sustained. On the ride into Barnstaple his mind had gone over all the possibilities, all the dangers into which he could fall and was confident that he was fast discounting them. At some time he knew the reaction would come. It always had with the robberies. It was the final signal of release from violence, marking the turning point back into everyday life. It hit him as he came down the ridge road by Long Holcombe. He drew into the roadside, went behind the beech-topped stone hedge and was violently sick.

*   *   *

The news of the death of the Foreign Secretary was held back for various security and police reasons until the morning of New Year's Eve day. Not many details were given. Sir Charles Read had been shot three days after Christmas while taking a morning ride on his Exmoor estate. He had died instantly. The assassination was a political one. An anonymous caller had passed a telephone message through the Press Association in London, claiming that it was the work of a German-based Arab terrorist group violently opposed to British policy in the Middle East and her historic role in setting up the State of Israel. The group was well known and no other communication had been received from them since the first call. Sir Charles Read's body had already been taken to London.

Grace heard the news on the radio as she was dressing. John Kingsford was told about it by Mrs Hurrell when she brought in his breakfast.

Ten minutes later Grace came into John. One look told her that he had heard the news. His breakfast was untouched and he stood by the window looking out over the lawns.

He turned and he knew exactly what was in her mind. He shook his head.

'No.'

'Thank God for that. Though I never for a moment thought——'

John came slowly to her and took her hand.

'Don't misunderstand. Because I couldn't do it makes no difference. You may find it a terrible thing for me to say, but the truth is that I'm glad. Just that. Does that change things between us?'

'No . . . I suppose not. At least it's honest. But it seems so fantastic that you wanted to do it and couldn't—and here it is.'

At this moment Carlo came into the room and, surprised to see Grace, said, 'Good Lord—what's happened to you? Down for breakfast.' He grinned at John and went on, 'Good morning, John. Do we let her into what is strictly a male preserve?'

John said, 'Carlo—we've just heard that Sir Charles Read—you know at Pitt Wood House—was assassinated, shot, two days ago while he was out riding in the morning.'

'Good Lord! You mean the Sir Charles . . . where we were going to the party tonight?'

'Yes, the Foreign Secretary.'

'My God—that'll put the cat among the pigeons. Do they know who did it?' Carlo had known this moment would come, had wondered why it had not come before; but he had never bothered to consider what his reaction would have to be. It came naturally. Just that touch of a little more concern than would have been there for any other comparable celebrity. After all he was—had been— a neighbour and they had been going to a party there tonight.

'Some anarchist group or the other from Germany,' said Grace.

At this moment Mrs Hurrell came into the room.

'Excuse me, Mr John. You're wanted on the telephone. It's a gentleman, a Mr Wardle.'

John went to the telephone in the study.

'Kingsford here.'

'Oh, Mr Kingsford, my name's Wardle. Mark Wardle—we have met once but you probably won't remember me.'

'No, I can't say I do.'

'Well, that doesn't matter. I presume you've heard about Sir Charles Read?'

'Yes, of course. A little while ago.'

'I'm at Pitt Wood House, Mr Kingsford—if I say on official business I think that will be enough. I'd be glad if you could make it possible to come over here and see me at eleven this morning.'

'What on earth for?'

There was the faintest suggestion of a chuckle and the voice said, 'Well, I hope perhaps to help us a little. I don't want to say any more over the phone than that. Sir Charles's mother has gone to London. There's no family here.'

'I see. Yes, of course I'll come.'

'Then perhaps you would give me your car number? The press are already scrubbing around. I'll see that you're let through. Oh, and would you be good enough at your end to say nothing of where you are going?'

'Of course.'

John gave the man his car number and then sat down at the desk. Wardle? Mark Wardle? The name meant nothing, raised not even the ghost of a memory. He dismissed it from his mind and leaned back in his chair. So Sir Charles Read was dead. And he had told Grace that he was glad, and glad he was. It would have been useless to lie to her. If he were to marry again he would want it to be someone like Grace, Grace herself maybe, for she was marked as now he had been marked as outside the need for love. With that thought in him, he wondered for the first time whether Elizabeth might long before their marriage have been so marked. Had something happened to her which had turned her towards him as the substitute for something for ever lost to her? Given that, she might have felt free to work for him even through deceit, putting her political ambitions for him in the place of love. The idea had never occurred to him before, and it came only now, he accepted, because he, too, had discovered new truths about himself which made him ready to try and understand what might have happened to her.

Later in the morning he drove over to Pitt Wood House. A dozen or more cars were parked alongside the road before he got to the drive gates. Close to the gates was a TV van and crew, a police car, and a small knot of pressmen, who closed about his car, calling and shouting to him in the few moments before the drive gates were opened and he motored through. The news of the event had been kept back two days; the world was hungry for details, and John knew that he would not escape. Well, if they came pestering around Darlock they would get short shrift. Sir Charles Read was dead—and that was an end of the man as far as he was concerned.

He knew the house and had always liked it. It had an elegance which had escaped Darlock. Sheltered by its ring of surrounding trees and the high garden walls, plants and shrubs grew here which would have shrivelled and died at Darlock. A policeman opened the car door for him and took him into the house. He was asked to wait in the hall and the policeman disappeared. Men and women came and went down the hall, moving into and out of the rooms he knew, the lounge, the dining room, and the library. There was no sign of any of the servants he knew from over the years. Tonight there was to have been a party here to which he would have brought Grace and Carlo and (at Grace's suggestion) Birdie Carter. Sir Charles would have had no objection to that. He knew the Carters, good yeoman farming stock. They escaped the net of any snobbery. At one time he had thought of making some excuse for not coming, but had decided against it. At some time he would have met him.

A girl came out of the small study next to the lounge. For a moment he heard the clicking of a typewriter and the slightly distorted sound of an incoming voice from some radio receiver. Outside on the lawn a tall, temporary radio mast had been erected. Brushing her lips with the sheet of paper she carried, the girl went into the library. John stared at the mask of a fox mounted on one of the oak wall panels. Underneath were details of the run and the kill and the date. It was a long time ago. In his father's time. A father he had never known.

The girl came out of the library and crossed to him. She was the kind he knew well from his brief days as a Parliamentary Private Secretary in a Junior Ministry. The height of the preferment achieved for him by Elizabeth.

The girl said, 'This way please, Mr Kingsford. I'm sorry you had to wait.'

She took him to the library door and opened it for him. He went in and the door closed on him. The eyes of an Elizabethan ancestor of the Read family met his from the oil painting over the stone fireplace. Forked beard, immaculate white ruff, crimson and green slashed doublet and a ringed hand on the pommel of a sword. The man was the spitting image of the dead Sir Charles.

There were two men in the room. They sat, comfortably spaced, around the large circular leather-topped library table. There was nothing on the table except a couple of ash trays and a large wire basket full of papers placed midway between them. One of the ash trays was untidy with cigarette stubs. The other was empty. One of the men who was smoking looked up at John, smiled, and nodded him to a chair on the far side of the table.

'Sorry to keep you waiting, Mr Kingsford. Do please sit down. Please smoke if you want to.' He reached out and slid the empty ash tray towards John. He was a plumpish faced man, in his forties, his greying blond hair falling from semi-baldness to a lank, untidy growth behind his ears and over his neck. The face was pleasant, florid, and with a fine net of broken blood vessels over his cheekbones. He went on, smiling, 'You obviously don't remember me?'

'I'm afraid not.'

'Some years ago. When you were a Parliamentary Private Secretary. A general conference on security matters which you attended on behalf of your Minister. Nothing really important. Remember?'

'I'm afraid not.'

The man shrugged his shoulders good-humouredly, and said, 'Oh dear—and one is always trying so hard to make a lasting impression. Wardle. Mark Wardle.' He pushed an official identity card across the table to John. It read— *Mark H. Wardle, C.B., Assistant Under-Secretary for State. Home Office. Police Department.* The card was numbered and carried a small head and shoulders photograph, embossed with an official stamp.

As John slid it back, the other man said, 'I'm Charles Grainger, Mr Kingsford.' He passed his identity card over. It ran—*Charles Grainger, M.C., C.B. Assistant Political Adviser. Foreign Office. Middle East Department.* The identifying photograph was a better likeness than Wardle's. A dark-haired, dark-eyed, white-faced man in his fifties. The face was expressionless, the lips a narrow, short bracket above a deeply cleft chin. Handing the card back John's eyes met the same face, still and cold. Wardle seemed all right, but nothing he felt would ever make him warm to this man.

Wardle said cheerfully, 'It's good of you to spare us your time, Mr Kingsford. You're probably wondering why we asked you to come?'

'Naturally.'

'Well, it's simply that Mr Grainger and I are interviewing all the people we can in this area who knew Sir Charles Read or were friends of his and who might have seen him recently. We want to talk to them because at the moment we're very much in the dark about this whole affair. One never knows when some small fact, something seemingly unimportant may not eventually fit into the . . . well, the pattern of his death. I don't have to tell you that significant facts often come in the guise of some apparently unimportant observation or remark, or even a moment's query about someone or something being fractionally noteworthy or puzzling.' He paused, passed a hand over his bald patch and added, 'Sorry—my conversation has a habit of turning into a speech far too often. By the way, I should point out—everything that passes between us in this room is confidential. You must say nothing of what went on in this room. Miss Todd—the lady who brought you in will give you a short statement which you can memorize for the crowd up at the gate if they come chasing after you. Which they will.'

'I understand.'

Wardle grinned. 'Good. I really should try and cultivate some of your excellent brevity.' He offered his cigarette case to John, who refused; then he lit himself a cigarette.

For a moment or two there was silence in the room and John had the feeling that it might be deliberate. Although they had wasted no time on deploring the crime, not even a passing noise of sympathy or conventional horror, he knew that they must be here prepared to spare no one in their search for truth. They were both career men and they would work together like a couple of matched hounds, ready to pick up the faintest scent. Wardle, he guessed, was only long-winded when he wanted to be. And the blank-faced Grainger's eyes would never leave the eyes of the person he was questioning. He felt uneasy because for the first time now he could foresee problems ahead. An innocent evasion of a question for personal reasons might take him into deep water. He had no wish to expose his intimate history. His private life was his own— and he wanted it kept that way. He saw that he would have to play each question as it came and make a decision without hesitation.

As Wardle, cigarette lit, put his lighter into his waistcoat pocket, he said, 'Charles.'

Grainger said, 'Thank you.' Then to John he went on, 'You knew, of course, that Sir Charles was down for the Christmas period?'

'Yes, I did.'

'Had you seen him since his arrival?'

'No, we hadn't met. But I spoke to him on the telephone. In fact he phoned me to say hallo and to ask me over to the usual New Year's Eve party.' He filled out his answer, smothering, he hoped, the difference between to see and to meet. If Grainger had noticed it he knew that the man would not reveal it right away unless it suited him.

'He was a very good friend of yours?'

'Yes, socially and politically. Myself and my late wife.'

'You've lived around here all your life. Know all the people. In winter particularly you'd notice strangers?'

'In certain circumstances I would.'

'Such as?'

'If they were off the beaten track, or doing something or other which was a bit odd. I imagine that's the kind of thing you're looking for. Frankly I've not seen anyone or anything like that in the last weeks.'

'No coloured or foreign looking types?'

'No, not that I remember.'

'When you leave here will you think it all over, Mr Kingsford. Something may come back to your memory. No matter how small it may seem—we'd like to know.'

'Of course.'

'Thank you, Mr Kingsford.'

Grainger gave him a little nod and said no more. Wardle stared out of the window as though he had no more interest in the proceedings. John waited for a moment or two for some polite phrase of dismissal. Getting none, he made a slow movement to rise, thinking the interview over. Their brief he decided was simply to see everyone around who had known Sir Charles and hope that something would stir in their memories which would help. But as he put his hands on the arm of his chair and began to rise, Wardle leaned forward, stubbed his cigarette out in the ash tray and shook his head.

John realized then that the pause had deliberately been designed to unsettle him.

Wardle said, 'Not yet, Mr Kingsford. You may be able to help us more than you realize at the moment. We are still, I confess, very much in the dark. We can't afford to neglect any lead. If we should end by embarrassing or annoying you, then I apologize in advance. So bear with us a little longer. Charles.'

Grainger leaned forward, elbows on the table, and rested his cleft chin on the pointed temple of his clasped hands like some Calvinistic preacher, dark and still, about to say prayers.

'Sir Charles was shot on the morning of the 28th December. The time of his death has been put at somewhere around ten o'clock by the surgeons. This is confirmed by the stableman who saddled up his horse for him. Apparently he almost always took his ride at the same time, and along the same route. Did you know that, Mr Kingsford?'

'Yes, I did. And so I imagine would most of the people around here. As a matter of fact I have in my time come over and ridden with him.'

Grainger nodded. 'His body wasn't found until well over an hour later. One of the house staff noticed the horse wandering loose by the river. So far as it can be reconstructed he had been shot first of all through the right side of his neck when he pulled up at the river gate. And then through the left temple as he lay on the ground. There was a third bullet mark in the gate post on the riverside. From these it seems highly probable that the shots were fired from the other side of the river and—given the angle of entry—from some considerable elevation. From somewhere on the top of the bluff where there are some ruined cottages.' He dropped his hands from his chin and clasped them over his stomach and was silent.

John looked from one man to the other. They were both watching him. He realized that nothing either of them had said so far was without relevance. They were going through a well-established routine. A routine just for him, he wondered, or for all the other local people they were going to see or already had interviewed?

Wardle said, 'Any stranger wanting to kill Sir Charles would have had to spend some time around here in order to establish his routine. But if he were killed by someone locally his routine would have been well known.'

'The news says he was shot by some terrorist group. I doubt if they would have any local members,' John pointed out. 'In fact, I'm beginning to wonder what it is that you two gentlemen want from me. The simple answer is that it could have been either. A well-briefed stranger who knew how to avoid attention. Or a local person.'

'Quite,' said Wardle, touching the top of his head as though he might hope to find his baldness gone. 'In your wildest flight of fancy, Mr Kingsford, is there any local person you could possibly consider as a candidate for that role?'

Indignation hit John suddenly. 'For God's sake—what a

question to ask! But if answer you must have, then—no. Of all the local people I know, there's no one.'

Grainger said, 'And what about yourself?'

John stood up quickly. 'Look, I've had enough of this. I don't know a damn thing about Sir Charles's death and I——' He broke off sharply.

'And you what?' asked Wardle blandly. 'Couldn't care less perhaps?' He smiled and began to reach for his cigarette case.

Grainger said, 'That's not a question you're expected to answer, Mr Kingsford. Please . . .' He motioned for John to sit down.

As John did so, regretting his outburst, Wardle said pleasantly, 'Bear with us a little more. One of Her Majesty's most important Ministers of State has been murdered. Mr Grainger and I are only one small part of the investigation process. Confidentially, very little progress has been made anywhere. Personally, since we're both professional men we'd like to think that we can beat the field. That kind of ambition means that we can overlook nothing. If there's the slightest fact for us to work from —then we must.' He smiled. 'And risk the justified anger of people like yourself. You see I am making a speech again, but that is only to cover my own embarrassment. Frankly, we have a theory. And also a few small scraps of fact which force us to pursue it. Also, I'm afraid, it obliges me to go on making something of a speech. So please be patient with me. Will you, Mr Kingsford?'

'Yes, of course. Anyway, I don't have any option, do I?'

Grainger said, 'That is so, Mr Kingsford.'

Wardle spun his lighter on the table before him and the morning sunlight reflected from it sent a brief flight of ragged, silver butterflies around the room. He picked up the lighter as it spun to a stop, and said, 'Good. Now that that's all been pleasantly settled we can get on.'

He smiled at John, and John knew that the man's pompous, long-winded manner was far from natural. It was a shield from behind which he worked his way forward to the point of sudden and effective attack. Although he had nothing to fear from them he knew himself to be uneasy and angry. And, more than that, hampered by a determination to keep from them any knowledge of the events in his life which had led up to that morning on the river bluff when he had discovered there was no power in him to curl his trigger finger back and shoot Sir Charles Read.

Wardle said, 'You've been a Member of Parliament, Mr Kingsford. And a Parliamentary Private Secretary. You know Westminster and, although you've forgotten the little conference which I chaired on security, you must be aware that, in far less than obvious ways, the Home Office and the Foreign Office look after their own. Particularly people like Foreign Secretaries. Security is a respectable name for many not so respectable activities. In the interests of the State we must do what we must do with sometimes very little regard for ethics or, regrettably, morals. Men like the Foreign Secretary are always in danger. And that danger doesn't always come from outside forces. Danger and risk are sometimes created by the man himself in his private life. Because of some personal indiscretion—sometimes reasonably innocent in character and sometimes not—he may lay himself open to peril of a quite unexpected kind. We keep an eye on these indiscretions or personal foibles. We make it our business—not a pleasant and certainly not a publicized one—to know about them. Sir Charles, as you know, was a man of robust habits.' He shook his head regretfully. 'An obstinate man, too. He usually insisted on taking his morning ride here without any protection. If only he had been wiser. However, I digress. He had an invalid wife, bedridden for many years, to whom he was devoted. But devotion stills few men's natural sexual feelings. This was an aspect of his life, of course, which was an obvious security risk.' He stopped and leaned back in his chair, not smiling now, his eyes on John, his face grave, almost sorrowful. 'Do I have to say more?'

'No. So he took his pleasure with other women. That doesn't surprise me.'

Wardle, shaking his head so that the loose locks of blond-grey hair rubbed the back of his jacket collar, said affably, 'No more than that? Just a general observation?'

John said, 'Sir Charles Read's private life was his affair.'

Grainger said, 'Not entirely.' He reached under the top paper in the wire basket, brought out an envelope and pushed it across the table to John.

Before he picked it up John recognized the handwriting as that of his wife. There was no shock in him. In some ways they had exercised their own kind of kindness, prepared him as much as they could with their oblique charity. He had not killed Sir Charles. They could not touch him. Quite calmly, learning a little now the art of their own game, he slid the letter from the opened envelope, wondering whether they had intercepted it in Sir Charles's post long ago or simply lifted it from his desk or safe. It would have been like the man not to miss it. He read it through without emotion. Elizabeth was beyond touching him now.

Where Sir Charles had frequently lapsed into an earthy directness, Elizabeth was more romantic, except in the one passage in this letter where she referred to the Honours List, making a claim for recognition in some way of her husband for his work on a departmental committee he had headed on a review of potential agricultural land still held for training purposes by the Army. Nothing had come of the review or the Honour. Sir Charles would have known how to handle her disappointment. He put the letter back in the envelope and slid it across to Grainger.

The man put it back in the basket to rest openly on the top now. He lifted his head, tilting his cleft chin up. There was a saurian stringiness to the skin of his throat. He said, 'When did you learn that your wife had been unfaithful to you for a long time?'

'After her death. Some weeks ago. I found by accident a secret drawer in her bureau. There were two packets of letters to her from Sir Charles.'

'And so?'

'I decided that as a point of honour I would shoot the bastard.'

Flatly, without surprise, Grainger asked, 'And did you?'

'No, I didn't! I went to the bluff to shoot him. But I couldn't. That was the morning before he was shot. And to forestall your next question—at the time you say Sir Charles was killed I was in the stables at Darlock with our local vet. One of the horses was sick. He was there from just after nine until half-past ten or later.'

Grainger, face unmoving, asked, 'And what did you do with the rifle?'

'Chucked it down the well. I never wanted to see it again!'

A little sigh came from Wardle and he said placidly, 'Well, that's frank enough. Our apologies for the way we have had to do it. Tell me, Mr Kingsford. What foreign languages do you speak?'

'None. Well, only a sort of bastard French from school.'

'Not German?'

'No.'

Wardle rubbed his plump hands together. 'I see.'

He rose and walked to a side table by the window which held a tray with a sherry decanter and glasses.

He filled a glass and brought it over on the tray to John.

217

'You'll excuse us, Mr Kingsford, but in view of all you've said, Mr Grainger and I would like a little time to confer in private. Yes, Charles?'

Grainger nodded, and rose.

Wardle as they went out said, 'Feel free to help yourself if we are over-long, Mr Kingsford.'

Chapter Eleven

THEY WERE GONE for half an hour. When they returned Wardle helped himself to sherry, and the two of them sat down. Wardle raised his glass to John and drank. Grainger sat bent over his crossed arms, looking like a well-preserved gargoyle. Outside on the large gravel sweep a police car drew away down the drive. High up through the top of the window John could see a kestrel hovering, wings flickering, broad tail down-pressed. Some vole or small bird was marked as victim. But nothing, John knew, could make him a victim. He had not killed Sir Charles. And what was more he had no damned interest in whoever had killed the man.

Wardle said, 'Now let us begin again. Certain very interesting points have arisen from the information you've given us. I'm sure you can summon up a little more patience with us?'

'Go ahead.'

Grainger said, 'Having decided to kill Sir Charles what plans did you make, and how near actually did you come to carrying them out?'

John said frankly, 'I came to the point of having him in my sights and my finger ready to press the trigger—and then found I couldn't do it.'

'No, no.' Wardle shook his head vigorously. 'You must give it in order, Mr Kingsford. You discovered the letters. You decided to kill Sir Charles. Now, as Mr Grainger has asked, what plans did you make? That *first* and then right up to the point of not killing him. I know this is going to be tedious for you, but not for us. We want to know everything in detail. So please, may we have it that way? And do forgive us if at times we have to press you about some particular point or fact. We are after all—no matter what our opinions of Sir Charles may have been—trying to discover who perpetrated this hideous crime.' He smiled, the humouring *paterfamilias*, and added, 'Take your time.'

John told them step by step how he had planned the killing. From time to time he was interrupted, either briefly by Grainger, or effusively by Wardle, when there was some point they wanted made clearer. They questioned him closely about the precautions he had taken to ensure his own safety, and it became clear to him from their questions that they already had a considerable knowledge about himself. He realized, too, that they had been up to the firing point by the old well.

When he finished there was silence for a while. Wardle lit a cigarette and Grainger unclasped his hands and reached out slowly and absently touched the letter in the wire basket.

Wardle said, 'Well, Charles?'

After a moment's thought Grainger answered, 'I think so. Everything fits up to a point.'

'I agree. Card by card right through the pack. Except, of course—there's no joker. Perhaps Mr Kingsford,' he turned to John and smiled, '—who has no cause for any concern about himself in this matter—after all it's no crime to wish someone were dead—can help us? Who do you think the joker would be, Mr Kingsford?'

Puzzled, John said, 'I'm sorry, I'm not with you.'

'No?' Wardle looked genuinely surprised. 'But surely you must be by now? The whole thing revolves around you. You were going to murder Sir Charles. You made quite a clever plan. Not that it would have worked as you must now realize. But no matter. At the very moment of action your conscience, your good sense, something kept your finger frozen. From that point you had no need for further precautions. You just got up, walked away and dropped your loaded rifle down the well. And the next day—in steps the joker. You see?'

John shrugged his shoulders. 'No, I don't. Except clearly the next day someone killed Sir Charles and possibly from near about the spot I had chosen.'

Grainger said, 'Mr Kingsford, Mr Wardle and I were present at first light on the morning after Sir Charles's death when that well was searched and dragged by a naval frogman. It was too obvious a place to overlook. No rifle was found. But it is well established by our ballistic experts that Sir Charles was killed by bullets of the same calibre as you were going to use. The same calibre, the same firing point—the same rifle, surely?'

John said, 'You can't seriously believe that someone knew my rifle was in the well, went down for it and . . .'

'Why not?' said Grainger.

Wardle said, 'There *must* be a joker in the pack. No organized terrorist group would have operated like that. On a fluke? On the chance turn of events? They would have had to have been watching you for weeks.'

'But you've had a message from them saying they did it.'

'So we have. And so far they haven't denied it. But if the message hadn't really come from them they might well have decided to let it be thought they had done it. After all—it's the kind of thing they would *want* to have done. So that brings us back to the joker.' He frowned a little crossly. 'Oh, come, you really must see it. It's much more likely that somebody, almost certainly locally, must have known what you were planning to do, and when you didn't do it, they did it.'

John stood up and walked to the window, then swung sharply round and faced them. He said firmly, 'The whole thing is ridiculous. They would have had to know about Elizabeth. They'd also have to be mind readers. And they would have had to be there to see me let that bastard go free and then chuck that rifle down the well. And a hundred other things. For God's sake there's no one around here like that.'

Wardle spread his hands. 'Our feeling is that there must be.' He smiled. 'I would almost say there has got to be. You should know that the message claiming the killing for the terrorist group was telephoned to the Press Association in London within an hour of the killing. It was made from Barnstaple—by a man. The Press Association are well used these days to handling that kind of message. They were helped by the fact that the caller gave them time for this call to be traced because in very bad English he insisted on speaking to someone in German so that he could read the group's communiqué. Who do you know around here, Mr Kingsford, who could read your mind, ferret out your secrets, and also who speaks German?'

'Not a bloody soul. The whole thing is ridiculous!'

Grainger shook his head. 'Strange—not ridiculous. You dropped the rifle in the well. It's gone. Sir Charles was almost certainly shot with it. Then the killer moved off to Barnstaple and made the phone call. He may still have the rifle or have disposed of it. Whoever it was, it was someone who had been taking a great personal interest in you, and was watching your movements—and that person, too, must have had a reason for killing Sir Charles.'

Wardle, nodding agreement, said cheerfully. 'It's really most intriguing. Unless we had known about your wife's affair with Sir Charles we should never have put you on a list of possible suspects—and so through you have come to this bizarre but quite tenable theory of ours.'

John came back to the table and sat down.

He said, 'Well, that may be so, but I don't see how I can help you any further.'

For a moment or two the men opposite him were silent. He had the uncanny feeling that even in their silence they possessed the power of communicating with one another, a power which had come from working together for a very long time. The odd thought struck him that while Wardle might well be from the Home Office Police Department it seemed inappropriate that Grainger should be from the Middle East Department of the Foreign Office. There was something about the man which made him hard to class as a political adviser. That could be just a cover for this particular job. He knew enough about political and governmental life to realize that people were not always what their identity cards proclaimed them to be. As these thoughts ran through his mind, Wardle turned his head slightly towards Grainger. The two men looked at one another, seeking some accord, questioning some move, so it seemed to John, and then Grainger nodded slightly, as though agreement had been reached.

Wardle turned to John and said, 'Let's just go back a little bit into the account you gave us, Mr Kingsford. It may be tedious for you, but I'm afraid that's unavoidable. You know—' he smiled affably, '—we often find that when people are asked to give an account of their plans and movements it's very easy to overlook minor, seemingly unimportant things in their narrative. After all, to take a small point in illustration, which I am sure is of no importance in this affair, you made no mention of the clothes you were wearing on the morning you went to the river bluff to shoot Sir Charles.'

'Well naturally. What difference could that make? You just wanted the straightforward, important facts.'

'Yes, we did. At that time. But now we have an entirely

223

different problem. We are looking for the missing joker from the pack of cards which has now been newly opened as it were and spread on this table before us within the last hour. So—now we're interested in every fact, every small detail of your recent past activities. You follow?'

'Yes. . . . Yes, I see what you mean.'

'Good, now let's take the letters from Sir Charles to your wife. Where were they kept until you destroyed them?'

For the next fifteen minutes John was busy answering the questions which came from both of them; small point after small point; keys, safe, rooms, details of his trips to the firing point, the layout of the gun room, and then, from Grainger: 'You're a good shot, Mr Kingsford?'

'Obviously.'

'Had you ever used the rifle before?'

'No.'

'Then even you would hardly go to the firing point without trying it first, I imagine?'

'No. Of course not. I wanted to check the telescopic sights and also to have practice in something like the same situation. . . . Oh, I see what you mean. Somebody might have seen me using it?'

'It's possible, isn't it?'

'I suppose so. Though I chose an isolated spot and used it very early in the morning.'

'Country people rise early. The sound of a rifle shot carries quite a way. How far from the nearest road were you?'

'About a quarter of a mile from the ridge road above Darlock.'

'Is it much used, early in the morning? People going to work?'

'No . . . no, not much . . .' But as he spoke, a thought came to him waywardly but sharply: Carlo had run it every morning during his training. He added quickly, 'I'm sure nobody spotted me. I was always careful about that. I had to be.'

'Well, we will let that go. Now let's deal with your staff. First the Hurrells. How long have they been with you?'

'Years and years. Ever since I was a boy. And the maid, Vera Thorn, for about two years. She comes from a good family in Bampton, the father's dead and the mother serves in a shop.'

'And that's the lot? No one else in the house?'

'No, of course not. There's——' John broke off, suddenly aware of the great gap between his way of thinking and theirs. They were ferreting away, determined to get any detail which might, no matter how trivial it seemed to him, mean something to them and their joker theory.

'There's what, Mr Kingsford?' asked Wardle gently.

'I'm sorry. I forgot. We've got a tower wing at Darlock. We never use it. But for long years we've now and then let it as a self-contained apartment. Usually in the summer. But this year, now as a matter of fact, it's let to two people. A Miss Grace Lindsay and her nephew, a young man called Carlo Graber. I should have mentioned that, I suppose.'

Unruffled, Wardle said quietly, 'That's all right, Mr Kingsford. This is being something of a morning for you, and we quite understand. So you have two, what shall we say—paying guests? Tell us about them.'

John told them what he knew about Grace and Carlo and they listened without interruption. When he had finished Wardle said, 'They came on your brother's recommendation—you'd never met them before?'

'No.'

'But you had met the boy's mother briefly, years ago you say?' asked Grainger.

'Yes. I can't remember her all that well. But I gather

that she used to talk about Darlock to Carlo. Miss Lindsay told me that he just got a fancy to see the place.'

Grainger went on, 'Miss Lindsay is English?'

'Yes.'

'How do you get on with Carlo Graber? What I mean is do you get on or don't you?'

'I like him very much. I had reservations at first. But being at Darlock seems to have changed him. He's taken to outdoor life and intends to go to agricultural college and become a farmer. He's lucky. He's got enough money to be able to afford it.'

'He's half Swiss. Does he speak German?'

'Not that I know of. French, yes. And Italian.' John stirred angrily. 'Look, if you think——'

Wardle interrupted. 'We have our duty, Mr Kingsford. An unpleasant one. You're now mixed up in it. You must face that. So let's go on so far as we can without emotion.' For the first time Wardle's face was as grave as Grainger's and his voice was cold and incisive.

'I'll try.'

Grainger continued. 'Is this young man a good shot?'

'Fairly, yes.' Carlo was in his mind, and now in theirs. His instinct at once was protective.

'He had access to the gun room?'

'Yes. But he could never have known about the rifle. It was locked away in a special cabinet with my Purdeys and so on. I have the only key and he never had it.'

'Does he own a car?'

'No. He uses Miss Lindsay's sometimes. But he has his own motor-cycle. A Norton I think it is.'

Wardle took over from Grainger and asked, 'Mr Kingsford, in the wildest flight of fancy you could imagine, can you think of any conceivable reason why Carlo would want to kill Sir Charles?'

'No. Absolutely no. It's a ridiculous idea. He could never

226

have known what I had planned to do. The whole idea is utterly out of the question.'

Wardle smoothed his hands over his bald patch. 'All right, Mr Kingsford. I think it would be asking too much from you for us to go on any further at the moment. You've been very helpful. But before you go, I must put one more point to you. You've been frank with us about your part in all this. Would you just consider for a moment whether there is anything you haven't said to us, a notion, some small fact, anything in fact which out of some loyalty, or personal embarrassment, you might have decided not to volunteer unless directly asked? Long-winded again, I'm afraid. But I'm sure you understand what I mean.'

John was silent for a moment or two. He could have mentioned Carlo's training runs, but he was damned if he was going to. He said, 'I think I've given you all the help I can. If I haven't I'm ready to stay here and answer any more questions you like to put to me, and to answer them quite truthfully.'

Wardle drew on his cigarette and stood up. 'I think we've put all the questions we want to at the moment. Thank you, Mr Kingsford. Please remember that everything which has been said in this room is entirely secret. Miss Todd will tell you what to say to the wolf pack at the gate.'

When John had gone, Wardle said to Grainger, 'Well, what do you make of our Mr Kingsford?'

Grainger said evenly, 'Unimaginative. Conventional. It doesn't surprise me that he couldn't fire at Sir Charles. Murder always demands a touch of fanaticism, or something abnormal. Kingsford had a wild dream—and woke up, glad to find it was only a dream.'

'And this Carlo?'

Grainger, a birth of a smile briefly showing, said, 'Interesting. Comes here in the middle of winter—when he could be in the South of France, Bermuda, Florida—just to see a place his mother visited donkey's years ago. Why?'

'Does it matter?'

'Maybe not.'

Wardle stood up and went to the window. Back to Grainger, he said, 'Political assassination is entirely acceptable. That makes Sir Charles a martyr. That's how it should be. Imagine the mess if it *had* been Kingsford! A trial and all the personal dirt coming out. A salacious handout to a sorrowing nation. None of our masters would have wanted to see that happen.'

'So—what's the next step? Carlo Graber? With a name like that and Swiss born the odds are that he speaks German. I'll run a check on him, his aunt and all the background.'

'And why should he have done it?'

Grainger turned. 'I'm happy to leave that until we know that he did do it. I'll have a word with our police friends here and get them moving quietly. Somebody could have seen him in Barnstaple. Big Norton motor-cycle. He's been here some time. Local people notice things like that. Let's be glad it wasn't Kingsford.'

The door opened and Miss Todd came in and laid a message form in front of Wardle. When she was gone Wardle picked it up and read it. He dropped it in the wire basket and leaning back said, 'They've jumped on the band wagon at last. I had a feeling they would because the opportunity was too good to miss. There's been a second communiqué from our Arab friends in Germany. Sent from Germany this time. Reaffirming that it was their act and then a lot of political guff and wind. They couldn't turn down a chance like this for prestige and publicity.'

Grainger came over, picked up the message, and read

it. He pursed his thin lips into the faintest shaping of a smile.

He said, 'We mustn't be ungrateful for any help.'

Wardle asked, 'Don't you ever get tired of sweeping other people's dirt under the carpet?'

'Not now. A long time back I had a few scruples. But not now. In an odd way I enjoy it. I wonder what that makes me?'

'Us,' said Wardle flatly.

*   *   *

John drove back to Darlock. As he left the car in the yard he noticed that Carlo's motor-cycle was not in the garage. Going through the kitchen—since it was now past the lunch hour—he told Mrs Hurrell that he had already eaten. He went up to the tower sitting-room and found Grace there.

He said, 'Where's Carlo?'

'He's gone over to the Carters. Since the party is off he's staying for supper there. Why?'

'I want to talk to him. But first I want to talk to you. But not here, not in the house. If you're not doing anything I'll drive you out somewhere.'

'John, what's the matter?'

'That's what I want to talk to you about. I'm not supposed to, but I'm going to. I've just come from Pitt Wood House where I've had . . . well, a not too pleasant time. Come on.'

He drove southwards off the moor a few miles and parked the car in a layby near some old mine workings alongside the river Mole. The same mine, he remembered oddly, where old Parson John had had trouble with the workers who poached his salmon.

Sitting in the car with Grace, he told her everything

229

which had passed that morning at Pitt Wood House. She asked no questions but sat listening and feeling the slow onset of an inner coldness take her. Long before he had finished speaking, although she could find no reason for the conviction, she knew instinctively that Carlo must have killed Sir Charles. Knew it, and silently fought against knowing it, and was unwilling to let her mind dwell on all the inevitable consequences.

When he had laid out the whole thing for her, John went on, 'I'm supposed to have kept all this to myself. But I don't care a damn about that. And if you're ever asked if I told you well then you must say I did. Carlo does speak German, doesn't he?'

'Yes. Fluently. Oh, God—what kind of craziness has he got into?'

John took her hand. 'Perhaps I shouldn't have told you.'

'Of course you should. I'm the only one he's got. I had to know. But what we can do, I can't think.'

'You think he must have done it?'

'I want to say No. But I can't.'

John said almost angrily, 'If he did it—and I'm going to put it to him—then we've got to help him. I've got to help him. I'm as guilty in a way as he is. I was going to kill Read and I didn't. Carlo—God knows why—did the job for me. How on earth he knew about it all and came to be there I can't imagine, but he's going to have to tell me. How the devil could he have known?'

'Knowing with Carlo is a passion. He always wants to know about people, and if he has any kind of reason personally for wanting to know he'll stop at nothing. When I first took him over he used to get at all my correspondence, poke about in my drawers and cases and be quite unashamed if caught. When he went into that stupid robbery trouble the whole lot of them had skeleton keys and God knows what. He could still have his. A locked door or safe would be a challenge to him, even if he weren't looking specifically for anything. But John, if he admits it, you'll have to tell them the truth——'

'No, I won't. If he did it, then I'm as guilty as he is. Those two over at Pitt Wood House have got to be able to prove that he did it, and that he had a motive for doing it. There's no reason why they should ever be able to do that. I'm not out to help them, I can't be. Carlo's the one who needs help. Carlo has got to keep his mouth shut and so have I. It will just have to be brazened out.'

Grace was silent. John was saying no more than she would have expected. But there was no confidence in her. There would be a motive. Carlo had wanted to come to Darlock. There had to be a reason for that beyond an idle interest arising from a moment-or-two's nostalgia on the part of his mother. She watched a kingfisher go hurrying up the stream, saw the white water creaming over the boulders and the wet pewter gleam of the leafless ash trees' trunks. Somewhere now Carlo was off with Birdie and there wouldn't be a moment's worry or, maybe, even thought in him about anything he had done. You did something, good, bad or outrageous, and then pushed it away and went on to the next thing.

She said, 'Would you rather I spoke to him?'

'No. This is between Carlo and myself. I can't even promise that I shall tell you what he says. That depends on him. I'll talk to him tonight, no matter how late he comes back. God, it's a mess. . . .'

He put his arm around her. The thought was suddenly in his mind that all this had sprung from Parson John's diaries. A Spanish bureau bought at a sale years and years ago and the mention of its secret drawer sending him idly to search for it. Against that kind of tragic thrust there was no shield. A few words once spoken or written, the smallest action absently made, they never died. They went on and on, forcing their consequences for ever. Wardle and Grainger, he thought, would know all about that. They were in the business of uncovering the past.

*   *   *

They left the motor-cycle in a cattle shelter high up on the Exford-Porlock road and, well-wrapped against the strengthening west wind coming in from the sea carrying scuds of rain with it, went off on to the moors for a walk. Late in the afternoon a path took them down into a deep valley which held a reservoir, full now to the dam top with the winter rains, the water cascading over it, the wind whipping it into white, ragged curtains and spumy screens of spray as it fell. They climbed a locked gate with a notice forbidding entry and by the edge of the water found an open-fronted shelter with dead, cut bracken piled in one corner weeks before to make a bed for some night-bound walker or tramp.

They turned the bracken with their feet, no words between them, and laid their coats across it dry sides up and then made love. Out of the wind it was warm, and lying afterwards they watched the little spray devils whipped up by the squalls go racing across the surface. On the far bank a heron stood, shoulders hunched against the weather, an old grey man lost in some eternal reverie.

With Birdie in the crook of his arm, her head against his shoulder, his free hand moulded across the swell of her bare shoulder, Carlo, relishing this closeness, both of them warmly cocooned in the aftermath of their loving, said idly, 'What exactly is a linhay?' He emphasized the aitch in the middle of the word.

'A Linney, you be meaning?'

'I suppose so, me little dear.' He faintly mimicked her accent.

Birdie laughed. ''Tis a shed or lean-to affair. Much like this. For storing hay and stuff or penning a few sheep. Why?'

He lied, 'It was in a book I read. A man made love to a farm girl in one.'

'It happens all the time round here.'

Carlo's fingers strayed and found the little locket and chain around her neck. *For Birdie for ever. Carlo.* That's what you had to have. Someone for ever. Or at least think you had, and then really believe you had. Though 'for ever', like love, was an odd quantity to bet on. The girl in the jeweller's shop in Barnstaple who had sold him the locket and made the arrangements for the engraving had given him that soft look which had nothing to do with love or for ever. Before Birdie he would not have wasted the opportunity. He was glad he had though. It meant he was maturing. Perhaps there was a kind of magic in and around Darlock and the moor. He had to come here to find himself, to begin to grow up and discover what he really wanted to do and what he really wanted from himself. He was a Kingsford. His body plainly marked. That could not be denied by anyone. But now, more importantly, not even by him. With a sharp little flare of perception he realized that the ambivalence of all his feelings about John Kingsford and Darlock had been no more than childish pique at times, a rejection of a truth he had now come to terms with. He was a Kingsford right to the marrow—and was glad of it. More a Kingsford, maybe, than John Kingsford, his father, because, barred from acceptance openly, he had reached for some act, some proof—like making the Run—which would establish himself if only in his own eyes as what . . . ? *Plus royaliste que le roi?* That, he saw, was why he had shot Sir Charles. His father's honour was his and sometimes a son must do what his father could not, would not, dare not do. Since that

233

moment deep contentment had been growing in him. He was glad he had ditched the rifle. No one would ever find it. And he had no need of it now. All that stupid business in his mind of putting it on the desk and making some melodramatic statement full of scorn. . . . Kid stuff. No, better some day when he had his own place, Birdie and children, to come back and quietly—man to man—make himself known. No self-pity; just an unruffled statement. He began to imagine the scene on that distant day to come at Darlock.

Birdie said, 'What are you chuckling about?'

'Nothing.'

He rolled over partly and lay looking down into her eyes. He could see his face in them, distorted but clear, tanned, planed down by exercise, dark hair untidy over his brow and although he was not like John Kingsford he could see the Kingsford bone shape there. He put his lips on hers and the need for her again stirred in him.

'No you don't.' Birdie laughed, and rolled away from him and began to stand up. 'We've got a long way back to go.' She grinned down at him. 'You've had your ration for this year.'

Without any real thought of Sir Charles, Carlo said, 'Thank God we don't have to go to that stuffy New Year's Eve party. We can see it in at your place, with your people.' He stood up and held out her coat for her. For Birdie for ever. Forever for Birdie. Picking up his own coat he began to whistle happily.

*   *   *

By midnight Wardle and Grainger, still working, had established some new facts. Grainger had gone up to the ruined cottages and from the firing point had looked around for the most likely hiding point for someone who

234

might have been watching John Kingsford. From across the river the patch of briars and bracken hid the well top from all angles. He eliminated the cottages because Kingsford had used one of them. Within a few minutes he had discovered the oak with its bower of ivy growth. He climbed it and was content. Here and there were small broken stems freshly wounded where someone had thrust into the growth. A large ivy branch was half snapped off to give an opening directly facing the well.

Wardle spent half an hour on the telephone to Interpol's main headquarters in Paris. As the last of the light of the old year was going, Miss Todd brought him, still to be decoded, the cipher message from Interpol. Although it gave him more than he had expected, he took little pleasure in reading it. Grainger went through it and slid it into the wire basket.

He said, 'By this time tomorrow we shall have turned up enough local stuff.'

'Including motive?'

'Have we never dispensed with it before?'

Wardle made no answer.

*   *   *

At midnight John raised his glass to Grace in the study. They drank and toasted one another. Then John moved to her and kissed her.

He said, 'You go on up and I'll wait for him here.'

'Are you going to tell me what he says?'

'I can't promise that. It depends on what he says, and whether he wants you to know.'

He went to the foot of the stairs with her and watched her go up. When she was gone he looked up at the portrait of his wife. A secret drawer in an old bureau. A woman substituting pathetic political ambitions for her husband in the place of love, because love was not there to be given. Simple lechery in Sir Charles Read. Not simply, he could guess, because of an invalid wife. More understandable, even condonable, a safety valve for the pressures of modern diplomacy and the stupid power games of the world. He had been a successful and an outstanding Foreign Secretary. His loss would change the course of history, must have already started to do that. In the event he had taken nothing from him. What had been given to him had never been on offer to the husband. No one existed isolated in time, immune from the unending game of consequences that was life. And now Carlo. Guilty or innocent? His own common sense told him the answer. The motive was hidden but opportunity, open to Carlo, denied to anyone else, made motive an unimportant thing easily waited on. Carlo would have his own battle to fight—and not, he prayed, without hope of winning. In a way it was the sort of fight Carlo would relish. Another Kingsford Run. A challenge because it was there and unavoidable, no choice now but a necessity. But that would only harden Carlo the more.

He went back to the study, poured himself another drink and waited. It was two o'clock when he heard the motorcycle come into the yard. He went into the hall and waited for Carlo to come through.

He came from the kitchen, crash helmet under one arm, his leather coat swinging free, his dark hair tousled, the firm, tanned face slicked a little from the rain which was still falling. Carlo said, 'Happy New Year, John.'

'And to you, Carlo.'

'I didn't expect to find you up.'

John said, 'Come into the study and have a drink.' He smiled. 'Not the first this year, I imagine?'

Carlo laughed. 'Not quite. But I always watch it when I'm driving.'

In the study John nodded to a chair and then poured a couple of drinks.

John sat down, nursing his drink, and faced Carlo. Over the last hours he had rehearsed this moment, but now that it was here all his planning went as he heard himself say, 'Carlo, when you first came here, although we both covered it up a great deal, I don't think we really took to one another much—do you?'

Carlo grinned. 'Well . . . no, I don't think so.'

'And now?'

'I don't know. I suppose I feel differently. I think the process of growing up isn't a smooth one. It goes by fits and jerks. Is all this in aid of anything?' Carlo sipped at his whisky and soda, watching John. He knew it was. One look at John told him it was. And waiting up until two in order to see him. Half-formed at the back of his mind was the idea that perhaps Grace and this man were thinking of marriage: 'Who's going to tell Carlo?' . . .

John said, 'Yes, it is in aid of something. But first let me say that I respect you very much for the change I've seen in you. I'd like to feel that I'm your friend, and that anything I say now is completely concerned with your good. So I hope you won't fly off the handle at me.'

Carlo smiled. It was all typical John Kingsford but no longer with any power to irk him. He said, 'I promise. It would be a bad way to start a new year, wouldn't it? Anyway, I can't wait to hear what it's all about.'

'It's about you. And it's no joking matter. I want you to answer some questions. And I promise you that no matter what you say I won't get steamed up about it.'

Carlo realized then that there was no question of anything between Grace and this man being discussed. He was silent for a moment or two, his mind flicking over the possibilities. Not old Carter worrying about him and Birdie? No, it couldn't be. And the other thing? He sucked in his lips, feeling the skin tighten over his cheek bones. Christ no . . . how could it be?

He said, 'Let's come to the questions then.' If it was the other thing he knew that his answers would have to be shaded or disguised on the prompting of each moment until he found the right pattern to follow. John Kingsford's first question shattered that design.

John said, 'How did you come to know that I was planning to kill Sir Charles Read?'

Carlo, eyes never leaving John, slowly put his glass on the side table. So there it was. The other thing. This slight interval now, surprise shadowing his face, offered him two choices. Tell the truth and he had to go on telling the truth. His own nature would force that on him. Tell a lie, and how much embroidery and validly seeming evasions would follow? He came out of the pause, refusing the lies which were forming in his thought, and heard himself say, 'It's a long and not very nice story. It began because of this thing I've got. I just like poking around, ferreting into other people's business.'

'Did you have any particular reason for ferreting into mine?'

'Yes, but I'd rather not go into that. In the end, if you insist, I'll tell you.'

'All right. We'll just stick to straightforward stuff. How did you come to know?'

'I saw you using the rifle one morning. That began it. I was on my training run. I had a look around your target. From the calibre I knew it was probably a rifle I'd already seen in your locked cabinet in the gun room. The one with the Purdeys and Hollands. I'd had a snoop there some time before. I've got a bunch of skeleton keys I acquired some time ago. I had another look to check up—and the rifle wasn't there. Neither was the box of ammunition. That set me off.'

Carlo paused. There was little feeling in him now. Once you got into something, you just accepted it and carried on. No good making a fuss either with yourself or anyone else.

John said, 'So you began to poke around?'

'Yes. I found the rifle in the bottom of your wardrobe. So I guessed you might be up to something.'

Carlo went on giving in detail the steps which had led him to the conclusion that John intended to shoot Sir Charles. When he told about opening the safe and reading the letters John was unmoved. Elizabeth and Sir Charles were dead; the letters were dead, destroyed. He could sit listening to this young man precisely outlining his movements, prompted now and then by a question from him, and nothing was touching him. He had no emotion for himself. Carlo was the one moving into trouble, and that fact had already created a responsibility and a loyalty towards Carlo which he accepted. Beyond all this, too, was the moment when Carlo would have to deal with the heart of the matter. Whether he would get the truth from him then he could not guess. He listened right through to the point where Carlo without any emotion admitted frankly that he had shot Sir Charles and had gone off to Barnstaple, disposing of the rifle and the other gear on the way, to telephone his message to the Press Association.

'And that's it,' said Carlo. 'I'd checked the rifle when I got it from the well. Knew there was a round up the spout. I covered him, just like you did—and then something just made me fire.' He drained his glass, and lit a cigarette, thinking that no matter how you had planned a thing, dreamt a thing would be, life imposed its own re-shaping twists and turns and you had to follow them.

John got up and refilled both their glasses. When he sat down he said, 'I couldn't shoot him. But you did. Why?'

Carlo shrugged his shoulders. 'I've thought about it a lot

since. At the time I just felt it was an irresistible temptation. A reflex action. He was in the sights and my finger was on the trigger.' He smiled briefly. 'But there always has to be a reason, doesn't there?'

'And yours?'

'You insist?'

'I must. God, Carlo—you've landed yourself in a bloody mess. All this is entirely between us, and it stays that way. But I have to know. The people looking into Sir Charles's death know what I was about. They know why I was about it, too. They knew about Sir Charles and my wife. They searched the well and found that the rifle had gone.'

'Are they interested in me?'

'They know about you. They won't overlook anyone. I'm on your side. You did what I couldn't do. They'll get no help from me. But I want to know why you did it. Was it a stupid, crazy impulse, or did you have a reason?'

'There was a reason. There has to be. Even if you don't recognize it right away. I did it for you. I know that now.'

'For me? How could that be?'

Carlo was silent for a while. He had nothing to fear from this man. A declaration of loyalty had been made, and he knew that John Kingsford would stand by it. As for the others . . . well, what could they prove against him? The rifle was sixty feet under water in an old flooded quarry. And for them, too, motive had to be paramount. Why on earth should he have killed? They had to answer that one. His hesitation now came not from doubt about the wisdom of revealing that motive to John. He would honour his word. More important was his own pride in being a Kingsford. Which did he want—to have it recognized, confirmed by this man, or to keep it to himself, a hoarded fact, like a stolen gem, to be enjoyed in secret for the rest of his life? For the first time since he had been in the room he felt the beginning of confusion creep into his mind. He suddenly decided, Oh, hell, what was the point of playing games, nursing secrets, and fiddling about complicating things which in themselves were so simple? Clear the air now, get everything behind him, so that he could go off to agricultural college, and on and on, to Birdie and a farm. . . .

He said, 'I did it for you. What you couldn't do, I had to do.' He laughed, briefly, nervously, and ran on quickly, 'Because you're my father. Though you couldn't have known it. That's why I came to Darlock. My mother told me. I don't think she ever meant to but she was drunk one night. She'd been on holiday here and . . . well, she named you. It could never have been Graber. He was impotent.'

John, held first by surprise, and then—since he knew that it could not be true—moving swiftly to an immediate concern for Carlo because of the dangerous position into which he had, from this conviction, this father and son myth, placed himself, said, 'My God, Carlo—you're an extraordinary chap! Just out of the blue like that—I'm your father? I'm sorry but you've got hold of the wrong end of——'

Carlo interrupted him quickly, 'I can guess what you're thinking. My mother was an alcoholic. What she might say in drink could have arisen from fancy, a muddled mind. But there's more than that. I've got the Kingsford mark like you on my hip. I read about that in Parson John's diary. You made a note that you had it. I may not look like you, but the family resemblance is there. And more than that, I feel like you. Though I disliked you and this place and the moor at first, in the end it all got to me. For a time I was bitter at being beyond all hope of recognition from you. Then I shot that bloody Sir Charles. Well, not even you can ignore that now. That's my real proof. I'm not crazy! I couldn't have done it otherwise.' He flopped back into his chair and in a changed, almost petulant voice said, 'I'd decided not to tell you for years and years. Perhaps never. You made me bring it out.'

John stood up. He said quietly, 'We've gone far enough for the time being. I want to think all this over, and then we shall have to talk again. But what I said at the start is still true, still holds. One thing, at least, is beyond dispute —I wanted Sir Charles dead. You killed him. So far as I'm concerned no one will ever learn that from me. As for the other—' he went over and rested his hand briefly on Carlo's shoulder, '—this question of parentage, I'd like to leave that for a bit. After all,' he smiled, 'the idea of my having a son without knowing it is something which leaves me up in the air a bit.'

Carlo stood up. 'It's true. I've got the mark. And you did sleep with her, didn't you?'

'Yes, I did. But I don't want to go into all that now. What I was going to say was, if it should be true—then, no matter what's happened, welcome to Darlock.'

Carlo smiled, moved towards the door, and then halted and looked back. He said, 'I'm a Kingsford. That's got to be true.'

John said, 'Does Grace know about this? The birth thing?'

'No. But she knows I wasn't Graber's son. My mother told her without mentioning you.'

'And what about Sir Charles?'

'Nothing. But if you want to tell her everything you can. She'd never let me down.'

Carlo gone, John sat down at his desk and pulled the telephone to him. It was very late, but that was unimportant. He wanted the truth. He began to dial.

Chapter Twelve

NEW YEAR'S DAY. Through the window, over the trees on the far side of the combe, Carlo could see the rise of the flat shoulder of Long Holcombe. Low over the heather and rusty grasses a pair of ravens were quartering low. Both of them he noticed were missing flight feathers from their slow moult. John Kingsford would have noticed that. No Kingsford would miss it. And now it came naturally to him. Once you were marked and known to be marked you came into the circle . . . found a home . . . yes, a welcome; that had already been given, and, more, a loyalty which was a shield always there. John Kingsford—no matter how he had failed with Sir Charles—would never go back on his word to another Kingsford. He was safe, safer now than he had ever thought to be. Nothing could touch him. And all the mess and confusion about himself and Darlock and the Kingsfords was behind him.

He laughed quietly and said aloud, 'Welcome home, Carlo.'

He stretched his legs under the covers and flexed his shoulders. No fat, no short wind, no shaky hands to spoil a shot. Sir Charles riding down to the river. Lovely. Rills of sunlight streaming over the chestnut mare like water falling. Sir Charles riding down to the river. Highly polished riding boots from the best shoemaker in London. Cap tipped at the right angle. Neck stock perfect. Tweed jacket comfortable from use over the years, a second skin. Sir Charles riding down to the river. And coming into his sights. They should write a ballad about it . . . *O, down to the river rode the doomed Sir Charles. O down to the river rode he.* . . . And so on. Maybe one day just for his own secret pleasure he would write it.

*   *   *

Grace came into the breakfast room just as John was finishing eating.

She stood across the table from him and said, 'You saw him?'

'Yes.'

'Am I to be told anything?'

John nodded. 'Yes. Carlo agrees. He trusts you to stand by him.'

'Which means he did it?' There was a heavy weariness in her body suddenly. Carlo—always Carlo.

'Yes—and the reason,' said John. He went on to give her an account of his talk with Carlo. She listened with an unmoving face.

He finished, 'After he'd gone I phoned Robert. I had to bully him, but finally he admitted that he had made love to your sister the same night as she had come to me. But even before ringing him I knew Carlo had to be his son because of the mark. For some genetic reason a marked Kingsford can't have a marked son. But a Kingsford without the mark can have both marked and unmarked sons. Robert has no mark.'

'I see,' said Grace, and then added uncaringly, woundingly, 'There would have to be something special about the Kingsfords, wouldn't there? So, he's a Kingsford—your nephew. I hope that means you're going to take him off my hands?'

'At this moment he needs us both.'

Grace said abruptly, 'No. I don't want to be involved

244

with him any more. He's old enough now to be on his own. In fact, he's got to be on his own. He's got to face things for himself. At least, as far as I'm concerned. I shall be leaving at the end of the week. Whether he stays here or not is up to you. I am not going to be involved.' She smiled thinly. 'I'm a coward really, you know.'

'I don't think so. I should know. I understand about that. But you must do what you feel is right. Carlo can stay here as long as he wants to. He has the right. I wouldn't deny him that. I wish I had the right to ask you to stay, too.'

Grace shook her head. 'You know it was never anything like that. You don't owe me anything. Or I you. We found a little comfort with one another. That's all. It would be a mistake to try and build on it.'

John stood up. 'Well, don't tell Carlo yet that you are going. Or about Robert being his father. Robert's coming down in a few days. I think that's the time for him to know.' He smiled. 'Who knows, you might change your mind. Things might be different then.'

'Things are never going to be different for Carlo. He plays a lot of parts, but underneath the real Carlo stays the same. But, if that's what you want, I'll say nothing yet.'

She went to the door and John held it open for her. As she crossed the hall and began to climb the stairs she knew that he was still standing there, watching her. For years now, on and off, this thing had been happening to her. As though she were fated always to be climbing an endless dune of shifting sands, making a little progress, then slipping backwards to take a little rest, a 'little comfort', before starting on the futile upward plodding again.

Ten minutes later John went up to Carlo's bedroom.

Carlo was lying in bed listening to the softly playing radio. He was propped against his pillows, a writing block resting against his knees.

He switched off the radio and said, grinning, 'You haven't come to turf me out? I felt like a lie-in.'

'No. I just wanted a few words with you.'

'Oh, I see. . . .' Carlo flipped the cover over the pad and laid it at his side and, seeing John's eyes on the pad, said, 'Literary work. I'm trying my hand at a ballad. Not much good I'm afraid.' He shrugged his shoulders and smiled.

For the first time John realized the familiarity in the smile and the shrug and wondered how blind he had been before. The gesture was Robert's. And in the face, too, there was a similarity, not strong, but true between the two. In the moment or two before he spoke he knew the slow coil in himself of a longing that it might have been the other way round, not nephew but a son.

He said, 'The Very Reverend is coming down in a couple of days. He can't manage it before. Until then I think, if you agree, that it would be better to keep things marking time. We'll go into everything when Robert comes. A family conference. I don't want to say any more than that now, except of course you will come as one of the family. All right?'

'Yes, of course,' said Carlo, pleasure feeding into him like a drug. Yes, of course. A family conference. That was the Kingsford way. He was a Kingsford.

'Good.'

As John turned towards the door, Carlo said, 'What about the other thing?'

'We'll face it if they do anything about it. If we stick together they'll get nothing to help them. But my guess is they won't bother us.'

'Why?'

'Because without a motive they haven't got a leg to stand on. And no Kingsford is going to help them get it.'

John gone, Carlo picked up the writing pad absently, smiling to himself. His body stirred with an arrogant, heady pulsing of nerve and blood. You could laugh at it, he thought, mock it—would do if you were not part of it—but it was true. The Kingsfords knew where they stood, knew what they had to do for one another, and he was a Kingsford. *O, down to the river rode the proud Sir Charles.* . . . *By the brawling stream he reined his steed.* . . . Good-bye, Carlo Graber! Welcome home, Carlo Kingsford! •

*　　　　*　　　　*

Grainger said to Wardle, 'He was in trouble some time ago at a discothèque in Barnstaple. He had his girl friend with him. I know about her. She's the daughter of a local farmer. One of the local town lads, Hell's Angels type, made trouble. Carlo beat him up viciously. The parents made a fuss to the police. The police traced him, but when they approached Kingsford and got Carlo's story they decided to take no action. With anyone else but Kingsford they might have. The local C.I.D. have done a good job for us. They keep their eyes on these types—they're the kind who like to hand out their own justice. They'd have an eye on Carlo whenever he showed in Barnstaple. Waiting their chance. The C.I.D. had a word with most of them.'

'And he was in Barnstaple?'

'Yes. Around eleven o'clock. Two thugs swore to it.'

'They would. That means nothing.'

'Not by itself. But the car park attendant remembered him, too. He saw him come in. Carlo, knowing he was marked, wouldn't leave his machine on the street to be smashed up. The attendant's time fits. The car park is the nearest one to the main post office. That's the only place with London telephone directories. Carlo wouldn't have known the number of the Press Association. What more do you want? He sent the message.'

'Motive, perhaps still?' Wardle fingered the edge of a morning paper which lay on the library table. The headlines were still screaming the news; articles, photographs, speculations and pundits exploring the political repercussions. Gab, gab, he thought. On the air. On the television screens. Three hundred yards away Sir Charles had died by the river, never to keep another man's wife warm in bed. A martyr. Westminster Abbey and a marble slab to hold him down. Dead by the river. (More years ago than he cared to remember he recalled that he had trout fished the river with his father. Summer holidays in Dulverton. The happy days of youth with life is real and life is earnest and all the tricks of the trade to be learned to come.)

Outside the sun was shining, and a thrush began to sing. Suddenly, he felt his throat knot. Although it was too early, he got up, went to the sherry tray and helped himself.

Grainger, patient, more familiar with this kind of situation even than Wardle, knew what was going through his associate's mind and found himself quite indifferent. He said, 'It won't be a political motive. He's no more connected with Arab aspirations than the man in the moon. Pity he's not a lunatic. That's happened before, and it's acceptable. Whatever you get from him won't be.'

Wardle finished his sherry in a gulp and then said, smiling, resigned, 'All right. Let's keep the people who count happy. Sweep the dirt under the carpet.'

*　　　*　　　*

The last light had gone from the sky. The air was sharpening with the first touch of frost to come. The fieldfares and redwings which had foraged all day over the top pastures, rising now and again in vast echelons to sweep with ragged conformity of flight to new grounds, were now all roosted in the bare hedgerows on the long slopes running down to the sheltered farmlands below Darlock moor.

Wardle sat in the little van, all lights off, parked on a waste strip beside the road well beyond the Sportsman's Inn. Fifty yards ahead the road forked. The left-hand branch followed the high ridge above the Sherndon Water, and dropped down to the bridge over the Barle at Landacre. The right fork, for Withypool, led out to Hawkridge Common and then dipped and curved eastwards to follow the dying contours of the moor to the bottom of the saddle at Portford Bridge where the long slope of Withypool Hill began its climb through heather and brittle whortleberry growths cut by pony and sheep tracks.

A car passed the van and took the right fork. It was the third that had passed in the last hour. Wardle watched the tail lights trace the line of the road and then disappear, cut from sight by the dip of the slope. With one hand he pulled the collar of his sheepskin coat higher about his neck. His other hand rested on his knee, fingers cold around the palm-fitting shape of the microphone. Vaguely, he realized, it reminded him of the feel of a hand grenade from his war days, a lump of cold metal, its guts seeded with death. An owl drifted across the road ahead of him. Eyes adjusted to the night gloom, he saw it, recognizing it as an owl, but was uninterested in its species . . . barn, short-eared, tawny, what did it matter? It was a bird of ill omen. If it knew its part it should perch on the distant signpost at the fork and screech its dismal signal. Crime and punishment. Nothing between. How many times had he and Grainger, following a familiar, dark brief, known these moments? Too many for his stomach. How many times had they played secret judge and jury? Crime there had been; punishment there must be, but no open trial to tarnish a reputation and titillate a scandal-hungry world. If the wrongdoer went free, who knew what arrogance would breed in him, what indiscretions begin to show their first growths? John Kingsford, who some few days ago had sat before them in the library, was lucky that cowardice or conscience had held him back, or he, Wardle, would be sitting here now in the car waiting for him.

From behind him, through the half-open window he heard the sound of the distant engine throb and grow through the cold air, caught the rising note and quick crescendo as gears were changed. From behind him, as the machine turned the corner at the ridge road, the long probing finger of a single headlight trembled across the darkness ahead and then steadied. Man was a creature of many routines, impelled by duty, work, love, pleasure. When he put himself in hazard they left him defenceless.

The motor-cycle went by him, fast, briefly clear in the backwash from the hedges of its own light.

He watched it swing to the right of the fork, then lifted the microphone, pressing the switch, irrelevantly aware for a moment of the faint crackle of static, and said, 'Coming now.'

'Right'.

Grainger's voice. Grainger would never admit it, but he found some kind of pleasure in this. He switched off the microphone and pushed it slowly into the open pocket before him. Without hurry he started the motor and, backing off the waste land, turned and drove along the road, away from the fork, past the Sportsman's Inn.

The owl came soft-winged over a hedge and floated down the road, eyes wide in the square face, watching for the small movement of a vole or the betraying plumage-shake of a roosting bird in the bordering beech and thorn growths of the moor wall.

Carlo drove fast. There were few nights now when he did not go to Birdie. But now—the thought was a warming drug in his blood—he went as a Kingsford. He moved the hand grip and the machine obeyed his impatience. To Birdie. To Birdie. But not to tell her. That must wait. A family conference. The Kingsfords in council. John Kingsford, the Very Reverend and himself. A family occasion. All Kingsfords—father, son, and uncle. And one thing never to tell Birdie . . . well, maybe some time, some time years ahead. *O, down to the river rode the proud Sir Charles.* . . .

He came fast down the slope to the Portford turns. As his headlight lost the line of the twisting road at the first bend ahead, he eased throttle and caressed the brake with a gentle pressure. His body swayed for the curve and the headlight came back, holding the road and the grey-white run of the stone parapets over the tiny stream. Body and machine one, the road and the night his to burn and eat up, and Birdie ahead, and ahead, and ahead; always Carlo and Birdie. Carlo Kingsford. Carlo, Carlo . . . Carlo coming home. . . .

He saw the wire, stretched from the top of one parapet to the other across the road; he saw it but never understood it.

His headlight smashed into the taut wire and it wrenched the handle-bars from his grip and then cut back into him, knifing into him, jerking him violently into the air, road and bridge parapet twisting madly beneath him. He went high through the air. The machine somersaulted into the right-hand parapet.

Grainger stepped away from the side of the car parked in the little layby by the stream on the right of the road. He untwisted the cable from its hold around one of the crenellated stones on top of the parapet. He walked across the road, gathering the wire as he went and freed the other end. He took the wire back to the car and coiled it in the boot.

Then he went down to Carlo.

There had been times when there had been more to do. But not this night. Carlo had been flung over the parapet and lay on his back among the rocks and heather at the side of the little stream where it flowed out from the under-road culvert. His head hung grotesquely towards the water, arms and legs loosely splayed across the smooth curve of a boulder, a puppet, all strings broken, his eyes fixed on the dark sky above the moor.

Without hurry Grainger satisfied himself that the night's work was done. He left Carlo by the stream and went back to the road. With gloved hands he pulled the motor-cycle off the road a little to free the corner from hazard to other traffic. Then he got into the car and drove away.

* * *

The Very Reverend Robert Kingsford conducted the funeral service. The headstone of dark Cornish slate when erected later bore the name Carlo Kingsford and the date of coming and the date of going. Twenty yards away lost in a tangle of weeds and briars against the Radworthy churchyard wall stood a much older headstone with the worn inscription—*Hannah Darch, beloved daughter of Thomas and Mary Darch of this* . . . and the rest of the words and the date mantled by a growth of rich green moss nourished by the wet, west winds from the Atlantic. Beneath John Kingsford's name on the mahogany board in the gun room, its fresh gold leaf bold against the dullness of the other entries, was inscribed—*Carlo Kingsford. 197–, December 6th. 2 hours 38 minutes.* Looking at it sometimes Grace wondered whether the child she carried would be a boy and hoped for John's comfort that it would.

Comfort she had long decided carried its own virtues and was an honest refuge.

Birdie, after putting Spring, Summer and Autumn flowers on the grave for two years, married a farmer's son from Timberscombe and soon had no time or need for visiting. The gold locket she had dropped into the earth with Carlo.

Robert Kingsford knew that the ways of the Almighty were not to be questioned and that there was nothing unspiritual in being unduly gratified by them. And John Kingsford, if he could have proved the truth of Carlo's death, which he suspected, would have known no bar to the slow and steady pull of his trigger finger.